The Sun in Capricorn

Paul Rosenblatt

WATERMARK
P R E S S

Watermark Press, Inc.
149 N. Broadway
Wichita, Kansas 67202

Printed in the United States of America.

Library of Congress Cataloging-in-Publication Data

Rosenblatt, Paul
The sun in Capricorn.
I. Title.
PS3568.07886S86   *1989*   *813'.54 88-33832*
ISBN 0-922820-00-7

Cover Art: Salvador Estrada
Design: Kirsten Johnson
Production: Cynthia Mines, John Hiebert

First Edition

Dedication

For
Joan and Abram and David

Author's Acknowledgment

In this novel all characters who may have existed or may exist and all events which may have happened or may happen are fictional. I am pleased to acknowledge in the formation of my revolutionary protagonist, Verlande, the direct and substantive influence of Sanche de Gramont's article in *The New York Times Magazine* (November 15, 1970), "How One Pleasant, Scholarly Young Man from Brazil Became a Kidnapping, Gun-Toting, Bombing Revolutionary." In acknowledging my debt to this excellent source, Verlande still remains, as Verlande himself would be quick to acknowledge, in name and being, a work of the imagination.

"Let *not the sun* in Capricorn *go down upon thy wrath*, but write thy wrongs in Ashes. Draw the curtain of Night upon injuries, shut them up in the Tower of Oblivion, and let them be as though they had not been."

—Sir Thomas Browne

Fourmillante cité, cité pleine de rêves,
Où le spectre en plein jour raccroche le passant!
—*Baudelaire*

CHAPTER ONE

1

Borne on the breezy sweep of sunlight, Professor Jonathan was trying to cross Avenida Atlântica to get to the beach. He was watching the crazy traffic whizzing by and it occurred to him that it had taken him a good four hundred and sixty-five years or so to get to the beach. A long time, he thought, when he had told his wife only about an hour ago that he was just going for a swim.

First, then, he had stopped at a café. He had been sitting in his swimsuit in a cane chair and he had on his darks and he had flung his towel and shirt over a side chair. He had been smoking and drinking and watching the girls go by. He had been looking upon the beach and the ocean and the mountains rising like humpbacked whales in emerald waters.

He had been watching a beautiful mulata go by. She was wearing a g-string and there were beads of perspiration shining like liquid jewels on the cup of her well-rounded, beautiful ass. He was stirred all right as he squashed the lime of his *caipirinha* with his tongue.

He saw the morning billowing and rolling within the crescent hollow of a golden light. He knew he was a bit whoozy from the *caipirinha* and his eyes were wandering skyward upon a torn drift of a seaway of cloud. He could see the waves bounding high, a veranda of venal greenery and splashy marble at their crest. Simpering wens at the shore, he thought. He was thirsty and he could use another drink. He was going back in time.

The night had been bad and the day had begun in the dark. He had gotten out of bed carefully without disturbing his wife who, he felt with some irritation, needed her sleep and he had gone into his children's room, his two sons, and he had kissed the forehead of each. His legs were aching from behind the knees and his eyes were burning from sleeplessness. He had gone into the kitchen and made coffee without burning himself. He sat at the breakfast table and had a cigarette with his coffee and he waited there for the coming of light. Then Eugenia, the maid, was up. She went out for rolls and the *Jornal do Brasil* and he went to the window to see the light come up the street in splendid giant shapes, oblongs and rectangles on painted buildings.

At the window across the way he saw a long tressed mulata with her bare-chested man. They were leaning on the white sill and lazily puffing cigarettes. She was wrapped in a white bath towel. Jonathan could see into their room, the strewn clothes and the tousled bed with a streak of light across it. He whispered aloud in the thinking remembrance, "Oh God!" The waiter brought him another *caipirinha*.

In a good café, he thought, life is timeless. Back now. Back in time. Back, back, back, back, he told himself. The *caipirinha* was doing its work. He looked at the green lime and he swooshed the glass tumbling the lime. It's like a movie, he thought, watching the lime tumbling in the cloudy *cachaça*. Dissolve to. Flashback, he thought, or whatever it's supposed to say in a movie script. He was smiling. He looked out at the bay and he could imagine the scene: Amerigo Vespucci himself, the old voyager on deck, his lips parched, tongue swollen, eyes blanched, the sunset flowing, the mountains and rounded peaks of Corcovado and Pão de Açúcar sacred in the sun's rays, the broad leaved forest aglow in the last light, a green feathered bird the size of a pelican soaring above, gliding. The old voyager's ship becalmed, the Bay of Guanabara under the spell of calm, there is enchantment in the air as the title, barely if at all readable at first, makes its way from distant waters on to the front of the screen:

Place: Rio de Janeiro
Time: The Tropical Summer of 1502.

Jonathan was really having a good time thinking and watching the girls go by. All cinemascope. All right, he tells himself, the old voyager played by Burt Lancaster, bewitched by the unbelievable calm, the enchantment of the air, thinks he's at the mouth of a great river. Now for the musical effects. Some music coming in, very low at first, rising and insistent, maybe a samba increasing in passion and intensity, even a touch of fury, or wait, better still, something by the great composer Heitor Villa-Lobos, one of his Bacchanals. At any rate, Lancaster turns to his smelly looking, unshaven but stalwart aide whose owl eyes are also filled with wonder. "What month is this?" Lancaster asks his aide. "January," his aide replies. Lancaster turns slowly about. He raises outstretched arms toward the sky where the green-feathered bird is still flying around. "I christen this river in the name of God and Queen," he calls out to the world as the music is now reaching a crescendo, "to be known throughout all of time as the River of January!"

Lovely, Jonathan thinks. He watches the girls go by. He begins to wonder about the swelter of that January summer of 1502, about the old voyager, Lancaster, dreaming continental dreams of samba and *condomblé*. Then suddenly it strikes him. Wasn't it the explorer, Gonzalvez Coelho, who named the river? Wasn't Amerigo in Bahia?

CUT! Lancaster in his bunk in his cabin. He is sleeping, dreaming. Jonathan wonders, is the first night to be cool and damp with the breeze of the sea or shall I have it with the air still, the breath of night heavy as the old voyager dreams on, as Lancaster conceives through fronds of palm the coming of the first mulata, bare breasted and swaying, the drums from the shore, Lancaster restless, perspiration on his forehead, rolling behind her a montage of the land of Brazil, Lancaster dreaming the dream of a continent. The fruits of the sun and the wood of the land, Jonathan is thinking to himself, *pau brasil*, brasilwood, brazier, *Braza*, Brazil, entomological coals glowing under the skin of the mulata, the princess coming through the fronds of palm, she, for whom the heart riots and the body dances, Carnival, a tropical universe—CUT!

Jonathan's smile lingers. He can almost see the battered old ship in the bay. Then he looks around him at the girls in the bikinis and the strings. He whispers to himself, "Amerigo, Amerigo, what have you wrought?" The waiter sees his lips move and awakens him from his reverie.

"Senhor, one more *caipirinha*?"

"No more," Professor Jonathan said, "first I must swim."

2

Borne, then, on the breezy sweep of sunlight, trying to cross Atlântica to get to the beach, he notices a woman standing nearby with her two children. She was frightened as the cars, zigzagging and erratic, went shooting down the Avenue and she clutched her beach paraphernalia, mats and towels, to her breast. He smiled at her and laughed. She smiled nervously at him and laughed back.

"With your permission," he said in Portuguese with what he considered some gallantry in tone and phrasing.

She nodded gracefully as if granting him a favor. He took the hand of her daughter, she the hand of her son. They were standing a few feet from the curb and then there was a spacing of cars and he shouted in English, "Now!"

They dashed across. They were laughing, she almost losing a slipper in the scramble, and then they were on the beach together. He was thirsty and felt he could use another drink.

She was speaking in Spanish and Jonathan could follow it pretty well but she at first was having a little difficulty in understanding his Portuguese. Her children, though, knew English. The boy was twelve and the girl was nine and their English was very good so every now and then Jonathan would toss out the word in English and they would give it to their mother in Spanish.

"Your children are intelligent and beautiful," Jonathan said to her.

"Do you like to dance?" she said above the waves. "I am on holiday."

She offered him a cigarette which he declined. She looked into his eyes. There was a flare of match and eye and then she leaned back, inhaled, blew out the smoke and told the children to play at the shore.

"But who will translate for you?" the boy asked.

"Our understanding improves," the mother laughed. "Go now and be careful for your sister. No deeper than your hips. I warn you. The waves are high. I will watch from here. Is that clear?"

"Thank you, Momma," the boy said and he took his sister's hand and they ran to the shore.

"I also have two children," Jonathan said. "They're both boys."

"*Claro*," she said puffing on her cigarette and smiling, "but do you want to dance with me tonight?"

"They're eight and six," he said.

"*Claro*," she said with some amusement.

She told Jonathan that she was from Colombia and that her husband had to remain in Bogotá. "He could not get away, poor man," she went on, "so much into his business you know."

In São Paulo she wanted to shop on the Rua Augusta. She had never boiled an egg but she knew one thing about cooking. She knew beef stroganoff. She could make beef stroganoff with the best of them.

She stretched. There was just enough muscle tone to ripple her body's indolence. The easeful and selfless lollatry of her movements had its effect. Jonathan was now hard up and dying. She knew and was amused and she yawned. Jonathan turned his gaze outward. As luck would have it, there walking the shoreline was the mulata he had seen at the window sill and she was there with her man. Jonathan was distracted. He was at the dawn of his morning.

"But where are you?" the Colombian lady said.

"On that island out there," he said pointing.

"Ah," she said, "you must be a strong, powerful swimmer for that island."

She leaned toward him. She leaned still further. Her breasts were magnificent and they were almost coming out of the flimsy halter and she took off his sunglasses. She laughed and said, "But you are tired my vigorous swimmer. Your eyes are red."

Jonathan told her she was lovely. He could see she was pretending not to understand. He said it two different times and ways.

Finally, she said knowingly, "You cannot dance with me tonight, it is true?"

"My wife and I have an engagement tonight and so I can't, I'd love to, just can't dance with you tonight."

"Oh, but I did not know you are with wife," she said sounding to Jonathan as if she were saying he was with child and she was commiserating. She sighed and said, "What a pity!"

He pressed her hand and put on his darks. They talked awhile about the sights and nights of Rio and he told her about the best samba schools. He asked her if she cared to swim.

"Much later," she said.

He went into the water and played with the children. They took turns climbing his shoulders and diving. Then the three of them splashed around and took on a few waves. Then he went deep. He swam out beyond the waves and into the calm. He was alone. He faced the sea and treaded water. Then he floated. Then he swam back to the children and wished them a happy holiday. The little girl hugged him good-bye.

He returned to their mother. She was lying in supine idleness and again he was stirred. He went close to her and kissed her on the right cheek and then on the left and he said, "Another time for dancing?"

She nodded and her lips moved. She did not say it aloud, a bare tremor, "*Claro.*"

The sand burned his feet. With a soft erection he walked through armatures of light.

He was back in the café in the same cane chair. Green leaves, yellow sun, white sills of repose, he thought. Morning in Rio de Janeiro. The waiter asked, "*Caipirinha?*"

"No, whiskey," Jonathan said, his thoughts turning once again to Burt Lancaster, the continental dreamer, the old voyager himself, sailing into Guanabara Bay.

CHAPTER TWO

1

J onathan was high and he was having trouble at the service door trying to find the bell. The hallway of the servant's entrance was unlit and it seemed to Jonathan that the hallway was damp and sodden in its darkness. He knew there was a string for a light switch somewhere around and with a cupped hand he kept swooping the air above him trying to find it. The motion was getting him dizzy.

Then he felt a chill. He shuddered. That's a premonition, he thought. He figured he would have to find the light if he were ever to find that damn bell. Now he was sliding his hands over the molding and the door. He wanted a hot shower. He wanted the steam rising and he wanted a ring of naked maidens in the tub holding hands and skipping around the prismatic arc, so he thought, of his rainbow. He began giggling like a schoolboy. Ring around the rosie! Ring around the rosie! All fall down!

He discovered that he was leaning against the door with an out-stretched hand and he was pounding the door with his other hand. He thought he heard Eugenia's voice and then the door gave way and he almost fell in, but Eugenia had caught him by the arm. She was laughing.

He picked up the mat and towel and straightening up he presented them to Eugenia.

"It's a fierce world out there, Eugenia, something fierce. Thank God I'm home! They should do something about that hallway light. It's a miracle you haven't hurt yourself. You must have the eyes of a cat."

"But *patrono*," she began to say.

"How are you supposed to find that damn thin worn string in the dark?"

"But *patrono*, the string is no longer necessary."

"No longer necessary? No longer necessary? But how?"

"The string is from the past. When you come out of the elevator there is an electric switch and there is one by the door."

He stood for a moment staring at her. Then he smiled with recognition and he said, "You are a wise and wonderful woman, Eugenia."

"Oh, Senhor," she said a bit embarrassed and she smiled back and she was pleased.

2

"This morning he came home from the beach singing 'Columbia, the Gem of the Ocean,' " Carol was saying to Arthur.

"Is he crocked or sober now?" Arthur said.

"He was singing in the shower, I mean with evangelical fervor! The children just about split their sides laughing, particularly when he began in with 'Ring Around the Rosie,' " and she paused, laughed. "It was a scream," she said.

The three of them were standing in the foyer of Arthur's elegant apartment in Botafogo and Carol and Arthur were talking about Jonathan as if he were not there. Jonathan put his hands in his pockets and hunched his shoulders and sulked.

"I'm sure that Arthur isn't amused," he said to Carol.

"Remember," Arthur went on, talking to Carol, "the Ambassador asked me to look after our star. He is perhaps unduly sentimental about the old relationship." Then he turned at last to Jonathan and said in his rather stiff way, "He truly has an avuncular regard for you, Jonathan. Please be so good as to remember that, won't you my dear fellow?"

"What do you mean *unduly* sentimental?" Jonathan said.

Arthur looked hard at him. "You know goddamn well," he said.

They had walked into the salon and into a burst of color. The walls of the salon were filled with oil paintings by Arthur's wife, paintings done in Munich and Paris, Teheran and Tanganyika, Saigon and Rio. Jonathan was moved to take Arthur's arm affectionately, for he was now remembering that Arthur had been cultural attaché in Saigon and he was the last American diplomat out of that doomed city.

The salon was crowded. Everyone was very well dressed including the frocked waiters. There was food and booze and smoke. The conversations going on were chiefly in English or Portuguese or French and Jonathan loved it, the languages flowing like wine and giving forth an aroma, a bouquet for the soul. He looked about and saw that Carol had drifted off.

"Looks like a lovely party," Jonathan said to Arthur. "Funny day today. I had a chill, a premonition. And there were all these maidens running through my mind."

"That shouldn't be too much of a problem," Arthur said now leading Jonathan by the arm, "as long as you keep them there."

"Very funny? Where are you taking me? There are people here I want to say hello to."

"Come along," Arthur said. "The Ambassador is waiting for you in my study."

"Well," Jonathan said hesitating a bit, "it's been a time since I've seen Christopher." Then he gave in to a little run of panic. He looked at Arthur. "This sounds like a set-up," he said.

They were now in the long hallway leading to the study. Arthur said nothing and just looked straight ahead.

"Why the study?"

"His regard for you," Arthur said finally. "He is very disappointed."

"Disappointed?"

"Please, no more charming games, Jonathan. We now know. Do you understand? We know. I love you like a brother, Jonathan, but you are a goddamn shit."

"Now wait a minute—"

"If for no other reason, how could you do it to him? To him? Yes, a goddamn shit," and Arthur was knocking gently on the door of his study and then opening it.

The Ambassador was sitting alone in the lamplight of the study. He was sitting behind a large desk. He rose slowly and was smiling. Jonathan heard the door close behind him. He knew Arthur had gone and he felt himself standing it seemed ankle deep within the texture of the rug and his eyes took in the walls and ceiling where the lamplight had done its work, where there were shadowy maps continental and peninsular it seemed to him and their groping shapes struck him with dread and he felt the geography of his dreams was wavering on the walls and ceiling and he knew at once he had become a man awaiting a dark sentence, *banished,* he thought, and the Ambassador approached while Jonathan stood momentarily transfixed, the Ambassador's hand outstretched in greeting, the Ambassador saying, "The world still before you, Jonathan, the world still before you!"

3

"You have a wonderful wife, Jonathan," the Ambassador was saying.

"Thank you, sir."

"Of more natural grace and beauty than one is wont to find in women nowadays. Carol reminds us of the poet's truth that modesty is a becoming thing in woman."

"Christopher, you are incorrigibly old-fashioned."

"You mean chauvinistic."

"A charming whatever it is."

The Ambassador raised his glass of Scotch and he seemed to Jonathan to be looking thoughtfully at the color and then he took a sip and said, "I didn't think the embassy was appropriate for our chat. I wanted an occasion and place less official, more congenial for old friends."

"I appreciate that," Jonathan said and then he thought he would take a stab at it, "I suppose I know why I'm here."

But the Ambassador put him off with, "Now, now, Jonathan. The propriety of good Scotch just won't let us rush into things. It's to be savored, like memory itself."

"Yes, sir," Jonathan said wondering what was next.

"I was thinking only this afternoon of—how many years ago was it?—when we used to sit around at Columbia and talk the great things through. I remember you had just met Carol and, yes, all the world before you."

"Yes, sir," Jonathan said again, "all the world," his voice trailing off.

"Ah, I never thought you'd turn into a professor of literature. I thought I had saved you for history and politics. But then again," he said gently, "there was always a kind of idealism about you, a naïveté of a kind different from ours, one that sought its own reality rather than what was and," and here the Ambassador paused and said a bit sharply, "what is."

"I get the drift," Jonathan said. "I know where you're going."

"Of course you do. On balance you were the best damn graduate student I ever had and you had to go and turn on me and go into literature."

"I think I'll sidestep that one," Jonathan said.

"Yes, you went ahead and turned on me. Well don't look so serious. I'm half joking. Besides, I respect you more because you are a professor of literature. You know the meaning of the imagination. The public imagination, ah, that's the great thing to be moved. Only culture can do that, literature, but, but, I must say, I mean, there is also what is, Jonathan, what is before we get it into the imagination, don't you think?"

There was a knock at the door and a waiter entered bringing in a tray of two more drinks and some hors d'oeuvres along with the faint drift of laughter through the open door.

"There's a party out there," Jonathan smiled.

"Would you like a cigarette?" the Ambassador asked as the waiter left closing the door behind him. With the closing of the door the float of sound was stilled. "Some of this pink salmon? It's nice the way they curl it around some of that cream cheese there in the middle."

"I'll take a Hilton," Jonathan said. He took a cigarette and Christopher lighted it for him with his banged-up Zippo lighter.

"Some lighter," Jonathan said.

"North African campaign," the Ambassador said and smiled.

"Never failed in the desert," Jonathan said softly.

"I suppose if I lost this goddamn lighter, I'd give up smoking," the Ambassador said and then he leaned back in his chair and he looked into Jonathan's eyes and waited.

"Then I am to begin," Jonathan said, "that for which I am here?"

"Yes, as you so quaintly put it, that for which you are here."

Jonathan looked at the shadowy walls and ceiling and there was dread and also a kind of sadness and he said to the Ambassador, "Christopher, it was all so simple and you probably know it all. We haven't come down to cat and mouse, have we?"

"No cat and mouse," the Ambassador said, "so I'll begin and tell you the little I know."

"Thank you, Christopher."

"We begin then with Petrópolis, the City of Emperors, where I had gone to talk beans."

"Beans?"

"The coffee thing has me going right now," the Ambassador said. "In Petrópolis we talked beans. Brazil can't be allowed to sell us processed coffee at prices cheaper than those they sell us the raw bean for."

"In the glorious City of Emperors you talked about beans?"

"That's what I'm saying. To get your interest I'll throw in Thoreau and say I wanted to *know* beans."

"I'll throw in Eliot," Professor Jonathan said. "'I have measured out my life with coffee spoons.'"

"Good. Now that we've gotten rid of the academic shit," the Ambassador said suddenly and harshly, "I'll go on with Petrópolis. Do I have your attention?"

Jonathan realized then that he must have been looking blankly or elsewhere, that the Ambassador was working things up, working up a judgment on him, a sentence, and Jonathan knew he had to concentrate on what was being said rather than to anticipate what was likely to happen. Carol had told him that it had become an oddity of his lately, the way he would fade in and out, his laxity at times in, as Carol said, "attending," a school teacher's term, "attending," "paying attention." He felt it now, that vulnerability that was taking him from where he was sitting, this time and this place with the Ambassador in Arthur's study to the memory of another time and another place and he was thinking ring around the rosie—all fall down! The inner melody had been playing with him since the morning shower. It seemed to be taking him off balance like an infection of the ear. There he was in schoolyard days, his heroic age, walking off the far end of the football field, punchy, and he remembered the wavering lines of the crowd, the shouting and the hollering and what seemed to him the call of sirens when he realized that it was all but an echo in an empty locker room where he had been taken and through this room he had been taken to the still emptiness of the first-aid room and the morgue of a table where they had worked on him and he was remembering and at the same time trying to attend to the business of the lamplit room.

"Petrópolis," he said at last.

"Yes, I see I have your attention, Petrópolis. Dr. Monteiro was there, that son of a bitch."

"A son of a bitch if ever there was one," Jonathan said smartly.

"I appreciate you're trying to accommodate me," the Ambassador laughed.

"Mr. Ambassador, I assure you I'm with you," Jonathan said. "Besides you can't say it too often, can you? Monteiro is a son of a bitch. Truth bears repeating."

"Ah, Jonathan, it is good to see you again." The Ambassador paused. "Now see this, Jonathan, imagine it. I'm sitting around with Dr. Monteiro at that oval rosewood table, its surface shining like a mirror. Dr. Monteiro is leaning toward me. I can almost feel his chin on my shoulder. Very cozy and I'm not looking at him. He's telling me in his most confidential and apologetic tone, in his damnably correctly clipped British English how very much he regretted that unfortunate little incident, surely more accident than incident he says, that took place a little while back—two weeks back, Jonathan? Three weeks? An incident about which I didn't know, Arthur didn't know, no one at the embassy knew, not a damn American soul there knew a goddamn thing about. Ah, Jonathan, good Christ, Jonathan, good Christ," his voice trailing off.

His hands were tremoring and he tried to steady them by resting them on the desk blotter. He clasped them and went on, "Then that son of a bitch went fishing. He went fishing, not in English, but in his most ministerial Portuguese. He was using tenses and moods I didn't know existed. He had the hook in my gills. I was bleeding and he was reeling me in, slowly."

The Ambassador had gotten up from his chair and had come around the desk. He put his hand on Jonathan's shoulder. Jonathan half turned in the chair to look up and meet the Ambassador's eyes.

"I didn't look at him, only at that grinning reflection on the table top and there I could see him reach into his inner pocket and take out an envelope and out of that envelope the photograph and then I had to look up from the table top."

Jonathan swallowed hard as he remembered the flash, a shot of light, the flash and the shot of light, Verlande surprising him in that moment with an *abraço* and Jonathan remembering he had almost cried out God but he was hearing simultaneously, even as he felt the fear, thinking he was hearing the sound of a camera and he remembered thinking it is only a camera and I am alive.

"You and Verlande," the Ambassador was saying, "in one heartwarming fond embrace, *um abraço*. God, Jonathan, I'm proud of you! What the Brazilians wouldn't give to get Verlande in an *abraço*! There was Monteiro swirling his moustache and giving me his world-famous gap-toothed grin. I couldn't figure Monteiro's game and I couldn't believe the photograph. You and that gun-toting revolutionary. I mean that's high company, Jonathan, getting hugged by a guy who's on the top ten of the hit parade, everybody's most wanted. Yes, sir, Jonathan. I couldn't believe it. The photograph had to be a fake and I had the damn thing read by our people and what do you know?"

"No fake," Jonathan said.

The Ambassador patted Jonathan on the shoulder. "Yes, sir, the best damn graduate student I ever had."

He went back to his chair, picked up the Scotch and said, "You know, Monteiro's got his pecker in my pocket. I want him to get his pecker out of my pocket." He took a sip of the Scotch and sat down and leaned back. "I don't mean to be vulgar." He smiled. "Well, then, Jonathan? But I forget. How about a piece of this salmon first?"

"You want me to spill the beans, right Christopher?"

"Very good. We did begin with beans, didn't we?"

"This is good salmon."

"Now that you've been fed, I'm waiting," the Ambassador said a bit impatiently.

"It was a personal matter," Jonathan thought to say. "Remember, Christopher, I'm from the streets of Brooklyn."

"Remember what Hemingway once said? 'What you win in Brooklyn you lose in Chicago.' "

"Mr. Ambassador, I don't know quite what you mean," Jonathan said feeling his stiffness and awkwardness in the saying, "but it sounds ominous. This isn't Brooklyn and this isn't Chicago."

"And this isn't a personal matter and there are no personal codes," the Ambassador said. "Do you think Spears was a personal matter? Forgive me, Jonathan, but for a grown man you do have an extraordinary naïveté about some matters where there's no room for it. Frankly, it seems to me wondrous, a little bit of a miracle you are still alive."

Spears, Jonathan thought. "It's funny you mentioning Spears. I've been thinking about Spears lately, thinking and thinking about him. That wasn't Verlande now, was it? I mean I never knew Spears but I've been thinking about him."

The official story, Jonathan knew, was that Spears was on leave from West Point to study Portuguese language and literature in preparation for teaching these subjects at the Point. That was the story. Then one bright afternoon the Captain had just come out of his house in Gávea. He was holding the hand of his child. He was taking his son to a birthday party and his son was scrubbed and combed.

Jonathan had wondered at the time and had wondered since, even now as he was sitting in the chair in Arthur's study trying to attend, wondered how was the child spared? In God's name, miracle of miracles, how? He saw again and again in his mind's eye the whole terrifying scene. It came to him like a faded newsreel in sepia, the child too dazed to cry, his father's blood splattered all over him, his father limp upon the fender of the car, the hand that had held the child's hand fixed on a windshield wiper torn loose from its mooring. It had been a submachine gun.

"Was he CIA?"

"Spears?"

"Spears."

"Do you care whether you get killed from the left or the right? Spears is dead."

"Yes," Jonathan said half to himself, "I was thinking about Spears."

"Well, I'm waiting. The room is safe. Suppose you tell me all about it."

"Safe?"

"I'm waiting, Jonathan. There is a party out there for us to join."

"Then I am to begin?"

"From the beginning," the Ambassador said.

4

"I suspect that there isn't all that much to tell that you don't know already," Jonathan began as he took another cigarette from Christopher, "but to begin in the beginning, in the very beginning, well it seems I piss like clockwork before class.

"I don't know if you've been in that men's room at the *Faculdade*, Christopher, but I ought to get hardship pay for going in there. The toilet bowls don't have seats. Nothing ever seems to flush. There are both rats and lizards all over the damn place. The cement floor's a pitted uriniferous soil, the incontinent's Slough of Despond, the mushroom paradise of the world. I'm telling you, Christopher—"

"I heard there were five of them," the Ambassador said. "Now please, Jonathan, don't get literary. Get on with it, won't you?"

"Ah, then you have heard," Jonathan said.

"I haven't heard until you tell it."

"I saw four of them when I walked in. Their backs were toward me. I didn't see the fifth one. He let me know he was there. He clubbed me from behind. The bastard let me know he was there all right. He clubbed me and I buckled. I think I could've held up. I went down."

"You were smart enough not to hold up."

"I was smart enough to go down."

"They were careful not to knock you out. I see that now. They were careful not to hurt you, not too much, at any rate. Let's be thankful for little blessings."

"They must wash the floor with urine," Jonathan said. "It wasn't the blow that surprised me so much. After all, I'm a street kid from Brooklyn and the blow comes and you receive, amen, and you get the blow."

"Sure, it's better to receive than to give," the Ambassador said.

"I mean it was while I was falling I got the second surprise. As I was buckling and beginning to fall, I recognized one of them. He was my student, a damn good student, and he had on the most goddamn sorrowful and compassionate and forlorn all at once face, really something, Christopher, a surprise, my woeful student, and I tried to smile at him. Must have been a pretty weak smile but I felt for him."

"Good Christ!" the Ambassador said and stretched for a pencil and pad.

"No, Christopher, I'm not going to give you his name."

Jonathan paused and sipped his Scotch. He discovered he was breathing rather heavily. He put out his cigarette and felt himself sinking into his armchair as the Ambassador said, "Have some more of this salmon and cheese, won't you?"

Jonathan was thinking there are tales to tell of Arabian nights and desert days. Keep the tales going and you can stay the sentence. I'm telling the story and I'm in it, he thought. He smiled dumbly at the Ambassador.

"Are you all right?" the Ambassador asked. "Please go on."

"Without wounding love," Jonathan muttered.

"What? I don't understand you. Are you sure you're all right?"

"I was thinking of my student."

"I've got to press you for that name."

"'Forgive me Professor,' he was saying. 'Forgive us all, Professor Jonathan.' Wasn't that something, Christopher?"

"Spare me, won't you, Jonathan?"

"Then, Christopher, he goes on to say, 'You are a good man, Professor. I have love for you but it has been deemed there is too much of your presence here, your American presence. You are understanding me, Professor? You are clear enough to be understanding me? I bring the message as it is ordered and as it is deemed.' So you're going to press for his name?"

"*Deemed?*"

"Quite something, Christopher, the fervor and the compassion, his face distorted in a funny way as if he were about to cry. He was kneeling by me while the others hovered about. I don't mean outspread black wings and all. *Deemed.* Yes, deemed was the word he used and the oddity of how he'd come by such a word struck me then as it strikes you now and I had almost laughed and asked him where he learned the word, deemed, as if the gods and fates had ordained all but he was going on with the message, going on. CIA and all. 'Some claim you are CIA,' he explains. 'Are you clear enough to be understanding me, Professor?' "

"Your question then about Spears—"

"Yes, Spears came to my mind just like that when my student said CIA. *Spears* I thought. I got to tell you this Brooklyn boy had good old fear clutching at his heart."

"Well, it wasn't what you'd call a normal school day, was it now?"

"No it wasn't," Jonathan said trying to smile and in the saying he heard and felt the lamplit hopelessness of his own weary voice in that shadowy room as he went on with, as he was thinking, his fairy tale of violence.

"I told him I was a little dizzy but clear enough to understand. He was just kind of kneeling at my side with his woeful look. He wasn't cradling but sort of cupping my head in his hands. He was keeping it slightly off that cracked, stained, pardon me, Christopher, uriniferous smelling cement. 'You are not bleeding, Professor, you are not bleeding,' he says to me. He said it like he was complimenting me and expressing his gratitude at the same time for my impregnable head."

"How badly hurt were you?"

"The nausea was bad." Jonathan hesitated. "There was a bad strain. I mean there was pain between my shoulder blades and in the back of my neck."

"Yes," the Ambassador said. "Yes, well."

Jonathan knew the Ambassador was waiting for him to say that remembrance of his meeting with Verlande, the revolutionary Verlande, the terrorist Verlande. The bathroom tale was but a prologue and the Ambassador was waiting, trying to be patient, and Jonathan was thinking, I cannot tell him. If I tell him I will have to tell him of my complicity, of my acquiescence, of that moment of my witness to a murder, of the moment itself when the Luger jammed and how Verlande had said calmly and gently, "Who has the Smith and Wesson?" Jonathan was thinking, I will have to tell him all and then after telling him all he still will not know and he still will not understand and he will say, "Have some more of that pink salmon," and then he will say, "I'm not sure I understand," and then he will say, "Christ, how could you?" and then he will say, "Tell me again so I can understand."

There was a long, long silence, Jonathan and the Ambassador looking at each other across the desk.

"And your student," the Ambassador said at last, a slight smile of encouragement on his face, "the one whose name you won't let me have?"

"He said pretty much the way I'm giving it to you, 'You will go home, Professor Jonathan. You will please return to the United States for your very safety. It has been deemed there will be no more American influence on this campus.' "

"And then?"

"The son of a bitch who clubbed me? He cursed me. Said I was a fucking cultural imperialist pig. For emphasis, he spit on me. Pretty funny, huh? My student got pissed off at him and ordered him to stand by the door."

"And then?"

"I guess you know. My student had tears in his eyes and asked my forgiveness just before he drew back his foot and kicked me in the ribs. No damage. He had great control like a soccer player."

"And then?"

Jonathan felt very tired. He wanted to say to Christopher that he didn't want to play ring around the rosie with him anymore. There was a knock on the door and the waiter came in with two more drinks. Then there was another cigarette and a strained pause until the waiter had gone and then another moment of quiet. Jonathan saw that the Ambassador was staring at him, plain staring at him and waiting.

"That's about it," Jonathan said clearing his throat. "My student and one of the other guys helped me to my feet and got me to the sink. I wasn't feeling prime but I wasn't in bad shape. They even had smelling salts. How's that for A-1 preparation. They got me to take a strong whiff and that snapped my head back getting the pain going again down from the neck through the shoulder blades. I doused my head and the back of my neck with cold water. Okay? Finished. I mean do you want all of these details?"

"I want to hear about Verlande."

"There were no towels and no sunlight in there. I used my handkerchief to dry off. My student gave me a pocket comb."

"Verlande."

"That dumb son of a bitch who spit on me was drawing on the wall by the door, great big letters, NLF, National Liberation Front. NLF, NFL, National Football League. Sorry for that. Just a little humor, Christopher."

"So then you knew for sure."

"I now knew for sure it was Verlande who had done the deeming, so to say."

"And then you decided on some personal diplomacy."

"I didn't think of it that way and, as a matter of fact, I didn't think anything of it along those lines."

"In brief, you said?"

"Remember, Christopher, I wasn't thinking too clearly yet."

"In brief, Jonathan, you said?

"I said I wanted to see Verlande."

"Very good," the Ambassador said. "Yes, sir, the best damn graduate student I ever had and you had to go and turn on me, didn't you? You had to go and turn on me."

5

"Mr. Ambassador, I ask you not to blow it out of proportion. They just laughed at me when I said it and I went on to class, a little high, a little late, that's all, a little sore and I think I had a good class."

"The DOPS and a half a dozen other security forces have been looking for him for two years and you say you want to see Verlande. And then you tell me you think you had a good class! Good class? Good Christ!"

"Getting beat up is a very personal thing, Christopher, believe me. It calls for a very personal response."

"Must I remind you there is no personal response in matters of this sort? There is nothing personal about it, Jonathan, nothing personal at all. In these circumstances the personal is a luxury none of us can afford. The reality now, look at that. You see Verlande. He gives you a hug. The picture's taken and it's all over. Over, Jonathan. You fucked up. If the papers weren't government controlled and our influence what it is, that picture would have been front page. Are you understanding me, Professor? Are you clear enough to be understanding me? Isn't that what your student said?"

"Yes, that is what my student said."

"Verlande may still use that picture but he's already gotten what he wants. The Brazilians don't want a fuss. No publicity. They just declare you persona non grata, under the rosewood table, as it were. No official action by them is needed and nothing gets in the American papers. No diplomat expelled stuff or professor expelled stuff. I just sit here in Arthur's study with you and tell you you're going home. It's simple, isn't it, old friend? That unfortunate little incident—that son of a bitch Monteiro!—is over."

"Home? You are exiling me, Christopher. That's what you're really doing. Is that what you're doing?"

The Ambassador looked at him in disbelief. "Not exile, Jonathan, not exile. Home. You are an American, Jonathan! Are you all right?"

"Abandoned, then," Jonathan said.

"Abandoned? I don't know what the hell you're talking about. Are you sure you're all right?"

"The White Dove," Jonathan said trying to recover. "I'm talking about the building for the Center for the Literature of the Americas. My dream. The building I'm going to put it in."

"Of course," the Ambassador said, "that's what you call it, the White Dove. I forgot. Why do you call it that? I forget why you call it that?"

"The architecture," Jonathan said, "it will be flowing and white like the rise of a dove."

"Like the rise of a dove, ah, that's good."

"Among tan brakes and green leaves."

"It's good to see you again, Jonathan, and I will miss you, my dear friend, a personal loss. But won't you see this all as a temporary setback and not as the end of everything? That which we have done here remains here in Arthur's study, among the shadows, you know. There's nothing of record, nothing of notation, nothing official. Your Brazilian post has been exemplary."

"And the White Dove?"

"Arthur has spoken to me about it. He's assured me it will fly. Arthur, by the way, will see to your apartment. I trust you have a diplomatic clause in the lease. Which reminds me, speaking of your apartment, what the hell have I heard about it? But that's for later. There is too much to catch up on, much too much to say. You have been busy, haven't you? First, though, Verlande. Then we get to the party and I want to talk to your wife. Yes, let's get on with it. Some more pink salmon?"

"You want to be briefed about Verlande."

"I want you to tell me about the meeting."

There was a knock at the door. It was Arthur and Jonathan saw even in the lamplight that Arthur was grave and ashen. He was standing there with a courier and two starched marines, each with strapped belt and holstered pistol. The Ambassador stood up. He was grim.

"Excuse me, Mr. Ambassador," Arthur said. He beckoned to Jonathan to come to the door.

"Come along, Jonathan," he said.

That was all he said. He had taken Jonathan firmly by the arm and they were going down the long hallway toward the bright salon and as they were halfway down the hallway they heard the Ambassador call out, a cry of rage and pain, "Good Christ!" Jonathan knew that if he spoke, Arthur would not be listening. When they reached the party, Arthur turned on a smile. As he released Jonathan he said to him quietly, "The Ambassador will be leaving through the servant's quarters. Now why don't you try to enjoy yourself a bit for the rest of the evening?"

It was not until the following morning when the maid brought in the paper and Jonathan was waiting for the family to awaken and he was a little hung over, not until then did he read an ending to the evening. "The United States Ambassador to Guatemala," the banner headline said, with all the finality of its tense, "is assassinated."

In the jagged morning, the light fragmented, Jonathan, sitting motionless in his armchair in the study, the paper furled at his bare feet, remembered that Arthur had once been cultural attaché to the dead Ambassador.

CHAPTER THREE

1

With the late afternoon and the approach of evening, Harry Fox came to the apartment. He gave Carol a white rose.

Harry Fox had a long straight nose and hollow cheeks and bushy eyebrows and filmy yellow eyes. His was an elongated face and he had a small mouth filled with large teeth. He was thin and bony, long fingered and raw knuckled.

He had been living for twenty years not in Brazil but in Rio itself. He had never left the greater city limits, not knowingly left anyway, so it was said by others. He had come twenty years ago to study under a grant in Latin American history and he brought with him the prize and prized maidenhood of a sixteen-year-old girl who was so sensuous and so beautiful that young men could not look upon her directly without embarrassment.

"And pow!" as Harry would say dizzily, "pow, pow!" Harry told Jonathan that the blood of that maidenhood, faded and stained, was memorialized in the boned perpetuity of his swing or, to put it another way he would say, I always have a hard on and no desirable virgin of *Nossa Senhora de Copacabana* would ever while he drew breath reach the age of seventeen in the unravished state of jeweled holiness or, to put it another way he would chuckle and say, It is my fate, my destiny to fuck sixteen-year-old virgins.

No one except Jonathan seemed to take Harry Fox seriously in any way at all, not even most of the sixteen-year-old girls. Many people took him to be vulgar if they did not think he was altogether crazy because he had acquired the habit of squeezing his cock and balls in tribute to every good-looking girl who happened to saunter by. He also had loud conversations with himself from time to time at odd moments in crowded places.

His belt was a thick, hemp rope. When he'd go to the beach to join in the fishing he used the same strong rope to hitch to the net line anchoring himself with it as he leaned backward to pull. His pants would then be drooping a little below his hips and he'd have to clutch at them every now and then.

Sometimes Jonathan would join in with the men, pulling, then walking, drawing in, then walking, until they were upon the men who were advancing toward them, those who were towing the other part of the line. The net boat would now be quite close to shore and two men from the boat would spring into the water to furl the net.

Children would then come running with plastic bags and buckets to catch the silver swarm of the little fish the meshing could not hold. Many men would come now to help in the final dredge and occasionally a tourist or two would forget his camera to help tow ashore the heavy life of the net and then the maids and the housewives and always the same one elderly man would come and they would stand in a large circle around the net as it was unfurled. They stood with buckets of sea water and the bargaining for the buying of the fish would begin and the elderly man always bought one fish.

Through this fishing and desultory jobs of translating, and in the early years when the clothes still held through tutoring Americans, Canadians, and the English in Portuguese, and playing the guide, Harry Fox had made it for twenty years feeding himself daily on rice and beans and manioc. He was staying, Jonathan supposed, because Harry thought she was still here in Rio that twenty years ago sixteen-year-old Vesta of his hearth and fire.

Harry told Jonathan that when he came to Brazil the marriage took about a year for dissipation. He explained that he never knew how not to spend money, even how to care for the modest grant money, and she, Harry would pause here when he'd tell it, she was swinging in fine style working in a bar so they could get by. In that bar if the young men were embarrassed to look directly upon her, the older men who were suave with dough were not. They looked and finally one had of her and then two and three and on. In that downtown bar in the business section she became swell and there was booze and she had her first abortion when she should have been getting her high school diploma back in New York.

She had been living in New York with her mother in a shabby apartment no more than fifty yards from where the El rattled and ran when Harry, then twenty-five, first came to tutor her in Spanish because she was failing her course. Her mother was young and believed in education and ogled Harry. One night he had to finally screw the mother and the following morning when the mother awoke feeling good and ready for another turn, Harry was not there. She was disappointed but she went back to sleep. When she got up with a start and felt the stillness of the apartment, she knew. She moaned. She went to her daughter's closet and most of her clothes were gone. When she saw her daughter's pink Easter bonnet was still there, she wept. She made herself coffee and went to the window with the cup and she watched the trains go by. A month or so later, the first letter arrived and it was postmarked Rio de Janeiro. Harry told Jonathan that until his wife disappeared, she and his mother-in-law had kept up a close and warm correspondence.

He took her away in her sixteenth year and she thought of him as super. He was super this and super that, a super sophisticate and a super lover. He was taking her from the rumble to platinum stardom, so she thought, in her gum chewing, nippling way. The faraway movieland place she was going to was like the magazines said and she said yes to Rio de Janeiro and the Sugar Loaf and the Christ on Corcovado and Copacabana and the sidewalks serpentine in their sidewinding patterns of black and white stone. So it was at the age when she should have been graduating from high school she had had too many boozy days and the first of her abortions and Jonathan thought that even then she must have sensed and known her fate, mistress and motherless, but he never said anything to Harry about it. He would just listen quietly to Harry as Harry, like the ancient mariner, would tell the tale of those years.

And when people, usually it was the momentary concern of Americans, would say, "You cannot go on this way, Harry. Why don't you go home?" he would say, "But I'm on a grant to study the Vargas-Lacerda relationship," as if the grant had not been terminated and the years had not gone by.

So now they sat, Jonathan, a professor of literature and therefore, Harry had once said, a pretender of sorts to thrones and princesses, and Harry, an historian, the Historian of Pow as Jonathan had once dubbed him ceremoniously during a drinking bout. They sat in the grand living room with a view of the *favela* on the hillside one street away. They were drinking martinis.

Carol would come in every now and then with her martini. She would listen to the talk for a moment and then she would disappear to the kitchen to see to the dinner and to chat with Eugenia. The boys, who had been drawing, were now wrestling in the study. They were cautioned by Eugenia and then by Carol and they were now chatting and giggling quietly. Harry looked about wistfully and the shale of evening light was upon them.

Harry went to the window. He was watching the *favela*.

"You are right, of course, for when you are in exile," he was saying to Jonathan, "or expatriated or even dispatriated, you're always explaining yourself to yourself and to others. You can't escape that. You're always spinning a tale to tell yourself and other people why. You become a prisoner of your ego. It's a kind of disease where you're always trying to justify yourself, your life, and to others. Like I'm doing now, you keep repeating yourself. Yet I'm terrified at the thought of returning home. Besides, I know she's here and I don't have the option. I'll find her, Jonathan, I will, and maybe then, together, we'll, we'll, yes, return."

"With the Vargas-Lacerda study tucked under your arm," Jonathan said, "a dream, a nice wonderful dream we've got to have."

"And your dream, Jonathan? What dream are you going to have tucked under your arm when you go home?"

Jonathan was startled. What could Harry know?

"That'll be awhile," Jonathan said.

"You've seen Verlande and you're being sent home."

"How the hell do you know?"

"It's my business to know. I stand on street corners."

"I think I'm looking at you for the first time," Jonathan said with a slight smile. "What are you into?"

"Our friend Oleisky, that's all."

"I still don't see."

"The no question agreement on the apartment, remember. I must know how soon before you go."

Jonathan was remembering. He was going back. Harry had said it was okay when he had introduced him to Senhor Oleisky. Given the kind of character Harry was and who Oleisky was, Jonathan thought it natural they should know each other and be in cahoots of sorts on all kinds of strange things. What was wonderful and what had stunned Jonathan, the Professor of Literature, was that it came out that this beggar Oleisky had read the seventeenth century writer, Sir Thomas Browne. He had actually read and admired Sir Thomas Browne! Jonathan was remembering how it came about, all so odd!

"There could be a due date," Harry had explained. "I'm sure it won't rub against your pieties."

"My pieties?" Jonathan had said.

"You know, that which hangs between your legs. This gentleman is the representative for the apartment, the real estate agent. I know this surprises you. I know Senhor Oleisky does not look the part, what with no shirt and tie or, for that matter, shoes. Yet, believe me, he is the only one entrusted to deal with that apartment. Ask no questions. As a matter of fact, the only commission you may be expected to pay to him is if the day comes when he must call on you in that lovely apartment, you will accommodate him. That is, he will have a request. That is our understanding. As your friend, I assure you there is nothing to worry about. You are not to be compromised."

"A mystery apartment?" Jonathan had laughed. "Shit, how can I resist, particularly given the tight situation for good apartments and this one is wonderful. Shit, I can't resist. Carol will love it. Teak furniture and all! Besides, 'I love to lose myself in a mystery, to pursue my reason to an *o altitudo!*' "

"Sir Thomas Browne," Oleisky had said.

Jonathan was stunned and he knew that Oleisky was pleased with him and they shook hands on the apartment.

Before this meeting, Jonathan had wondered about Oleisky. He was a familiar figure to anyone who walked the streets of Copacabana. He was the man, as Jonathan had thought of him before being introduced, who spoke to the ocean. Of what Jeremiadic prophecy Jonathan did not know. Jonathan saw him as a handsome man of deep and dark semitic features, robust and strong. He had flowing black hair and a flowing black beard. He wore a shiny, pin-striped, double-breasted blue jacket on bare skin and his pants were tattered and shredded below the knees and he was barefooted.

He walked the avenues and the shores with a magnificent, healthy stride, a beggar of immense dignity. Give him the jawbone of an ass for his weapon, Jonathan had once thought, for he looks like a flailer of Philistines. Now they had met and now Jonathan knew that someday they would have business together, this man who read Sir Thomas Browne. After that meeting with him and Harry, Oleisky ever since would stride past Jonathan as if he were not there.

"Now there's a life," Harry was saying nodding toward the *favela*, "that even a guy like me can't enter. I'm poor enough for that slum, God knows, but I'm a white American. There are lovely young girls up there—see the silhouette of that stately water carrier, there, there Jonathan, you see just mounting the crest of the hill? Do you have to go?"

"What option do I have?"

"Can't you do something else? There's always something else to be done."

"Even if they don't revoke my passport, if only the diplomatic connection is cut, how can I support my family? How can I work? You know how the list works. I've become untouchable. The big U is branded on my chest. It's a scarlet letter."

"Your apartment's the only respectable joint left open for me."

"Will I have to accommodate Oleisky?"

"I suspect so but I don't know for sure. Jesus, I'll miss your martinis" Harry said running his tongue over his upper lip.

"How does Oleisky know? What's he into?"

"That you'll have to ask Oleisky. Who knows what anybody's into for sure in this country?"

"God help it, I just love this country." Jonathan put his hand on his chest. "I am a *carioca*, a citizen of Rio, here in my heart," he said.

Eugenia was a little fearful of ragged Harry. She once confessed to Carol, "Senhor Harry is an omen and I am afraid for the Professor."

The children were brimful and amusing and as it was the custom at dinner, the family spoke in Portuguese. The children at times would correct Jonathan's pronunciation and accent and it gave Jonathan great pleasure to hear their young voices speaking Portuguese so clearly and so beautifully.

After the children were in bed and Jonathan had finished reading to them, he and Carol and Harry went out for a walk. They walked down Souza Lima to Atlântica and they walked along for a while, Carol in the center holding their arms. They made a curious trio, Jonathan in his well-tailored sports clothes, standing lean and tall, Harry in rags, tattered and seeded, seemingly disreputable, bent in his stance as an old crone. Tourists in the restaurant-cafés stared and above all they could not take their eyes off Carol for her beauty was virginal, a kind of tumescent virginity as if the first warm lolling moment were yet to be and was now beckoning, as if each time were to be the first, as if she were a miracle of ever renewing virginity, seduced, fucked, and still the white rose, thornless and waiting in her fragrance and loveliness and tenderness, waiting to be plucked.

The breeze was fresh and the waves were high and strong. There were fisherman at the shore with long surfing poles. There were fires pitched here and there on the sand and you could see wavering silhouettes of dancers. You couldn't hear the Bantu chants but you could see the pouring of rum or wine and in the morning when he would run the beach, Jonathan knew he would see washed ashore the bedraggled flowers and the remains of the frail vessels that had been sent to sea by the devout.

There were places on the beach where the young gathered for the guitar, soft and gentle, and there were the lamplights curving with the Avenue and you could see them all at once from *Postal Seis* and you could see the entire crescent of Atlântica to the shadow of Sugar Loaf itself, the lights suffusing the night, a tender radiance above each lamplight, a kind of halo.

Jonathan and Carol and Harry found seats on the outdoor terrace of the old Miramar Hotel. This was a time before the terrace had been covered with glass. Jonathan ordered three cognacs and the waiter knew he wanted the cognac *nacional* unless he wanted the very good

French cognac and then he would tell him.

They had barely settled when she came by. She seemed not quite sixteen, a frail and thin looking whore who had a large global ass and she minced her steps and rolled her ass. Harry put his hand on his crotch, squeezed, and said, "I bequeath you my cognac."

He was across the terrace and down the steps. He stopped her and she looked at him once and seemed to want to go away but he detained her. Then he shot back up on to the terrace and he said quickly, *"Vinte cruizeros novos."* Jonathan, smiling, gave him the twenty. Just then the waiter brought the three cognacs. Harry said, "I hereby renounce my bequeathal." He downed the cognac in two agitated gulps as if it were a *cafezinho* and he was off again with the whore, arm in arm.

"Don't they make a fine looking couple," Jonathan said.

"Oh, Jonathan, she looks pitiful, doesn't she? She can't be more than a child."

Jonathan said nothing. Carol went on, "And Harry, dear Harry, why must he?"

"Oh, Lord, forgive us a little trespass," Jonathan said.

"This is not amusing," Carol said softly. "I know Harry is hurting."

"I guess you're right. When you think about it it's not amusing. Why think about it then?"

"Jonathan, that's not you. You're angry. Why are you angry?"

"Shit."

"Jonathan?"

"Last night," he said. "You let me walk into it. My own wife. I know things haven't been too great but after all. Why Carol? Why the hell didn't you say something?"

"I didn't know."

"You must have had at least a premonition. Arthur and you are such good friends. He adores you. He adores you enough for you to have had at least a knowledgeable premonition, something he mentioned to set you on."

She placed her hand tenderly on his forearm. Her touch surprised him. Their eyes met. He could not remember when she had last touched him with love. She never moved toward him for an embrace and yet there was always about her an emanation of feeling, of warmth, of tenderness.

"I did not know," she said. "It was after, that is while you were with Christopher, that Arthur told me we are going home. He told me that if we stayed your life may be in danger. Jonathan, you have asked me. What is it that you are not telling me?"

He was surprised by her touch and he was moved by it. He paused. He said, "How about a good fuck?"

"You bastard," she said and tears came to her eyes.

"My life is not in danger," he said. "Let's go."

On the way back to the apartment, she broke the silence. "Jonathan, what are you thinking about? Will you tell me?"

"I was thinking," Jonathan said hugging her arm to his side, "how you can't discuss certain things because if you did they would be explained away forever."

2

Carol was in bed in the dark thinking of Harry Fox. She wanted to sleep but she was so awake that she thought she heard the light of the study go on. She heard Jonathan scuttling about, now in impotent rage, now with a stifling weariness. She knew the routine. She thought she heard at times the turning of pages and the keys of the typewriter. She sensed his pain. She knew how tangled and cavernous the nights could become for her husband, his flight from her side, the keys of the typewriter and the whiskey to control the rage and finally, inevitably, the whiskey would do its work and drown him in sleep.

Now she was thinking thoughts of Harry Fox's yellow eyes, of rooms of straightbacked cane chairs and pitted chrome bedstands, of unpainted and peeling walls crawling with roaches. Then she was seeing Harry in chromes of yellow and green and red, in lurid and unwithering lust, seeing him wet mouthed in sensuality, the way he had at dinner of licking clean his long fingers from the joints to the nails and then smiling, his teeth glistening. Then she was thinking of streams and meadows, of a light clean and of clover.

And she was thinking and thought that it was like something they used for the tonsils, that which can now be done legally, impeccably, without that terror and the furtive terror of her bus journey from New York City to that little town outside Philadelphia. All these years she had been living again and again in the nightmare from which she knew she had never truly awakened. There had been the cautious phone calls, the thing that was not said, the word that was not said directly on the phone. She would see again and again, membraneous against the darkness of her dreams, that furry little doctor with the vampire teeth who had said when he saw her, "My, my, are you sure? Are you sure you're not a virgin?"

She was terrified and yes, it was like something they used for the tonsils and she remembered she had cried out, "Oh, my baby, we are pretty no more!"

She had been seventeen then and a brilliant student who was already in her junior year at the university. Later in life she would come to think upon her precocity, think of it sadly and without self-pity, think of it almost clinically, intellectualizing it in a kind of distant way, formulating it in a language having to do with plants and flowers, that upon the stem she had ripened and fruited before the leaves appeared, that she had blossomed and flowered before the foliage, that she had become an odd and single and spurious inflorescence. So she told herself in that kind of language, told herself so she could keep the pain in the mind, outside, where it would not touch the heart.

The morning after the abortion she saw the doctor. He told her everything was fine and she should take it easy.

That afternoon she was on the bus back to New York. It was a rain-streaked and ferrous day. She was dazed with weakness and medication. She was pale and she was trying not to weep even as she was saying to herself over and over again, "I am really no more." The man in the seat next to her whom she had not noticed said, "Is something wrong? May I help you?" He had looked at her in simple and worried concern and she saw that his lips were pressed and his skin tight upon his face and she was appalled at his earnest innocence. As she turned to him there was a smirk on her wan and tear-stained face. The man was Jonathan.

He helped her as they rode along. At a stop he brought the coffee to her, she being too uncertain to descend from the bus. She learned that he was a graduate teaching associate and they were both going back to the same campus, she at Barnard and he, Columbia. At the bus depot they shared a cab back to the University and he helped her up the steps to her lodging.

She remembered how when he had passed her on campus some days later, he invited her to coffee. He asked after her health and he asked if she were studying too hard, if she were getting enough exercise. He told her he was twenty-seven years old. She was amused and pleased by his assumption of age and experience and as the conversation went on he said to her, "You strike me as a girl who is just coming out of the end of her first love affair." She was able to laugh at this and she was struck again by his assumption and his innocence.

In time, in her eighteenth year, she had fallen in love with him, had fallen in love with him strangely because the desires of her body were seemingly gone. She could not bear to have her breasts touched.

They were married the day after she graduated. She thought it was just like Jonathan that they should go to Cuba on their honeymoon. They loved Havana and they saw Hemingway's boat, the *Pilar*, in the harbor and there were sandbags and machine guns on street corners and the university was shut down and Castro was in the hills. She saw that there was a romantic awe about Jonathan, a wonder. "What better place for love than crisis?" he had joked with her.

In the shuttered hotel room even as they kissed and twined she resisted him. She tried not to. He was hurt and baffled and she could not. She tried to respond and she could not and so they fumbled and yet he held on to love with hope and tenderness and when they returned from their honeymoon he was still accepting, waiting, confident she loved him, and some nights it seemed to him to be hopeful and an awakening was about to take place and he was certain that in time she would respond to him with passion. When their first son was born after five years of marriage the doctor said to him in surprise that she had a good deal of scar tissue.

Jonathan looked at her and knew at last what she had not and he believed should have told him and what he himself should have guessed. He knew at last what the bus trip had been about. He knew but said nothing and she, she was waiting for feeling to return to her body, even tonight, like waiting through dull and humid summer days for a rain shower or like waiting for yellow eyes in a feline darkness.

CHAPTER FOUR

1

In the morning, at the edge of the shore, a score or so of jelly fish were melting in the sun. Jonathan was running the beach and having a go of it with Dom Hélder Câmara, Archbishop of Olinda and Recife. He had read in the *Jornal do Brasil* that morning that Dom Hélder supported the *Humanae Vitae*. He was supporting the Pope's stand on birth control. It was hard to believe.

Jonathan had never met Dom Hélder, but the Archbishop was one of his Brazilian heroes. Jonathan saw in his writings the preserver of simple joys and anonymous virtues. Dom Hélder was a child of Abraham, one who hoped against hope. He had once written that dead ends house the sanctity of humble love. Jonathan didn't know exactly what that meant but he liked it anyway. The line would come to him at different times and places, unsuspectingly, and Jonathan would think, dead ends house the sanctity of humble love. It was a melody of sorts.

Jonathan was thinking of Dom Hélder, the organizer of the *campesinos*, the man who preached revolution through love. Jonathan was thinking of how that would-be assassin at the last moment, quavering gun in hand, told Dom Hélder he could not kill him because of all the good the Bishop had done for mankind. And now, Jonathan was thinking, here is Dom Hélder saying that birth control is a First World plot against the population of the Third World!

Jonathan felt his breath leaving him. In his anger and disappointment he had been running fast and hard. He was saying to himself, nonsense, Dom Hélder, nonsense! Every sexual act is open to conception? Nonsense!

He was walking loosely now and his eyes were moist. He had run from Arpoador to Leme. He was remembering that it was here last week at Leme that a whale had been washed ashore. It had been a windy and sea swept day and it was too late for anyone to do anything. He was feeling sorrowful and lonely and he turned back towards Copacabana. He was walking slowly now.

He watched a game of volleyball. Then he watched the surfers. He watched the children and the beautiful women. He looked for the Columbian lady and her children but they were not there. He took a swim. He played with the waves, getting them at their crest and riding them into shore.

He was sitting on the mat thinking that there didn't seem to be anything to do but to wait. There was another time of waiting, he was thinking, and that was in Brasília. He was thinking that somehow that time in Brasília had led him here to this state of sorrow at the water's edge, to this rendezvous with jellyfish and beautiful women and children in the sun. He was going back in time.

2

The conference in Brasília was on Brazilian and American literature. Jonathan's lecture was to open the conference and it was to begin at nine in the morning. He had been unable to start until 10:40 because as it turned out the American flag on the platform was a little larger than the Brazilian. There had been diplomatic objections and a flurry. The search was on and at last two flags were found, much smaller than the originals but of equal size.

The flags were unfurled upon the platform to the good-natured applause of the audience. The TV cameras began to roll. Jonathan began with Walt Whitman's line, "Welcome Brazilian brother—thy ample place is ready." He read on to the ending lines of the poem:

. . . thou brilliant lustrous one! thou, learning well The true lesson
of a nation's light in the sky, (More shining than the cross, more
than the Crown,) The height to be superb humanity.

This greeting had stirred the audience. Jonathan felt it. They were ready. He could now get down to textual matters.

Even here on the beach on his mat alone in his state of sorrow Jonathan had to laugh in spite of himself to think that while he was lecturing to professors of literature on variant texts in Walt Whitman, the Supreme Court was meeting a couple of miles away to see to the legal transfer of power of the Presidency, the President having died in office. Jonathan learned later in the day that the proceedings of the

Court had been halted by the military entering the Chamber. The General had announced to the Justices that Congress itself was hereby suspended. The General told the Justices that a purge was now in effect to save Democracy, to save the Revolution of 1964. So now after five years the military were back in full control if ever they had been out.

Jonathan had gone down for the papers the following morning and the man at the newsstand looked at him in wonder and said of course there were no newspapers, none in the country. "Closed! Censored!" Then he offered Jonathan a newspaper and Jonathan smiled until he saw it was the sporting news.

Early that afternoon he waited at the airport. He was trying to get out of the capital. He remembered his dear friend Dr. Jorge saying that the airport was the most beautiful building in Brasília when it meant you were leaving Brasília.

Jonathan had already been stopped twice on the street for identification. He was very tired. He felt old and his walk had become a shuffle. After the third time the military police stopped him, he felt the earth wobbling on its axis.

Now at the terminal he had to deliver his passport for a security check and it was taken from him. He explained to the military police that his passport was signed by the Brazilian Second Secretary, the *segundo secretário pelo Embaixador* in Washington, that it had a quasi-diplomatic status, a *Vista official*, that he was here on an official cultural mission for the Department of State.

"Here, here, read the stamp," he had said.

"Your stamp does not have ribbons," one of the policeman had said.

And so the passport had been taken from him and he felt lost and a little concerned. He was waiting at the airport and he was looking about at the posters. There was one tattered poster whose panel on the left portrayed Soviet tanks in Prague and the people on the cobbled streets were huddled in fear and under the panel was the caption

Comunismo
Opressão e incerteza

and the panel on the right showed two school children, a healthy boy and a healthy girl, skipping hand in hand through meadows and the caption read

Democracia
Confiança no futuro

There was another poster, fresh, new, without pictures, as if it had just been put up, shining with large black letters on glossy white:

A Revolucão
De 1964
E Irreversivel
E Consolidariá
A Democracia
No Brasil

He was waiting and looking at posters. Plane after plane and flight after flight had been preempted by military and politicians or had been cancelled. The afternoon had become evening and the evening had become night and Jonathan had fallen asleep on an airport lounge and at dawn there was a plane. As he entered the plane an owled official, a weary and rumpled old man, handed him the passport.

At Galeão he took a taxi and he rode along Atlântica and in the bright wave of morning sunlight he saw the people on the sea swept beach and there were people in the cafés as they always were and the whole of the scene was as if nothing had happened. Something should have happened, Jonathan thought, should be happening, to time itself, at least a stance, a daze of time in which the world stood still and held its breath.

"Is the revolution over? Who is in? Who is out?" the cab driver asked him when he learned Jonathan was coming from Brasília. "Did the Americans make this revolution like the one of 1964?"

It was as if nothing had happened beyond gossip, as if their newspapers had not been denied them and their vote taken from them and as if the people had not been deprived of their political rights. He knew the rights of livelihood would be taken away for some of them and he knew some of them would be going to prison and some of them would be tortured. It was all as if nothing had happened. The light of normalcy was awful and he felt like a mooning adolescent. He was out of step with the world. He stood forlorn at the window of his apartment. He was gazing upon the *favela*. He drank his scotch slowly through the evening and he welcomed the night and he went to bed without dinner.

When the censored newspapers appeared late at the newsstands the following day, he began to learn a new and fearful word, *cassação*, and the verb *cassar*, and the adjective *cassado*, words accompanying the lists in the newspapers of deprivation, *cassação*, the cassation, the cancellation, the annulment, the abnegation of all political, of all civil rights for those people whose names were on the lists.

By the end of the week he was waiting for the American magazines, for *Newsweek* and *Time*, so he could get news of what was happening, happening, he thought, in my own neighborhood. To his amazement the magazines had been gone through by hand. They had been razor cut. How could this be done, he wondered, thousands of issues by hand? Every story and news item on Brazil had been cut out.

On the mat, alone and lonely, he realized that he had been living with the unvoiced question these past two days since Christopher had spoken to him. Whose list was he on? On what tattered poster had he been framed? Was his tissue being cut out by someone's razor? Had he been aborted and in what way and by whom?

Humanae Vitae, Jonathan thought. He rose from the mat to once again take on the high bouncing waves.

3

When he got back from the beach, Jonathan called Arthur and Arthur told him he had been trying to get him.

"Where were you? We've some things to talk about."

"I was in Brasília," Jonathan said, "retreating into memory. It keeps me busy."

"Oh," Arthur said. "Where shall we meet?"

"After all," Jonathan said, "the evening with the Ambassador had in a way been suspended and I agree, there are things for us to talk about."

They met for lunch at the Majorica, a *churrascaria* on Senador Vigueira. When they sat down the waiter brought olives and pâté and quail eggs and bread and butter. Jonathan and Arthur drank whiskey and then they had *linguica* and *lombo* of pork and chicken and thick french fried potatoes and *farofa*. They drank *chope*, a good draft beer, with the meal.

"That apartment of yours really didn't help matters," Arthur was saying, "not with our Brazilian friends who thought the worst. You see, the Ambassador asked me to look into your apartment and I did. Did you know when you rented it that it was owned by the wife of that cabinet minister, you know, the top aide who went into exile with Goulart, Malgahães?"

"I didn't know she was the wife of Malgahães when I rented the apartment but if I had known, if I had put two and two together and made the connection, I still would have rented it. I was happy to get it. It's been a lovely apartment."

"I assume it's been a quite exciting apartment, particularly when Malgahães returned to Brazil a few weeks ago. Jonathan, why do you think he returned?"

"Well, when the President died or when he heard about the President dying, I guess he wanted to test the waters for Goulart, don't you think? He wanted to see if it was okay for Goulart to return. As far as he's concerned, Goulart is still his President and the President of Brazil. He had to see first hand what he could get going for his old boss, to see if he couldn't get him back on a white horse."

"That's the way we read it, but what bothers me is that it's logical and makes sense. Do you think he was trying to join hands with the Maoists, with Verlande's group?"

"You're the people who ought to know," Jonathan said.

"This much is clear, anyway. He didn't count on the military take-over and he got caught by it."

"I heard he's in prison."

"If you want to call it a prison. I understand it's a very comfortable bungalow by the sea and the guards are as much waiters as they are guards."

"But still in prison. Suppose we say incarcerated. That better? The first word I got on the whole thing was when AP —God bless the American press!—Garvey, I think it was, called my apartment and told me Malgahães was back and was about to be arrested. Wanted to know what I knew. I told him I just lived there. He didn't believe me."

"The government doesn't want him incarcerated, to use your word. They've offered him an escort out of the country. He's too big to fool with. He's also one of your people, as I understand it, a scholar, big time, a cultural anthropologist, isn't he? Why doesn't he take them up on the offer and go?"

"Arthur, have you ever heard of love of country? I don't mean patriotism. I just mean he's a Brazilian and these are his people and he couldn't stand exile. That could just be another kind of prison."

"Okay," Arthur laughed, "have it your way. And the police, the phone must have come off the hook with the police, friends, reporters."

"It was a bit wild, even a little scary because the police called and wanted me to come down to the station for a talk. I refused to go. I was afraid to go. As a matter of fact, I even almost called you about it. For a while I was expecting them at the door of the apartment. I haven't heard from them since the call."

"We know," Arthur said. "We learned about that. It was wise you didn't go."

"Why the hell are you people always asking me things you already know?"

"Besides, they are probably tailing you anyway," Arthur went on, "right now, as a matter of fact, as we lunch."

"I don't believe that. You're putting me on. Who are they?"

"Believe as you will, you are tailed. Or shall I say you are under protection? That apartment of Malgahães and then Verlande, you poor innocent son of a bitch. You have taken on guilt by association. How's that for justice? Is there anything more, anything we don't know? Anything more about that apartment?"

Jonathan didn't answer. He kept on eating. Did they know about Senhor Oleisky? No, they did not know about Senhor Oleisky, he decided.

"Okay," Arthur said. "Jonathan, you know I love you. I confess not as much as I love Carol. I apologize for calling you a shit the other night. However, you have been one hell of a dabbler. What is Verlande to ex *presidente* Goulart or ex *presidente* Goulart vis a vis Malgahães to Verlande? Presumably nothing, although I have my suspicions. Yet you touch both bases in your remarkably naive way. God, I think you ought to be tailed."

"It's funny, isn't it?"

"Well, we don't know the ending yet, do we?" Arthur said.

The *Reitor* of the University came into the restaurant with his entourage of five. He gave Arthur an *abraço* and in that embrace he looked beyond Arthur's shoulder into Jonathan's eyes and Jonathan saw the *Reitor* was amused. He shook hands with Jonathan and gave him a fatherly pat on the shoulder.

"We will miss you. You will be back," he said in a warm tone and with a smile of comfort.

Arthur watched the group move to the table that had been reserved for them and as he watched, he spoke in a low and even tone, "A divine mystery. As the young bridegroom said to his fat, fat wife on their wedding night after he was sweating and grunting and clambering in frustration over her folds of flesh, 'Fanny, give me a hint, won't you, dear girl? Where's the hole?' "

"The divine mystery?"

"So far we're giving two lucrative, I mean lucrative, scholarships, so-called scholarships for Fanny's children, one at Harvard and one at Amherst. At least they're bright kids. We're still not sure, though, of the *Reitor*."

"You still can't seem to find the hole?"

"Put that way it is rather vulgar, isn't it?"

"Yes, it is," Jonathan said and paused. "Look Arthur, I want a stay of execution. Let me at least finish out the semester. I need more time."

"*Cafezinho?*"

"*Cafezinho.*"

"Cognac?"

"Why not?"

"Precisely," Arthur said. "To look at the bright side of things, we are getting your Center for the Literature of the Americas at the end of all of this. To sweeten things, we've even tossed in the funding for an English Language Lab at the *Faculdade*. That was the penultimate commitment. The Ambassador and the Minister are ready to sign for your White Dove. The Dove is just about ready to fly. It's about to soar."

"Doves don't soar," Jonathan said reaching for his cognac, "do they?"

"They don't? I could've sworn they soar. What kind of bird is it anyway if it doesn't soar?"

"I think a small bird, Arthur, one that ought to stay close to earth."

"Why, how high do they fly?"

"I gather, then, that after the penultimate we have Jonathan the Ultimate."

"Precisely. As far as the Brazilians are concerned, you're persona non grata, only they want us to take care of it. I'm sure the Ambassador went over that with you."

"I'm a political leper."

"You've become a temporary liability. Jonathan, for God's sake, be reasonable. Here you have the forces of a government looking for Verlande and you go by and say hello to him. That picture of the embrace, looked at from one particular point of view, is, I suppose, a kind of taunt. The Brazilians aren't going to deport you. That's gauche. On top of it all, you're a scholar of some standing and if they deport you, it's messy. It makes a story in the *New York Times* and the *Washington Post*. It's in the *Los Angeles Times* and it goes international in the *Trib*. The intellectuals, your colleagues, get all heated up. No, we send you. We send you in the way we're sending you."

"And if I refuse the role of Jonathan the Ultimate?"

"You know that's nonsense. You realize the Ambassador loves you like a son. He's doing all he can to protect your future and your interests. I thought he told you, or suggested in his way, that when he was in Petrópolis he was given to understand by Dr. Monteiro—"

"A son of a bitch if ever there was one," Jonathan said.

"Was given to understand there would be no White Dove unless you were taken care of expeditiously. Of course they know that if you remain in Brazil you will be taken care of anyway, one way or another. When I see the Minister next week, you will be in the States. The Ambassador can always formalize your deportation and you don't want that, not with your friend, Christopher. We must help our Brazilian friends. We must save them unpleasantness or fuss. We must close the Verlande episode in this rather informal way. Do you understand, Jonathan? You seem to be elsewhere, distracted. We must close the Verlande episode."

"I want to see the Ambassador," Jonathan said. "The evening never really ended and I have things to say that might change his mind."

"I have something for you," Arthur said, "something for you to look at."

Arthur gave a sidelong glance at the *Reitor's* somewhat distant table, reached down and opened his briefcase, took out an envelope and said, "Here's the photograph."

Jonathan unwound the string of the manila envelope. He slid the photograph out.

"Keep it flat on the table," Arthur said. "It's time you looked at it."

"*Ave, Caesar, Imperatur, Morituri te Salutant.*"

"Your Latin's good," Arthur said, "but try to understand that if the papers were not government controlled, that *abraço* would've made their front pages. It could have circulated underground, but that's not Verlande's game. He's too intelligent. You've got to give him credit. This is so much better than a propaganda shot. And it's so much simpler than killing you. I mean he's gotten rid of you, hasn't he?"

"I've got to see the Ambassador."

"I heard you the first time." Arthur waited a moment and then said, "By the way, you should also know that you were on a kidnapping hit list by another group, international, associated with the Tupermaros. I regret to inform you, at the risk of damaging your self-esteem, you were a mere sixteenth on the list."

Jonathan looked up from the photograph and smiled. "How did you make out?" he said.

"Not too badly," Arthur said and he smiled back. "It is a badge of honor, you know, a matter of prestige. I was second. I will say this for these Latin Americans, they sure as all hell appreciate culture. Why, the military attaché and the commerce attaché were ninth and tenth. The Latin Americans know what the politics of culture is all about."

"Number one?"

"Number one, of course," Arthur said.

"Yes."

"The Ambassador, it's a dreadful possibility even with all precaution. He won't be intimidated, you know."

"Arthur, may I see him, please?"

"Not unless you go to Washington," Arthur said. "The Ambassador to Guatemala had been a career officer. I think you know he once served here as Minister. He and Christopher were good friends. The Ambassador has left for Washington to attend the funeral. While he's there, he also wants to get in to see the President. He wants to talk with the President directly, that is, if he can get an appointment of sufficient length to make it worthwhile. This will probably take a couple of weeks to arrange, if it can be arranged at all."

Jonathan, sliding the photograph into the envelope, felt all at once a sadness and a hopelessness and he tried to smile and he said, "May I keep the photograph?"

"A *memento mori*? No. I'll send it to you later on."

Was there anything else that ought to be known? This is what Arthur wanted to know as he put the envelope back in his briefcase and as the waiter brought the check.

"I don't think we want anymore surprises. Does the Ambassador know what you and Verlande talked about? Did you get around to that? Is there anything, anything more we should know?"

"I'll pay the check," Jonathan said.

"No, I'll pay. I've got the business account."

"No, I insist," Jonathan said. "Let's put an end to this silliness. I insist because I want it to be all personal."

That was the way the lunch had ended and now with whiskey and ice at hand in his study, Jonathan was thinking, can it be only four o'clock in the afternoon? Are the birds singing? What am I to do with this sadness touching upon melancholy?

CHAPTER FIVE

1

Jonathan floated. Upon the shroud of his imagination there appeared an image of the mulata, long tressed and warm, leaning towards her man and they were at the window, at the white sill of repose, and they were watching languidly the geometry of light, the light of dawn upon painted buildings. "Oh, holy, holy, holy," Jonathan whispered.

Had Eugenia heard him? He sensed she had. He sensed she had entered the room.

"Professor, when you were taking lunch with Senhor Arthur, a little while back the Commission called," she said. "I did not know you have returned."

"I didn't want to disturb you, Eugenia. Where's Dona Carol?"

"Senhor Fox came by. They have gone for a walk."

"And the children?"

"*Patrono*, they will be late in school. They are preparing a play."

"Thank you, Eugenia. Will you make me more whiskey and ice?"

He looked at the large painting on the wall above the couch. He could see it through the archway of the study, blacks thick from the palette groping on the rough canvas of thinner reds. He turned from the painting. Eugenia brought the whiskey and ice and he toasted her, "*Saúde!*" Eugenia smiled shyly and backed out of the room. He sighed and dialed the Commission thinking again, can it be four o'clock in the afternoon? Four thirty? Are the birds singing?

Jorge's assistant, Dona Aila, answered the phone saying, "Oh, yes, he wants to speak to you very much, Professor Jonathan. Can you hold?"

As Jonathan waited, his thoughts wandered. Perhaps it is best to just go quietly, he was thinking. The repression and the violence was getting to him. Still, when he thought of Brazil the images that came to him were those of a sleeping giant of sunswept and ocean sprayed loins, of barefoot rhythms in the sand and breathless gyrations in the air. Above all in his mind there was the image, sacred for him, of the *mulata*. He would think of fronds of palm and tropical flowers.

Jonathan looked out on the *favela*. He could hear the traffic of the streets. He could hear the sounds of sirens. There is torture and violence in the land, he was thinking. Where are the songs of Carnival now? Still they sing the songs of Carnival. Ah yes, he was thinking when he heard the voice coming through the receiver, still they sing the songs of Carnival. "Are you there?" Dr. Jorge was saying. "Jonathan, my dear friend, are you there?"

Then he was speaking to Jorge de Ponte, the Executive Secretary of the Bicultural Commission.

"Yes, yes Jorge. I'm sorry. I was distracted, temporarily I hope."

"Dona Aila said it was you. I have been trying to get in touch with you."

"I can tell it's bad, Jorge."

"A setback, my friend," Dr. Jorge said. Then breaking into Portuguese he said, "When classes resume tomorrow, you are not to go to the University."

"What is it this time?" Jonathan said speaking Portuguese now. "A protest or strike? A hostage threat?"

"No, you are not to go to your classes anymore, not even to say good-bye. They will not have you, my dear friend."

"Who will not have me? Surely not the students?"

"Of course not your students. Your students love you. The *Reitor* has called the director of your *Faculdade*. Very political. It is certain the edict came from the Ministry of Education."

"So I really am finished. There's nothing left for me to do here. I just saw the *Reitor* today."

"No, you are not finished. A temporary setback. We'll see what we can do."

"Jorge, you are being kind. You are being a Brazilian. Worse, you are a *carioca*. You must know what's going on. Do you know everything?"

"But of course. It is very bad but it is only a very bad temporary setback. You are a friend to all Brazil. I will see what I can do."

"Jorge, is there anything you can do?"

Jonathan waited.

"I will try more. There is nothing I have been able to do. Anyone but

Verlande. It is a very bad setback."

"Thank you for trying, Jorge. I know you would have tried every-thing before calling me. I am grateful."

"Do not be despondent, my dear friend. Remember, Jonathan, God is a Brazilian. Somehow we will work something out. It is our genius to work something out at the last. That is the way Providence operates. Come to see me tomorrow or the next day. We will take out the whiskey and think."

"Yes, I will come to say good-bye."

"Only a setback," Dr. Jorge said.

"*Ciao*, Jorge. Jorge, do you think my phone is being tapped?"

"Everything is possible," Dr. Jorge laughed.

"And thanks, Jorge."

"Until tomorrow," Dr. Jorge said in English and then repeated it in Portuguese, "*Até amanha!*"

Jonathan put down the receiver, looked out the window at the *favela*, took a sip of whiskey and said, "So God is a Brazilian?"

Jorge's brother, who was General of the Army, was destined for the Presidency next go around. Jonathan knew that Jorge probably had not tried his brother. If he had, would they have found a way out of this Verlande matter? Was it really true, he wondered, that Jorge would not ask anything of his brother, would not even speak to his brother until his brother declared himself on behalf of the *abertura*, the opening up of freedom for all of Brazil? Probably so. There were people Jona-than knew who said that the General would do this when he became President, that there would be an end to terror and there would be parties, *festas*, at the airport to welcome back political exiles.

Jonathan thought the General would do this when he became Presi-dent because the General and Jorge had spent a good part of their boyhood in exile with their mother and father. They had been forced into exile during the final years of the Vargas regime and Jorge never forgot those years of exile and he worked skillfully his influence and contacts to secure refuge and work in Brazil for persecuted exiles from all over the world. Jorge, Jonathan was thinking, the journalist, the dramatist, the novelist, the critic, the raconteur, the gourmet cook, the former Brazilian cultural attaché to Paris, saver of souls and my own father confessor, I will miss you.

I will miss you very much, Jonathan thought. Yes, the General cannot be that much less than Jorge. He will open things up. Circum-ambient the world. Ring around the rosie. I will go and I will return.

He looked about the living room flooded with the light of the late afternoon hour, the bowl of fruit on the rosewood table, the lavishness of fresh flowers and leaves. He knew Eugenia was in the kitchen steaming the rice and listening for his call for more whiskey and ice.

He turned on the phonograph, the record of the Salgueiro School, samba, the songs of Carnival, and his soul was richly laden with light and fruit and flowers and leaves and aromas and song and he thought of the Columbian lady, *Do you like to dance?* Well, he was thinking, not if it's open to conception.

His thoughts were running with the whiskey. *Humanae Vitae.* Our marriage has been tender in its fashion. *But do you like to dance?* We don't say the things which must be said. I want joy. But do you like to dance? I want the eloquent and laughing joy of the soul alive, the soul animalized. Oh, dance on the hot sand under the wayward palms, he whispered. Smiling beautiful faces, he thought, oh, lovely breasts, oh, lovely asses in lovely movement and barefoot rhythms. Bra tropism.

It was almost as if his own body were turning and bending and curving. He was listening to the music and drinking whiskey and thinking I am dancing in Carnival, dancing down Avenida Presidente Vargas, an array of color and costume and sound, dancing beyond the phantasmagoria of color and costume and sound, beyond the frenzy, beyond the banners and pennants of the orgiastic, beyond the heat oh sweet sweet Black Orpheus, dancing beyond light itself to the preternatural, to the altar of the mulata princess, she to whom all motion, all nature, to whom the breath of life itself is directed. Back, back. He was back in time with a hard on.

At two in the morning she had squeezed into the space that wasn't there in the tightly packed stands on Avenida Presidente Vargas. She was wearing white jeans and she was full breasted and she was wearing a necklace of flowers and she was dark haired and beautiful and joyous and laughing. They watched the samba schools dancing by and there was the pop and ices and the lacy movement of her pink tongue curling over the strawberry ices.

They drifted along the streets and they were alone among the dancing crowds. They went on to República do Chile and to the great Cathedral that was under construction. The bribed and drunken security guards gave them a good-natured warning not to steal everything. Among the scaffolding and the sounds and the movements, there in the darkness with other lovers, they loved. She told him they were consecrating the Cathedral.

With the dawn they returned to Avenida Vargas and they watched the samba schools still going by into the summer heat of day and by noon the parade had ended. He had three matches left in his American matchbook and she took one match from it and threw it away and she kept the cover and its two matches and she kissed him good-bye. She walked away into the afternoon with her souvenir.

And there was the image of the princess and he saw her everywhere, along the avenues and in gatherings and at the window sill at dawn.

He had stood among the empty benches and he had watched her go and he had remained and her image had remained.

He turned off the music and he stood by the window looking out on the *favela* and drinking whiskey.

Then he heard the door open. He turned around to Carol and Harry and the children.

"Harry and I walked to school to meet the children. I didn't know you would be home so early, dear."

"Where was I supposed to go?" Jonathan asked. "How did school go today, boys?"

"It didn't go. You had to push it," the older boy said.

"Oh, my God! That's a terrible and ancient joke, prelapsarian," Jonathan said. "Do you think you might remember that word? It means before the Fall in the Garden of Eden."

"Hey, Dad," the younger one said, "I've been promoted in the Christmas play."

"Christmas in sunny Brazil?" Jonathan said. "Is Christmas coming upon us? Isn't this October? Or have we moved into November? Or are we really in December? What were you promoted to?"

"I'm going to be one of the three wise guys."

"You are! That's just grand!"

The children came to him for a fatherly embrace. He looked around at the apartment that had become their home and at Carol and Harry standing there and smiling and at Eugenia coming to say hello and he smelled the aroma of her wonderful cooking and there was the beginning of dusk in the apartment. He felt great, like the luckiest man in the world. His eyes filled with tears. His soul was singing. *Humanae Vitae*, he thought. He embraced his children. He formed a circle with them hand in hand.

"Let's play ring around the rosie!" Jonathan said.

"You're crazy, Dad. I'm too old!"

"Oh, Dad! Come on!"

They went around and around, faster and faster.

"All fall down!" Jonathan cried boisterously, madly. "All fall down!"

"Oh, God, stop it!"

He saw Carol shouting at him.

"Stop it, Jonathan! Stop it!"

CHAPTER SIX

1

A t about 6:30 the following morning Jonathan ran along the shore. He ran from Arpoador to Leme and he walked back. It was a magnificent morning of bright sun, high waves, a clean sky. He had worked up a good sweat and he ran into the water and he dove and he went beyond the waves to the swells of calm and he floated there awhile and then he rode the waves back in and they battered him a bit and he came back onto the shore laughing and feeling new. He dried his hands and lit a cigarette and settled on his mat. He watched two elderly men playing chess. Then he stood up and rolled his mat and went back to the apartment.

Eugenia met him at the service entrance and took the towel and mat. The children had left for school. Eugenia told him that Dona Carol had gone with them and then was going to the open market. He told Eugenia he would take *café da manhã* in the kitchen. He showered and shaved and put on his robe and came into the kitchen. Eugenia had the *Jornal* at his place. He had papaya and some pineapple and he had a coffee with boiled milk and a roll with jelly. He smoked a cigarette and read the paper beginning with the soccer news. Then he went into the bedroom and dressed.

Then he went into the study. He looked over his papers. Then he knew he had decided what to do.

First he would stop off at the Commission as was his custom before going downtown. There he would take a *cafèzinho* with Dr. Jorge. There would be music to talk about, perhaps painting, maybe the theater or literature, the new ballet company, or food and women, or politics and soccer, or maybe even about each other's work. Then he would have to bring the talk around to Verlande. He knew he must talk about Verlande. He must tell his father confessor everything, that he had been a witness to murder, no, no, that he had been more than witness. Jorge must help him by listening to him, by giving him the purgation of the telling and by giving him the wisdom of his advice, what he should do next. He would talk it all out with Jorge. More than witness, Jonathan had to say to himself over and over again. It was a mournful incantation of the soul. More than witness.

He would avoid talking to Jorge about the University. He would not compromise Jorge by telling him that he was then going to the University in spite of the injunction not to go. He carefully packed his lecture notes and his books into his briefcase. I've got to get out of memory, he was thinking, and into doing something.

"Oh, I didn't hear you come in," Jonathan said. "How was the market?"

Carol was holding long-stemmed, fresh-cut flowers in her arms.

"The cookie lady asked for you," she said. "I think you remind her of her wayward son."

"Yeah, I'm as wayward as a stranded whale, a beached whale."

"My leviathan," Carol said. Then she said, "I thought the two of us might spend the morning together, the beach or shopping, and then we might lunch leisurely along Atlântica."

"The flowers are beautiful," he said. "I've got to go to work today and now. I'll stop off to see Jorge."

"Jonathan, we have things to say to each other. There are things we must do for our return."

"Not now. I've got to go."

"Darling, you know you are not to go."

"I've got to go. What else am I going to do? This is what I know and love and am good at. At least one more lecture and a few words of farewell. At least a few words of farewell to my students. That's not asking for much, is it?"

"Your presence will create trouble. You know how fond the students are of you."

Jonathan leaned back in his desk chair.

"I've got to go. Remember how when we came here there was that terrible student strike caused, you remember, in large part by the encyclical of that U.S. Commission on Education. That report if implemented was to reform the Brazilian universities along American lines and the students were shouting cultural imperialism and Yankee go home, remember? And I walked right into it at the University. Yes, yes," Jonathan paused and smiled in the memory.

"Now as Harry would say, 'Pow! Pow!' Carol, remember when Arthur told us we were to be sent home? Yeah, they were afraid of a kidnapping, that I would be taken hostage or worse. And Dona Aila, God bless her, saying, 'You Americans are so innocent. You think it is all a game. You think nothing will happen to you.' "

"I remember," she said softly, "and so?"

"How things have changed, don't you see? I made it work down there at the *Faculdade*. I'm among friends. I'm swollen with memories. I must go down at least to say good-bye."

"Verlande," she said.

"Verlande won't bother with me anymore. Why should he?"

"My flowers will wither," Carol said. "I must put them in water."

"They're very beautiful," Jonathan said rising from his chair.

"Exotic."

"Exotic."

They paused

"There is no reason for it now," she said. "The game is over. It's time to go home. You are acting as if nothing has happened and everything has happened."

He moved toward the door with his briefcase.

"Jonathan, you don't realize how distracted you've been lately. You don't attend. It has been almost, well, eccentric. You just seem to fade in and out. You don't know what all this is doing to you."

"Images," he said with a smile.

"Images?" she said in a sad, murmuring voice. "You seem so strange."

"The not attending. The fade in and out. Images. Christ on the Cross. A white dove rising among tan brakes and green leaves. A beautiful mulata rising from her sleep in a misty dawn. Don't you understand, Carol? I said images. Like the Virgin with an armful of fresh flowers from the market or even the Virgin with one rose will do. That's what we give our lives for, images. You are absolutely irresistible with your large brown eyes and your armful of flowers. You, my dear, are an image."

"You bastard," she said and tears came into her eyes.

"Right you are," he said and he kissed her on the lips but there was no response.

2

He left the apartment and he was in the elevator and then he was saying good morning to the *porteiro*.

"Professor, it is going to make much heat today," the *porteiro* said mopping his brow with a red bandanna.

Jonathan turned on to Avenida Copacabana and there were the shops and the traffic and the people and the mosaic sidewalks. He was in love with the movement of the Avenue, *o movimento*. He remembered during his first days in Brazil on his first visit to the Commission that it had been raining, a light and warm rain, and that time and again along the crowded Avenue he had locked umbrellas with strangers.

Memories of the heart, he thought. A vertigo of the brain in heat, Carol dearest, forgive me. *Mea culpa*. Mosaic sidewalks, he thought, mosaic memories, the Mosaic tablet, patterns of remembrance, fragments and chips of remembrance. He had to have a drink. How sly and cunning the thirst has come upon me, he thought. A *chope* would be fine. Perhaps a gin and tonic would be better. The heat was all consuming. The porter was right.

He was thinking that the black and white stones of the mosaic sidewalk seemed to be rising like the swell of a wave. He thought that if he didn't get a drink soon they would rise. He turned toward Atlântica.

What am I doing, he wondered, sitting in a café, gin and tonic in hand at ten in the morning? He began to feel a bit light, a bit comfortable, a bit at home. A time to wait, he thought. They also serve who gin and wait.

Measure the time, he thought. Measure. Be careful. Ten twenty, more or less. Can't tell the window from its frame, a network of tracery, bright stones in the window of the Cathedral, love and loving. Why are the damn things never finished? he wondered. Then he remembered the day his students had smashed the windows of the Embassy.

He remembered that he had been late for class and he had taken a cab downtown instead of taking the bus and he had come up the back way and Dr. Dahglian, the Director of the *Faculdade*, said, "Professor Jonathan, I am your only student today. Go home. I tried to get you by phone but it was impossible. You Americans are on the moon and we cannot get a phone call through from downtown to Copacabana. How did you get through downtown?"

"I missed it. I came by taxi."

"The fighting is not good. The students have smashed the windows of your Embassy. They have smashed the windows even of the Embassy library. They are at the Museum of Modern Art itself. It is not good. There are two tanks in the streets. Barricades and truncheons and tear gas. They are fighting over by the bridge by the Museum. Go home. I am your only student. Why do they send your General Westmoreland here? Why do they send the General of Vietnam here? Why do they do this? Why does the Organization of American States have a meeting here of the military? Have we not enough military of our own? Why do they send Westmoreland?"

"Patience and calm, Dr. Dahglian," Jonathan said.

"Paciência e calme, hein! How you talk like a Brazilian! Are you sure your mother was not Brazilian?"

They had smashed the windows of the Embassy and Jonathan thought that this should be enough and he should go home but he was waiting and he decided to keep waiting.

When he had just come to Brazil there was that strike against that encyclical going on, the reformation of the universities along American lines. Jonathan would stand and wait in the dark anteroom of the old Portuguese exhibition hall where the *Faculdade* only recently had moved its campus. The classrooms had not been completed and the student strike seemed to be getting ugly and there were no faculty offices except for the temporary office of the Director, Dr. Dahglian, and Jonathan was upset but not discouraged to find the whole place in such a state.

He remembered standing in the dark anteroom day after day to meet with student representatives and he told them that he did not and would not interfere with their internal politics but he had come thousands of miles to talk with them about Emerson and Thoreau and Hawthorne and Melville and Whitman and Dickinson and James and Fitzgerald and Hemingway and Faulkner and Bellow and Stevens and Williams and Frost and anyone else they wanted to read and talk about and would they not want to begin? Then the third year group said they would. Then the second. Finally the fourth year representative said, "*Bem*, Professor Jonathan, we will hold classes."

They sat in folding chairs in the grand hall. Behind Jonathan was a large portable blackboard. He could see and hear the workmen on the balcony level banging away on the classrooms. The heat was intense. Occasionally the class would be joined by one or two large, very large, rats. Jonathan thought you could've put a saddle on them.

Jonathan was remembering that there in the open hall one day, about twenty-five yards from his class, some two hundred students were holding a strike meeting. They kept looking over at him, the *Americano*, but they did not interfere with him or the class and every now and then the sound of their voices would rise to an agitated pitch, to a swell above the clangor of the workmen. The student strikers were denouncing American imperialism while he was talking to his class about the world of Emily Dickinson's garden and explaining to the students of the tropics the climate of New England and its landscape and he was reading the poetry of Miss Emily. The only classes going on at the University were these American literature classes taught by an American professor and Arthur had said to him one day, with a kind of wry amusement, "While this strike lasts, the University of Brazil is in fact an American University."

"Maybe I'm doing the wrong thing," Jonathan had said.

"No," Arthur had said. "The personal equation is the strongest of all equations with the Brazilians. They must like you very much. They are giving you, *um estrangeiro*, their all in hospitality. When you think about it, there is really a delicacy to it. The decision to go to class is their decision. Yes, they must like you very much. They are very brave to go to class during the strike, particularly an American taught American literature class!"

Of niceties and delicacies, Jonathan was trying to remember, yes, it was the second strike, the one before the strike against the military of OAS and Westmoreland and the USA, when the classrooms had been completed. They had no sooner been completed when Jonathan saw the posters going up in the classrooms that still smelled of carpentry and paint. Mao communism was very strong on campus. There were anti-war posters and slogans, posters depicting American soldiers bayoneting Vietnamese children and pictures of napalm victims. In his classroom there was one of those posters of an American soldier bayonetting a Vietnamese child. One student got up from his seat and tore the poster off the wall and said, "Professor, you do not have to suffer this in your own classroom," and he returned to his seat.

"Thank you," Jonathan said trying to control the emotion in his voice. "I know it is not true and I thank you very much, my friend."

3

He made out the time, eleven-thirty. Yes, he was thinking, I came upon the scene with a flourish. Verlande might have been thinking what Arthur had said, that this professor had turned the University of Brazil into an American university. How many strikes had there been anyway? he was thinking. If I count it will keep me sober, he thought. Do I count the mini-strikes, a morning, an afternoon, a few hours, a day or two? Should I count them? he wondered. The count was blurring. He was now on martinis. The first martini had been bad, too much vermouth in spite of his injunction to the waiter, *"Martini americano, muito sêco, por favor."* He had even followed it up in English, "An American martini, very dry, please."

Now, above all, he was back to remembering the day the students had smashed the Embassy windows. The *Faculdade* was on República do Chile and the street itself looked bombed out. It was being torn up to make it a major connecting thoroughfare and across the way from the *Faculdade* the great Cathedral was under construction. Jonathan would begin and end his school day with the memory of that night of Carnival, with the image of the mulata princess. From the terrace of the *Faculdade*, the outer shell of the Cathedral looked to Jonathan like a soccer stadium, a *maracanazinho*.

He had just left Dr. Dahglian and he was wondering if he should keep waiting or if he should, as Dr. Dahglian had told him to do, go back to Copacabana. He was worried about his students and he was thinking that maybe he ought to get up to the fighting at the Embassy, the bridge, the Museum. Then in the distance, coming along the mosaic sidewalk that ran above the embankment of the thoroughfare, there they were, a large group of stragglers, a ragtail army. A breeze awoke and Jonathan felt chilled. He went back inside the building. He went to the auditorium where he held his large survey class. He remembered that he did not go up on the platform. He leaned against the edge of the apron near the entranceway and he waited. He remembered distinctly that he had checked the time and his class would normally have begun an hour ago.

They began coming in slowly, filing past him singly and in pairs and in small groups. Jonathan's heart was breaking as they came by, their spirit aloft. Some had all the weary signs of exhaustion in their faces. Many had scrapes and bruises and cuts and wounds. Some had their clothes torn and there were two or three whose shirts were just about shredded. Most tenderly for Jonathan were the eyes of those who had gotten tear-gassed. The students had known pain and fright and terror and their spirit was still aloft like streamers and banners in the breeze, so Jonathan thought. Most of them were still carrying their books and this is what made Jonathan's heart break above all. He walked up on the stage and slowly made his way to the podium.

No one had said anything. His class was about three quarters full. Then a student called out, "Professor, we are all here. Some students are not here because their parents would not let them go downtown today because of the disturbance. You may begin."

"Yes," Jonathan said, "I understand there was some trouble downtown."

There were smiles and echoes of slight, nervous laughter.

"In fact, I understand there was some fighting around the American Embassy."

There was more bodied laughter now.

"I also understand that a good many windows at the American Embassy have been smashed. God, the whole building is glass!"

There was a gathering rush of laughter.

"I know that none of you were involved. You're too grown-up. You all know that when you throw stones at glass the glass shatters."

There was a pause.

"Shame," Jonathan said stroking his forefinger at his audience, "shame, shame!"

At this the laughter rose like a wave and burst upon the shore and Jonathan knew they were released and ready. "Let's get started," he said.

He had been lecturing on the Colonial Period and he was talking about the poet Anne Bradstreet. He was trying to round out the image of the Puritan and he was explaining to the students how one sees in the poetry of Bradstreet that the Puritan woman enjoyed a good home, good furniture, loved children, loved, indeed, passionately, that the somber, dark, stereotyped portraits of the Puritans were but partial portraits, lineaments of a whole.

The Bradstreet poem he had chosen to read was "A Letter to Her Husband, Absent upon Publick Employment," a poem in which she writes of frigid cold now that her husband is away, of her need for his warmth, of the comfort that she takes "in this dead time" from her children who are images, likenesses of their father, "fruits through which thy heart I bore," of how even though he was away and she was at home, parted, "Flesh of thy flesh, bone of thy bone," they are "both but one" through their children.

Now Jonathan did not know what to do about it, his students there, responding to the sentiment and the nuances of the poem, calling aloud in Portuguese terms of endearment as he read the poem to them. Lovely, they said. How true, they said. How beautiful this love is, they said. Now what do you do about those faces of pleasure, Jonathan wondered, those students just arrived from the barricades, from the truncheons and the tear gas, from the field of tanks and shattered glass, those faces of pleasure as they sang aloud their love for this poem by this minor American poet of the seventeenth century? Now what was he to do about the tears coming into his eyes? He took a lesson from his students. He kept the tears back and he kept going.

He remembered when he left the auditorium, the Director's secretary was waiting for him at the door.

"Professor, the Director wishes to see you in his office for a moment if it is is not an inconvenience."

He followed her up the stairs and through the empty hall. He waited a moment in the anteroom and then he was shown in to Dr. Dahglian's office.

"So, Professor, we had a lecture today!"

Jonathan felt very tired.

"Good," the Director went on, "that is very good. Very, very good. We must keep the University going at every cost through every time. We must keep our work going. Strikes are ruining the universities everywhere. But you must be on your way, I suppose, so I will not detain you."

"Then?" Jonathan asked.

"That's right, ' Dr. Dahglian said, "I must be getting old. I want to tell you. We are in the process of naming rooms at this time. The classroom 23 on the right from where you hold your seminar we are naming the Camões and the lecture room 19 on the left is the Machado de Assiz. I think we might call your seminar room 21 the Mark Twain. Is this all right? Or do you think we should name it after another American writer, dead to be sure."

"Oh, yes," Jonathan laughed, dead writer to be sure. "Funny, how when you mentioned Twain there came to mind a time I was lecturing in Argentina, actually in Mendoza. I remember Jorges Luis Borges telling me that the first full-length book of fiction he read in any language was *Adventures of Huckleberry Finn*. Then he said he went on to read *Roughing It*. Twain will do splendidly. I am touched by your gesture to the literature of my country by naming a room in this great University in honor of Mark Twain."

"Between Camões and Machado!" the Director said growing in pleasure. "We will get a fine photograph or painting of your Mr. Twain. Will you help us locate one? Perhaps your Embassy?"

"My shattered Embassy," Jonathan said. "It will be my pleasure to help you locate one."

"So you had a lecture today! That is very good. *Até logo*, my friend."

"*Ciao*," Jonathan said.

4

It was one-fifteen and the waiter was asking him if he wanted lunch, a brochette with *arroz a la grega*, perhaps. Or a nice filet? He said he wanted a telephone and a bathroom first. He hugged his briefcase very tightly and moved his way inside the bar. He thought he had asked permission to use the phone on the bar counter.

"*Quem fala?*" the voice on the other end asked. It was customary to answer the phone by asking who's speaking and you're supposed to give the number you're calling because wrong numbers are quite common.

"Two, seven, twenty one, thirty three, hike!" Jonathan said.

"Oh, Jonathan, I was worried about you," Carol said.

"Verlande's pal here, Carol baby. Did you lunch, did you? I thought I'd take you up on the morning this morning, the invitation for lunch on Atlântica, you know. I'm at the Cabral waiting for that lunch. Where are you? The brochette is good here, lamb and shrimp and all that sort of stuff."

"Jonathan, are you with Dr. Jorge? Let me speak to him."

"No, never made it with old Jorge. Had to keep the stones down before they came up. Fragments of them everywhere, the whole god-damn sidewalk. Brilliant diamonds and emeralds and rubies and lamb and shrimp."

He heard Carol laughing.

"Why are you laughing?" he said. "This is serious. Besides, I need to be conveyed. I need to go to the bathroom."

"To the where?"

"Don't you hear? I've got to relieve myself."

"Great," she said. "Then order us a meal. I'll be there in a jiffy."

"All right, but be careful of those stones. They'll get you like hard snowballs. And you got to look out for the shattered glass from the windows. They're stalactites now, you know."

"Stalagmites?" she asked.

"No, stactites," he said, "or something."

He knew he was good and drunk but he also knew he was all right. At first he bounced around a bit in the bathroom hitting the sink and the wall and he was laughing. Then he finally steadied himself enough to hit the toilet bowl. He washed with cold water. He carefully checked his zipper. Then hugging his briefcase again he made it back to his table, ordered two meals and began devouring the rolls and popping in the olives and chewing the carrots the waiter had placed on the table. He was becoming anxious. Where's Carol? Would she make it in time? And Carol was there. He smiled broadly.

"I love you, Carol. You are so true," he said.

"You are so drunk," she laughed.

"Why are you laughing?" he said. "Have a carrot. They're soused, pickled, or whatever's in them."

"Only your carrot is pickled," she teased.

"I am just a little high," he said with dignity. "You have never seen me drunk. The children have never seen me drunk. Just a little high, that's all."

They had a good lunch. He thought he felt more steady and he allowed Carol to help him into the cab and he thought he was indulging her. He placed his briefcase carefully on his lap.

"República do Chile," he told the driver.

"Jonathan, you can't go to the University," she said good-naturedly. "Besides, you are in no condition."

"Come on," he said. "I just have time to make it. You're going to hear a damn good lecture. I feel bright. I feel so damn bright you're going to love every minute of it. It's going to be sensual, sexual, divine. Really divine. No shit. I mean divinity. I'm going to fly. I'm going to be the very apothecary, I mean the apotheosis, of The Lecturer. I'm going to rise."

"*É certo,*" the driver said.

"República do Chile," she repeated.

"This is the way the lecture will go. You know, I'm lecturing on Henry Adams and it's the Virgin and the Dynamo. Some chapter I'll say. Medieval times. The Virgin in Her Compassion, Love, etc. is the moving force."

"I like the etc."

"I won't say etc. Carol baby, this is just a rundown, okay? Mankind worships Her and it is this adoration that brings the princes and the paupers together to build the great expression of an adorable binding, the communal adoration, the great Cathedral of Chartres. Now measure that Virgin creating, that unifying building cathedral force against the great force of the twentieth century, okay? This force is the Dynamo, big D Dynamo. Mute, silent, well maybe a low hum. We pray to it because it's the force for our time just as the Virgin was for hers.

"Terrifying, Carol, absolutely terrifying. We pray to a machine. We pray today to nuclear force. That's primary. Well, you know what I mean. That kind of force splits the soul. The soul's just atoms, what the hell. No more love like the Virgin. No more force like that nohow. Okay? Nothing new so far. Now—why are you laughing?"

"Go on," she said. "Go on."

"Okay, you can laugh if you want to only I don't see what's so funny."

"Please do go on."

"Well, all right, but pay attention because I'm giving a test at the end of this. Now, Brazil in all of the twentieth century is different from all other nations of the West. Of course we don't measure with the Virgin here. You know that, I'm sure. Nope. It is, guess, Carol, it is? Come on, take a stab at it. Guess."

"I give up."

"Why, it is the mulata. I'm surprised at you. It's the mulata princess who's the unifying force of this exotic country in the tropics. It's she for whom the soul of the nation dances, etc. She turns our eyes to the stars."

"And who, may I ask, is the mulata princess?"

"Yes " Jonathan said, his voice beginning to trail with fatigue, his eyes lowering, the words sounding softer and softer, moving more and more into a murmur. "The Dynamo has not won the soul of Brazil. The new Cathedral has the shell of a *futebol* stadium. It's soccer, Carol, pure soccer. Nobody plays it like the Brazilians. The mulata princess is the Holy of that shell. Maybe not a shell. Maybe a skull. We revolutionize and have religion and politics under a skull.

"Not base but of the spirit, of the good old divine human spirit. The soul of Brazil is not metallic. The shiny electrodes of torture, the parrot's perch—all instruments of the Dynamo. They can't win. Brazil hasn't lost yet, baby. The world cup, baby. Carol baby. Where am I? Why are you smiling?"

She cuddled his head at her breast. She kissed his forehead. He remembered they had been riding the beautiful *atêrro* into the city when he kind of fell asleep and he thought he heard her say, "All right, driver, you may turn around now."

He was too tired to care. When he awoke they were back in Copacabana. They were rising rapidly out of the underpass and on to the corner of Souza Lima and Rua Pompeia.

He was in bed and she was at the edge of the bed. He moaned.

"Hush," she said gently.

"I have betrayed my students."

"Hush. Sleep, my darling."

"I have betrayed my students. They came from the barricades, from the tear gas and the blows of the truncheon. And I couldn't make it from the Cabral. Isn't that funny?"

"You were not to go," she said.

"I have let them down. I have betrayed them. I will try to sleep now. I'm very tired. Thank you, Carol, Carol dearest."

He did not remember sleeping. When his eyes opened, the evening light was in the bedroom. He blinked. I am still alive, he thought.

CHAPTER SEVEN

1

Professor Jonathan lay in bed in the evening light thinking of lines from Sir Thomas Browne. From *Hydriotaphia* he remembered, "The great Antiquity *America* lay buried for a thousand years; and a large part of the earth is still in the Urne unto us." The doorbell chimed. "The Urne unto us," he repeated to himself. Chimes and a voice. What a fine coincidence, he thought, thinking of Sir Thomas Browne and now Oleisky at the door. It had to be Oleisky. He knew it in his bones.

They were there. Jonathan divined and finally heard the voices of Oleisky, the barefoot Jeremiadic flailer of Philistines, of Harry, the Historian of Pow, of Carol, the Virgin of the Unborn Child. Sweet Carol and her scar tissue, Jonathan thought. Sweet, lovely, large brown-eyed, tender-eyed, oh Carol, luminous eyes, eyes of the soul.

He wondered if he were still high. He did not think so. His stomach was not good, but his head felt clear. Although he had stumbled out of bed, he was standing aright. He splashed cold water on his face and neck and he combed his hair. He slipped into a pair of tans. He didn't bother with a shirt or shoes and he made his way to the living room and on the way he saw the look of terror on Eugenia's face as she passed him in the corridor.

"Eugenia what is wrong?"

"It is not the Senhor of Good End," she hurriedly said and she was gone into the children's room.

So there they were.

"Senhor Oleisky, how happy I am to see you," Jonathan said extending his hand.

"I am sorry if we have roused you," Senhor Oleisky said. "Your wife said you were asleep."

" 'The Huntsmen are up in *America,* and they are already past their first sleep in Persia,' " Jonathan said.

"*Garden of Cyrus,*" Olesiky said. "True?"

"Yes, it's from the *Garden of Cyrus.* I don't believe it. How many lovers of Sir Thomas Browne are left in this world?"

Afterward, he knew, Carol would say, "You were manicky. Absolutely manicky."

"And have we all met?" Jonathan said. "Please sit down."

That is what she will say afterward, he thought. He saw at once there was a restless air about her, restless more than surprised or confused, and he watched her take her first cigarette in months.

"I was telling Carol," Harry was saying, "when you—"

"God, talking about Sir Thomas Browne in Brazil," Jonathan said interrupting.

"Brazil is a surrealistic country," Harry said. "The only surprise is if there is no surprise."

"I was reading in the *Jornal* only yesterday," Senhor Oleisky said, "about a police chief who was commenting, I forget the intersection, I think maybe in Flamengo, or was it Laranjeiras? It was Botafogo. He was talking about the numerous accidents which occur at this certain intersection. He said, 'The problem is that this is the corner where two parallel streets meet.' "

"Pow!" Harry said. "See!"

Oh, Carol will have something to say afterward all right, Jonathan was thinking. I can see by the nervous way she's handling that cigarette. The cough, a very light, polite child's cough.

"I see," Jonathan said, "two parallel streets with an endless traffic of Volkswagen beetles, a honking beach-side heaven, a screeching burn of tires, exhaustion. I feel for that police chief."

"They meet at the corner, pow!" Harry said.

Jonathan stared at Harry unbelievingly. Then after a moment he said, "I was going to the University today but I'm afraid I didn't make it."

There was a quiet space, a long and uneasy pause.

"He was not to go, of course," Carol said with some hesitation. She was glancing at Senhor Oleisky.

"That's all right. Senhor Oleisky knows everything. He knows who you are," Harry said.

"But we don't know who you are" Jonathan said. "Your English, for example, is more British than American and yet neither."

"Senhor Oleisky also speaks French, Italian, a true Spanish. His superb, one might almost say native, Portuguese you can judge for yourself," Harry said with great satisfaction. "He speaks broken pieces of German. He speaks Hebrew, and of all things, Roumanian. I cannot vouch for either his Hebrew or his Roumanian."

"I gather then you are not Brazilian," Jonathan said.

"I come from the old country," Senhor Oleisky said. "I was it seems always an orphan, that is until I grew up. You cannot be a grownup orphan, can you?" he smiled. Then he went on, "I know I am a Jew and I know my parents as of a memory too dim. They were murdered in Auschwitz."

Jonathan was seeing Carol and he could see that as she was listening to Oleisky, her restlessness had given way to something that was for a moment almost beatific. Her eyes shone. How beautiful she is, Jonathan thought. She went to Senhor Oleisky. She swayed toward him and kissed him on the forehead.

"I hope you do not mind," she said. Then she smiled and said, "Would anybody like a drink?"

Scar tissue, Jonathan was thinking, a kiss for the world's victims.

"You see to hunt Nazis," Harry was going on without surprise. "That is why he originally came to Brazil."

Senhor Oleisky was not listening. He was looking wonderingly at Carol. "We are so fast a friend?" he said.

"So fast a friend," she said. "And now a drink? Jonathan, dear, will you do the honors?"

"I'd be glad to do the honors," he said trying to understand Carol. Then he thought, she is going to carry it off splendidly after all. "I should have told you," he would say afterward, "Harry was the contact for the apartment and a condition had been placed upon it."

"Had they told you why at the time? Had they told you what the apartment held?"

"No, they had not told me. You see, I thought it unlikely that Oleisky would have to be, well, accommodated. I think that's the word. But you were so great this evening, Carol. You were superbly great."

"The truth is, darling, I thought you were manicky at first. Absolutely manicky. Then you gained control. Were you still high? Are you high now?"

"I attended," Jonathan said proudly. "By God, I attended."

2

"There is a safe in this apartment you do not know about. I have come for that safe," Oleisky said. "I hope my interrupting you is not too inconvenient."

Senhor Oleisky was sipping tea and eating a torte. Harry and Carol were having martinis. Jonathan was drinking beer. Under Eugenia's care, the children were taking early dinner in the kitchen.

Jonathan was trying to understand and believe that what was taking place was in fact really taking place. He knew he was not back in the bedroom dreaming the whole thing up. He was having trouble understanding and believing that he was in this thing for real. What safe? He was a professor of American literature, an academic, and Verlande and Oleisky and Malgahães, politics and revolution, this was a fable and that he was in it constituted, well, he thought, made another fable. There was another safe in the apartment, one he didn't know about. Jesus Christ!

The conversation, casual and amiable, had shifted to some seriousness. Senhor Oleisky, speaking of the press of time, that he must be gone by seven, had risen. Barefoot, in his tattered clothes, his cloth of history, Jonathan thought, Oleisky had risen ever so formally. "Time's press," he said with regret.

Harry and Carol and Jonathan, in single file and in silence, followed Oleisky into the bedroom. Oleisky knew exactly where the safe was. Carol removed some hangings laying the clothes on the bed so that Oleisky could have some room as he sat on the slightly elevated platform of the closet.

"I know the combination of your safe, but I do not have the key with me," Oleisky said. "There is the other in the back of the safe you use. The back metal, the wall of your safe can be released and there we find the other."

"The other?" Carol asked.

"Safe," Oleisky said. "The second safe."

"Oh," Carol said, "the second safe."

"Yes, naturally," Oleisky said. "We will now bring the safe into being. But first, yes, the duplicate key."

Jonathan detached the key from his key ring. The combination was dialed and now the key was turned and Carol removed the passports and jewelry from the safe.

"Yes, so simple and natural," Senhor Oleisky said as he took a pitted tool from his jacket pocket, a dull, thin blade with a two pronged curve at the end. He seemed to fit the prong into a seam, a scarcely noticeable joint where the roof of the safe seemed to meet the rear or panel wall. The panel was released by the tool and shot upwards. There stood the second safe. Senhor Oleisky returned the key to Jonathan and he took another key from his jacket pocket and he turned it before dialing the combination of the safe that was there where a wall should have been.

There was a stuffing of American bills inside, not a neat piling or a wrapping or a tabbing. It was as if the one hundred dollar denominations had been carelessly thrown in, clearly a very large sum of money, thousands upon thousands, or so it seemed to Jonathan, and he smiled.

"Pow," Harry said softly.

"Yes, this is a performance, is it not?" Senhor Oleisky said. "If they were *cruzeiros*, the performance would be ruined. What would they be worth? So the prop I need at present, if you would not mind, Dona Carol, ah, but you are frightened?"

"No, I am all right," Carol said. "What do you need?"

"If you would not mind, a large paper bag, like from the *supermarcado*, and if it is a little soiled, so much the better."

Jonathan knew Carol was very upset, but she was carrying it off. And why should she not be frightened? he thought. Had he not implicated her without her knowing, without her consent?

"You bastard!" she would say to him later through tears.

Senhor Oleisky said lightheartedly, "You are all my accomplices." Then he said, "I regret more than I say that this must be so."

He asked for a second bag as a precautionary lining for the other bag. He tossed the money into the bag with the carelessness and ease with which it must have gone into the safe.

There was still time for another cup of tea for Senhor Oleisky and Jonathan realized that Harry had never let go of his martini glass through the whole thing. Quite something, Jonathan thought.

"Senhor Oleisky," he said once they were back in the living room, "why now?"

"I will tell you. In my heart I am sorry you are leaving shortly. I am more than sorry to see you go. The police will not be sorry. That is why now. The DOPS will not be sorry. That is why now. Agents will be over this apartment, every inch, the moment you leave. They are sharks. They are devil fish."

"Will they confiscate the apartment when we leave? Won't they do that?"

"I do not think they will do that. I do not think they will confiscate property. I do not think they will do any damage. It would be a bad precedent in a country where you may be in one day and out the next and back in on the third day. Also, the wife of Senhor Malgahães is very well connected through family with the foreign office."

"Where is she now?" Carol asked.

"With family," Senhor Oleisky laughed. "In the States, in St. Louis visiting family. She has family there, I think his in-laws. Maybe that is why he is anti-American."

"But aren't we, Senhor Oleisky, aren't we spotted now as we sit here?" Jonathan said.

"You are, on and off. Surely your Embassy has said so to you. Is that lovely man, Arthur, your cultural attaché? Or CIA? Soon you will be watched tighter. But I am so well known, so familiar a beggar of Copacabana with a soiled bag, that I go unnoticed, how do you say, someone who looks in garbage cans, a rummager? I am a rummager. No one sees me. I am invisible. I am so familiar I am invisible. I go by the service entrance. I go by the stairs. And it is really time now."

"Wait," Jonathan said anxiously, "Malgahães? Something?"

"You have been so kind," he said looking at Carol, "that I will tell you something. You must know that Malgahães came back to test the reaction, yes? The government seemed on the verge of collapse. What you may not know is that when you saw the late departed not lamented President, ten days, you might notice if you can see those newsreels again, ten days there were pictures of him in the newsreels and papers, never television except file tape, the President sitting at the table with his cabinet or in other conferences before he died, but he was already dead those ten days. You never saw his lips moving. You saw sometimes a fixed smile but never a laugh. The government needed time. He was actually dead. Imagine! The body was treated and propped at the conference table. The military had to have those ten days. Collapse was imminent with the death of *o Presidente*. The power needed time to generate, if that is the proper English word, and it got time with a dead body. Do you not hear the flapping wings of the vulture?"

They listened and then they heard the laughter of the children coming from the kitchen and they heard the laughter of Eugenia.

"And Malgahães came back to test the reaction, but the power had been generated," Senhor Oleisky said. "As you must know, just as he returned to feel if the air might not be clear for Goulart's return, the act was invoked suspending the Congress. The Judiciary was warned, or shall I say, advised."

"And Malgahães was arrested and imprisoned. That I know," Jonathan said.

"A homelike and comfortable quarters he has, a notable political prisoner. He swims and fishes every day. He is, you see, at the water's edge. It is very funny, this special lodging of his, this bungalow, because he is a legendary swimmer, a swimmer of great strength. I think he can do the bay. Maybe he can do the English Channel. Holding him is such an embarrassment for this government in the world that I think they want to see him just swim away like a dolphin. They offer him exit from the country you know," Oleisky laughed. "Now I must go. It is time."

"Too soon," Jonathan said. "Christ, we must talk. We haven't even spoken about Sir Thomas Browne! At least a word."

They all moved toward the service entrance.

"A word?"

"Yes," Jonathan said.

"A word of Browne's then. 'All things began in order, so shall they end and so shall they begin again.' "

"Great. You're a seventeenth-century man," Jonathan said, holding him at the door.

"I think in one way maybe this is so, that I am seventeenth century. I think that I have seen enough to feel like Browne that it is late in human life, in the history of the planet. I think it odd in this most odd world that we should meet on Browne. That is a hope. But you are a man of letters, a scholar. There is history." Senhor Oleisky took Jonathan fondly by the arm. "I have seen the sequence of forces. I have seen the dialectics, Marxian, Hegelian, what have you. What do you want to buy? I have seen Clio, the Muse of History, turned into a storekeeper measuring weights. Cliometrics. But this I believe, in all that I have seen, in all that your Sir Thomas, our Sir Thomas, has taught me. This I believe, that truth is not dialectical, that truth is essentially of a non-dialectical character, that is the truth that interests me. You understand what I mean, no?"

"I understand and so I then don't understand how you can be a revolutionary," Jonathan said. "Senhor Oleisky, we are first getting started now. Please don't go yet."

"I must," Oleisky said. He embraced Carol. He looked at Harry and said, "You I will see."

He smiled sadly at Jonathan. "Perhaps we will meet again. It will be a joyous occasion, I am sure," he said and then holding the soiled bag against his chest, he began the six floor decline of steps.

He turned a moment, smiled a bit grimly this time and said, "Do not be alarmed. I must talk aloud. It is my guise, a part of it, of my guile. Man of letters, I am putting on the antic disposition. I must perform." And at the landing below he began and Jonathan knew it was for his benefit the Latin, the strong voice solemnly cadenced, *Ipsa sui pretium virtus sibi.*

"What is he saying?" Carol asked softly.

"Virtue is her own reward," Jonathan said. "Sir Thomas Browne tells us, and old Oleisky knows it, that that's a cold principle."

"It sure as all hell is, Professor," Harry said and startled them in the saying. "Isn't he a remarkable man? He's going to help me find her?"

"Her?" Jonathan asked.

"My wife," he said squeezing his genitals. "She was seventeen."

"Yes," Jonathan said looking at Carol, "and there goes one revolution in a soiled sack."

3

Carol was not amused. Harold Garvey from Associated Press had called as she was preparing for bed. Jonathan had answered the call and spoke to him. He came into the bedroom and he was brimming over. He reminded Carol that Garvey was the same reporter who had called when Malgahães had returned from exile. "You know, the one who told us Malgahães was going to be arrested and he wanted to know if we knew where he was."

She was putting lotion on her legs. She was trying to stay calm while he was luxuriating in his telling of his conversation with Garvey, in the grandness, she was thinking, of his emotions, as if he were to be part of, oh, the whole great thing whatever that is and she thought it is Cuba all over again, as if the years had not intervened, the children, the career, and on and on. To the hills he would go if he could, she thought. When will he grow up? she wondered.

"That goddamn Oleisky," he was laughing, "can you imagine? Garvey told me that at seven o'clock this evening, Malgahães, that legendary swimmer by the account of our friend Oleisky, he walked out of his bungalow by the sea for an evening swim and he swam into the sunset. And he swam, Garvey said, and he swam. Garvey didn't know if he did the bay or had a boat waiting or if the government gave a shit anyway and if the guards just looked the other way to get rid of the embarrassment or what."

Jonathan, sipping scotch, was going on while Carol, applying lotion to her breasts, her hands circling her breasts, was listening and waiting.

"It's turned into a great day," Jonathan said. "Didn't look too promising this morning but it's been a fine day. Did I know anything about it, Garvey wanted to know. Did I? Did I? In strictest confidence, of course. Would even go off the record. I told him nothing. That goddamn Oleisky! I love that seventeenth-century bastard!"

"And what does Garvey think?" she said at last as she buttoned her pajama top.

"What Garvey thinks I don't think is so," Jonathan said. "He thinks Malgahães is seeking Verlande. Seeking is the way he put it."

"Verlande. Malgahães. You. Who knows?" she said.

She put down the tube of lotion on the night table. She tried to smile.

"Malgahães could be more left than we think, but he wouldn't fool around with the kind of Chinese communism of a Verlande, would he? Although the communists and Goulart probably had some pleasant times together, I don't think so."

"Perhaps we'll never know," she said indifferently. Then she said, "You were a mark from the beginning, Jonathan. Now that I know how we got this apartment, and got it for this low rent at that, I wonder how Harry could have done this to us. How could he? Does he believe that dear Senhor Oleisky will find him his seventeen-year-old jewel as a reward? Is this why he did this to us? I don't mean to be nasty. I love Harry. I think I do need some sleep."

"You're going riot," he said. "It's your imagination that's thinking."

"Lights, please," she said.

"Yes," he said. "I'll finish my drink. I'll have another one in the study."

"You didn't have enough today? Sorry for being a bitch about it. You are celebrating, though, aren't you?" she said and she turned away with closed eyes.

In the middle of the night, he awoke and he knew that she was weeping. He turned toward her and embraced her. A swift, damp breeze came into the room.

"Shall I close the window a little?" he said. "I think we'll be having rain before morning."

"You were having such a good time, you and Harry, like little boys in a mud pile." Her voice was muffled.

"I suppose so," he said. "Do you hear that, the tires on the pavement? It's raining."

He went to the window.

"It's coming down straight—"

"And ever so gentle," she said. "How beautiful! I can smell the rain now. It's as if I've been waiting a long, long day for the rain and now at last."

"The streets are glistening," he said. "Come on over to the window? God, the glistening of the pavement, the darkness, the rain, the feel of the air,—"

"Yes, well you better come away from the window," she said.

"Darling, I don't know if I can go back with you," he found himself saying. "It's too soon. Too sudden and soon. Things are first beginning to happen. I have a premonition about it. Things are first beginning to happen and I've got a part to play, something to do and something to happen."

He could see now that she was sitting up in bed. She stretched for the box of tissues. She was dabbing her eyes and she blew her nose.

Then he heard the low quaver of despair and anger in her voice: "That finally is it. I have just about had it. I'm afraid to let you walk the streets with your own sons. I fear for their safety. I think of poor Captain Spears and of his child and I am afraid. I don't want you to, no, I won't allow you to walk the streets with them, to take them to the beach, to take them to school, to take them for ice cream. I am afraid for them and you cannot even take them for ice cream, as innocent and as natural as that is, no! I will not allow it. And you say too soon!"

She was sobbing. He came to her to embrace her, to protest, to comfort. She would have none of it.

He lay there, his eyes closed deep into the night unable to sleep. The two of us, the old sadness, he was thinking. And then it came like a refrain and he puzzled over it. Dead ends house the sanctity of humble love. What did it mean? He went into sleep at last mumbling it as if it were a thought to taste. Dead ends house the sanctity of humble love.

CHAPTER EIGHT

1

D r. Jorge gulped the rest of his *cafèzinho*. Then he leaned back, offered Jonathan a cigarette, and took one for himself.

"This is precisely what makes men like Verlande so dangerous," Dr. Jorge said. "Their behavior conforms to their ideals. There is not one centimeter of deviation. There is no void, no terror of space in their moral consistency. This type of revolutionary is, inevitably, logic demands, the apostle of violence."

Jonathan wandered over to the wide window and looked out into the sunlight. From the sixth floor of the Commission's office he could see the jutting third floor terrace below with its soft nude statuary and beyond the terrace he could see a verandah below and in the garden beyond there was a cluster of palms and beyond the palms there was the play yard of the Hebrew school where boys wearing skullcaps were shooting basketballs.

"Now the good Dom Hélder at home in Recife does not believe, Jorge, there is a just violence. Our Archbishop believes in revolution through peace. I remember that lovely saying of his, 'Be revolutionary like the gospel, but without wounding love.' How can that be, Jorge? I guess you're right. It's a question of moral coherence."

"There is a smugness about the phrase, moral coherence, isn't there?" Jorge said.

"Perhaps there is less so for an American ear than a Brazilian ear. You organize the *campesinos* and they become a power and you tell them revolution through peace. But the regime cannot allow that power of the *campesinos*. It is a very dangerous power for the regime and the regime fires upon them and love lies a-bleeding. Love is wounded and you have wrought the guerrilla, the *guerrilheiro*. His creation is the ultimate logic. He is the tiger of your consistency, the lion of your morality. Peace is dead."

"Yes, yes. Verlande now, he was trained by the Jesuits, you know. In São Paulo. He was to be a Jesuit. It was wonderful that he had you brought to the unfinished Cathedral for your meeting. What a sense of things! I must admire his imagination. He has the touch of a poet."

"Ignatius of Loyola. Soldiers of Christ," Jonathan said.

"A Manichean sensibility, a world of light and a world of darkness, of good and of evil, the imagination of extremes, of fascists and revolutionaries. The imagination of war, of combat."

"For a while I thought of him as a soft and gentle man, a scholarly type almost," Jonathan said. "But not at first and not afterward."

What do you think, hey Professor? Verlande had said.

"The jeep, mounted with a machine gun stood at the midpoint of what is to be the nave," Jonathan said to Jorge. "The foreman was prostrate before the scaffolding of the altar. His face was swollen and bruised. He was sobbing and his body was shaking. The laborers were standing around or sitting on their haunches and they were laughing and smiling. The *guerrilheiros*, there were five of them, were chatting with the laborers and passing out cigarettes and there was Verlande in the dim, interior sunlight. That light had taken its color not from heaven, Jorge, but from the dust and the rock and the soil and the plaster of labor and the earth.

" 'See that armchair elevated on the altar,' Verlande said to me. He was pointing to the altar, his arm fully extended. 'Yes, there where this foreman has enthroned himself,' he said to me. 'As if he were God, you understand,' he said. 'A vasselage. The *favelados* are his slaves. They must pay tribute to him or they will not have work. They will be told to starve. This is the lowest of scum. We have not yet decided whether to kill the foreman. To kill him would be the greater lesson than a mere beating. It would be instructive for these *favelados*. The boss they do not see or I would kill him. It has to be concrete. Lessons have to be visible, hey Professor? The *favelados* will understand the lesson. They are now our friends. Yes, I think we will kill this blasphemous, self-styled god of the altar. Then we will build the Cathedral with our foreman. What do you think, hey Professor?' Just like that Jorge. Mad insane and just like that."

Jonathan trembled even now at the window, even as he was speaking to Jorge. He had trembled at the first words of Verlande. The day after he had been assaulted in the men's room, his student who had kicked him and begged forgiveness, had come up to him as he was getting out of class. He took him by the arm and walked him hurriedly across the thoroughfare. They moved through the rubble of construction into a cave-like opening and inside into the shell of the Cathedral and down what was to be the nave to the jeep with its mounted machine gun. And there was Verlande in battle fatigues and without introduction, without the ado of any words, Verlande pointed and said, "See that armchair elevated on the altar?"

From the window of Dr. Jorge's office, Jonathan could see that the children in skullcaps had warmed up. They had become two basketball teams and they were charging up and down the court haphazardly and Jonathan saw someone sink a basket off the wooden backboard.

What do you think, hey Professor? Life and death just like that. Thumbs up, thumbs down. The Coliseum. He thought of Oleisky and of his story of the dead President propped up at the conference table. He sighed. He came away from the window with tears in his eyes.

"Are you all right?" Jorge was saying breaking the silence. "Jonathan, the morning is young."

"I have trouble attending," Jonathan said.

"Attending? Ah, distraction my friend, that is natural because you have sorrow."

"I float in time as if I have no chronology."

"All this talk of Verlande in the tropical country. It drives one mad. But since you can be sure that in Brazil everything will come in its own time, you do not need a personal chronology," Jorge said with a smile. "That is the art of relaxing."

"I feel coaxed," Jonathan laughed. "I feel so coaxed I will take a gin. As early as it is here, I know it is the proper time for cocktails somewhere in the world."

"I will give you a whiskey."

"No."

"I will give you a tonic then of gin."

As Jorge went to the bar, Jonathan returned to the window. He was watching the game. Then Jorge joined him.

"We are all children of Abraham," Jorge said. He handed Jonathan the gin and tonic and looked out on the children. "Yes," he said, "Brazil is New Christian. That was our settlement from Portugal. We were Old Jews and then we were New Christian."

"And now?"

"Just look at us," Jorge laughed, "a syncretic people, from Buddha to Voodoo all in one without a contradiction."

"That's your genius, your humanity, your incredible charm."

"But of course!" Jorge said and laughed again.

They stood by the window now in silence watching the game.

What do you think, hey Professor? Jonathan was remembering.

At first he had been totally confused, made stupid almost by this question. The question appeared to be neither rhetorical nor mocking. It was a question to be studied before an answer was to be given. The question and the event itself, the circumstances under which they had met, had thrown him so off-guard that *his* circumstances, why he was there to see Verlande after having been clubbed and kicked, why he had been marked by Verlande for deportation, the questions and circumstances he had planned for Verlande were now at once totally subsumed by Verlande. They were subsumed by Verlande's presence, by Verlande's circumstances, by Verlande's momentous question.

Well, Jonathan thought, as the Ambassador had said in his toss of Hemingway, What you win in Brooklyn, you lose in Chicago.

Jonathan was remembering. "This Cathedral is the vestibule to Hell," Verlande had said angrily. He had said it after the Luger had jammed. Lugers, he had explained to Jonathan, were never supposed to jam.

Jonathan looked at Jorge's wise, round face, his owl-shaped eyes, and he knew he was now finally going to talk about it, to say something to Jorge.

They had moved from the window and Jonathan told Dr. Jorge that he must speak a little bit more about Verlande, of that meeting in the shell of the Cathedral.

"Cathedral? A *futebol* stadium or an Aztec temple," Jorge laughed. "Yes, I will be your priestly psychiatrist."

"Princely psychologist," Jonathan said.

"Then I will charge you less," Dr. Jorge said.

"This then I suppose is my farewell to you until next time. I leave you with my burden."

"I accept your burden. I accept it gladly."

Dr. Jorge was sitting at his desk in that small office that was piled high with papers and books. The bookshelves on the walls were crammed. The top file drawers of the cabinets were slightly open with the overflow of paper, sheaves of paper. The typewriter by his desk had a sheet in the roller. There was a Jenner seascape in blue on the wall above the couch. Jonathan sat on the couch tinkering with the lime in his gin and tonic.

"Now Jorge, what it is really important to understand and what I had not understood is that there is no center to this revolutionary movement, to this National Liberation Front. There is no formal organization. There is rather a gathering of forces, a mobilization. It's a matter of action leading to action, violence to violence as the cells, that's what Verlande calls them, metastasize. Each cell consists of five or six people. They are mobile. They strike at banks. They strike at foremen and overseers and landlords. They shoot and dynamite the visible. Each cell acts independently on its own. Their targets must be visible because the purpose of this terror is to destabilize the government, to force the government into actions of reprisal that will lead to political consciousness, actions that will make those outside the system, the millions of marginals, politically aware of the system.

"Verlande told me that the factory workers, the laborers, the *favelados*—for them you must create the act as example. They at first do not think of a system that is oppressive and responsible for oppression. It is a foreman they think of, an overseer, a landowner. Not a system. Too early. At this point Verlande is not interested in the political development of labor, in pamphlet writing and meetings—no, Jorge.

"So the interest is in cells and in new cells arising, new cells being formed to kidnap, to, well, dispense terror, your neighborhood apothecary. They are loosely connected, multiplying, floating, more and more urban. You know for yourself, Jorge, that there's a great floating population of *guerrilheiros* in the big cities, in São Paulo, in Rio, in Recife. More than half the population in São Paulo, Jorge, think of the enormity of it, have no documents, no official identity, no address.

"This is no rural warfare Jorge. This is no Regis Debray or Che Guevarra. Verlande is in the cities. They are not coming from the countryside to surround the cities. They are in the cities. The warfare is urban. The horse is Trojan. Revolutionaries walk among the undocumented, among the officially unidentified and they hide among them when they must. The ordinary police of the streets do not want trouble. They do not want to die for this regime. Whenever they can look the other way they do.

"And now Verlande, himself, Jorge. I come to my complicity for which I must make confession. You must forgive my long way around this thing, but you've got to get what was working on me."

"Would you care for another gin and tonic?" Jorge said.

"Thank you, no, Jorge. I want to do this sober. Remember that time he was caught? They had him on the parrot perch. It hangs in what they call the violet room. They had him on that iron bar with his hands tied over his knees and they put the electrode to him. He was screaming. 'Hear the Polly scream,' they said. 'Does the Polly want water? Does the Polly want a cracker? Let us hear the music of the Polly.' I didn't ask him. I didn't know you'd say Polly here and then I thought while he was telling me this, must be the influence of Walt Disney. Funny, isn't it? Polly want a cracker and they put the electrode to him again and again.

"Verlande told me they all had their turn at him one way or another, the São Paulo army, the political police, the Rio de Janeiro army, naval intelligence, the army secret service. He showed me the wrinkled grape purple skin of his ankles and the burned serrated flesh on the thigh of his left leg. Finally they had to send him to the hospital to keep him alive."

"It was a DOPS hospital, wasn't it? I have heard," Jorge said.

"Yes it was, a DOPS hospital, smart and gleamingly modern. The doctor in his stainless white coat noted on the chart as he spoke to the nurse, 'Nurse, what was it? Electric shock? What stage?'

"They treated him with gentleness, skill, and care. Finally one sunlit day at his bedside, the doctor smiling with satisfaction, said to the agent of the DOPS, 'We have the patient in good shape. He is fit to be returned to torture.'

"The doctor and the agent shook hands. 'Thank you, doctor. You have done wonders,' the agent said."

2

"He had skirted the edges of geometry and luminosity," Jonathan went on, "I suppose seeking a cleanly ordered world. He told me that as a youth he had sought the harmony of the good. He told me he had sought an architecture for the soul. I'm not being fancy about this. I'm using pretty much the words he used. You're right about that touch of the poet in him. There was about him the melodrama of the Gothic, the conflict between absolute good and absolute evil. You're right again, Jorge, a Manichean sensibility.

"He had been babysitting his friend's apartment in São Paulo when he underwent a moral crisis. He had been agonizing over the callings that he felt were drawing him to a life in the priesthood when his friend returned unexpectedly from the Amazon. He had the supervision of a road crew there. He came up to the apartment with three prostitutes. 'This one is for the snake bite I have received and this one is for the gigantic mosquitoes and that one, with the great tits, is for protection from the poisoned darts I will yet receive from the *indios*,' his friend had said.

"He did not spend the night in the apartment. I see him, Jorge, walking the streets of São Paulo that night. I see him sleeping on the grass in the park. I see him lingering, huddled in the doorway of the apartment house waiting for dawn, stretching out the rheumatic feel of his body in the chill dawn, saved from the evil women, saved from the prostitutes, murmuring upon the stickiness, the crust of his underwear, the nightly emission of the dream, the dream of a beautiful nude mulata with a long-stemmed rose in her hand, smiling with pity and compassion.

"He returned to the apartment. The prostitutes were having coffee in the living room. They offered him coffee. They were concerned over the plight of one of them who had to be home to feed her children. She finally appealed to Verlande. She said to him. 'I have to go now. I have to feed my children. I must wake him but I am afraid that he will be very angry if I do this. Do you think I can wake him? I must be paid'

" 'I will wake him,' Verlande says. 'I will get you paid.'

"So simple, so straightforward, and yet however slight an act, still for the Jesuit in him, an act of complicity, Jorge, the first of which he was painfully aware. He got the money from his friend and he paid the prostitute. She could not feed her children until she got paid. She had become a prostitute in order to feed her children. What else was there to do? Verlande understood this. Were her children to starve?

"What was he to do? She was a good woman, not bad as the Jesuits said prostitutes were bad. Oh no, she was doing what she was doing so she could feed her children. Her husband had no job she told him. Be good and her children die.

"Jorge, the *guerrilheiros* have the marginals mapped. They are an elite, these *guerrilheiros*, intelligent, often intellectual. The elite are the fighters. Politics and the military are one. They are demographers of the dispossessed. Those outside the system are increasing at a startling rate. They're having all the babies. Procreation has become a destiny."

What do you think, hey Professor?

"I'm coming to it, Jorge. One more thing to give you a sense of it all. You know bank robbing is their apprenticeship to revolution, their entrance exam for admission to the struggle. They steal a car for a bank robbery. Then they notify the owner. They tell him to report the stolen car or he will be held by the police as a conspirator, an accomplice. After the job, this now wonderfully tuned up car, in mint getaway condition, is returned to the owner with a full tank of gas. Only in Brazil!"

What do you think, hey Professor?

"What was I to say, Jorge? I mean I guess I didn't think. I couldn't quite believe what was taking place. I couldn't believe that I was in it. Verlande and I had been talking, this remarkable man and I, him telling me some of the things I've told you. We were talking and the logic, the coherence of it all took on an inevitable meaning. I said after we talked, after the personal and the social and the political and the economic talk, after all of this I found myself saying that I could understand why he did what he had to do. I answered his question, 'What do you think, hey Professor?' I understood why he had to do what he had to do. I mean as if, well, yes, *shoot the foreman. Shoot the son of a bitch.*

"When the Luger jammed, he said angrily, 'This Cathedral is the vestibule to Hell.' Jorge, I cannot speak of the terror of the foreman or of the horror of my witness. Lugers, Verlande explained to me, were never supposed to jam. Then he said very calmly and very gently, 'Who has the Smith and Wesson?' "

3

"I was dazed. Verlande gave me an *abraço* and there was the flash of the camera, Jorge, the now famous picture. They covered the machine gun with only a canvas and they were gone. The sight of that armed jeep going up the nave was almost ludicrous, funny. Quickly my student took me by the arm and we left as we had entered.

"We walked rapidly, almost running, across the thoroughfare to the *Faculdade*. At the landing he said, 'You see the situation, Professor. You did not discuss your situation with Verlande. What for? He saw that it was not necessary that you do so. Now you see that it was not necessary. Now you will go home. It is much clearer than discussing it, no?'

" 'Will someone notify the police?'

" 'By now Verlande has notified the police. *Até logo*, my favorite professor, *áte logo!* ' "

4

"There is no complicity, Jonathan," Dr. Jorge said to him firmly. "You have spoken at length and I will draw a breath and speak. 'What do you think, hey Professor?' Now Jonathan you leave me no burden. No burden at all. I will not accept your fakery, your literary quackery. I know you, you professors of literature.

"We are dear friends so I may speak. I do not know what happened. You do not tell me what happened. 'What do you think, hey Professor?' Who did you shoot? And how could you have prevented the shooting? Don't be a fool. Has the Senhor of Good End visited you? Has he visited you with the bowlines, shot them forth to stigmatize the palms and the feet? Stigmata, hey Jonathan? Let me see your palms.

"Enough of these great and awful Jesuits. They have made enough history for the world. Do you expect me to understand, my friend, my dear friend, that there is a parallel between that delicacy of our Jesuit revolutionary with the prostitute and that maidenly delicacy of yours, this, your complicity in the brutal murder of the foreman? No, Jonathan, no burden.

"I say to you in Portuguese now. Your language makes me stumble in language. I do not believe in violent revolution. I do not believe in terror. I do not believe in a just violence. Whether or not you were there, the foreman would be just as dead. Shall we split the hairs of morality? Shall we count the angels on the head of a pin?

"There are no truths, at best half-truths. We live, my friend, with failure. Successful revolutions do not make its leaders poor. It leaves the poor people poor, maybe poorer, God forbid, and it makes its leaders rich. You cannot change the centuries overnight, not even in this age when you Americans are on the moon.

"Our reality is failure, the vacancy, the void, the spaces, the centimeters of deviation from all absolutes. Terror, yes. Most instructive, yes, when we are talking about Pascal's terror, say, the terror of infinite space. This is our reality, this is our anguish, our pain and confusion. The infinite spaces. This is what we cry about. This is what makes us devout. This is what makes us artists. This is what makes us human. Enough of the Jesuits. I give you a good old Jansenist, Pascal: 'Man is neither angel nor brute, and the unfortunate thing is that he who would act the angel acts the brute.' No more angels of revolution in our time, please!

"Let us hear the last of moral coherence, my friend, of logic, of consistency. We are drowning in our causes. We become dehumanized, brutalized by our strict, I might say behavioral, conformity to our idealisms. Let us relax, my friend. Let us stretch and breathe awhile the good air. We need not be hypocrites to accept the seasons without trying to change them, to accept all things in their own time.

"Your princely and priestly psychologist will not let you fall victim to sadness, worse, to melancholy, a sin in and of itself. Such a sin violates nature. It violates all that is good in life. It is the sin that leads to suicide. There is no burden. There is no moral complicity, Jonathan. Do you understand? 'What do you think now, hey Professor?' No burden on Jorge's desk, no burden at all. Let me see the palms of your hands. So! They are clean! They are clean after all!"

CHAPTER NINE

1

Jonathan walked around the block to the playground of the Hebrew School. The boys were gone. He could hear the singing of the birds. He stood alone and then he realized he was not alone. He raised his eyes and there at the office window was Dr. Jorge. Jorge waved and he waved back, farewell, farewell, and Jonathan took to the streets.

The morning was darkening. A swirl of clouds had come in with the gathering breeze of the sea. He shrugged his shoulders. There we have it, he thought, a voyage home.

Carol, he was thinking, was probably now at the *Escola* high in the hills of Gávea taking care of things for the boys now that they were really leaving. It would be hard for the boys in a way. He remembered how excited his sons were their first days sitting in a classroom from where they could sometimes see squirrel monkeys swinging from the large leafed trees. Carol was now probably getting their school records and seeing to the transcripts and necessary certifications. Back to the States. Home. Jonathan knew that back home in some school somewhere his sons would turn to the window on a long and hot afternoon to dream of giant ferns, of the lushness of a foliage that was no longer there for them, of golden monkeys swinging through sunlit patches of an old rain forest high in the hills of Gávea.

On the hillside there was a *favela* across the road from the school. He did not know the name of the *favela* and he wondered about it. He was thinking of the touching ballad by Elizabeth Bishop about the criminal,

Micuçú, and of the names of the *favelas*, the hills of slums, one called the Chicken, one the Catacomb, one the Kerosene and one the Skeleton and one the Astonishment and one, Bishop saves it for last because it is where Micuçú meets his death, the Hill of Babylon. What was the name of this *favela* across the road from the school? he wondered.

He began to think of another hill, this one in the Tijuca Forest. He was thinking of how once upon a time he had come up that narrow winding road through the *mato*. It was dusk. He had come to the *Vista Chinêsa* from whose deck there were no *favelas*, no tyrannies, no *o movimento* of the great city below. There were the first lights of evening twinkling like low lying stars and there was Sugar Loaf, Pão de Acúcar, aureoled in the palest vermilion. There was Corcovado, how gentle the purple of Corcovado, and the tropical sea slowly, almost imperceptibly, was shifting its colors from emerald to turquoise. He could hear only the soft breeze from the sea and the sounds of the flight of tropical birds in the thick *mato* and it grew darker and a chill came into the air and with it the lowering of the shade of the early sky of evening and there was darkness and it was a blue night.

The blues of *saudade*. He was wondering how you can explain that word in English. You probably can't, he thought. *Saudade*. Nostalgia and homesickness for all our dreams, he was thinking. This longing for this paradise of place and soul that was and that was never in a time that is yesterday, that shall be today, that was tomorrow, *saudade*. "They strip me of the veils that befit me," Jonathan whispered, remembering the lines from the poet Murillo Mendes. Oh, Carnival, bejeweled, bemasked, befeathered, the naked dance, the samba of the night, the burning furnace of our dreams, our *saudade*, the sadness of all our gaiety, the tears of our laughter, the futility of all-souls, of all hallowed souls, Jonathan thinking, the mulata, even as her body sways, her arms upraised rounding her bare nippled strawberry nippled breasts, I strip the veil and it is morning here in Copacabana on Avenida Copacabana.

I walk. Jonathan said to himself I walk on the borrowings of the sun. What must I give back to the sun? There, suddenly, a few heavy splotches of rain. It looks like it's going to be heavy, he thought.

He ducked into the entranceway of a boutique. As he did so a large rat came tumbling by him. The dead rat was being broom swept into the gutter by a young well-dressed man.

"This is what the ocean and the beach give to us," he said grimly to Jonathan as he went back into the boutique, "rodents, bulging rats that defy the godless exterminators."

"Maybe they come from the hills, from *favelas*," Jonathan said.

"The authorities should burn those hills," the storekeeper said in parting.

The large, scattered drops of rain had thickened to a heavy shower, a tropical downpour. The force of the rain hitting the pavement and the swirl of wind had the effect of a spray and Jonathan had to move more deeply into the entranceway. He was joined by others who were scurrying from the rain. There were smiles and laughter and good-natured fellowship in the crowded doorway. There was the smell of damp clothing and perfumed bodies.

In the beginning is the end, Jonathan thought of a sudden as he sensed his presence. He had sensed him in the good nature of the crowd, in his, Jonathan's, discernment of the other's glance. Jonathan had caught the reflection as he had turned and looked inside the boutique, a reflection on an oblong column of smoked cut glass. It is my reflection, he had at first thought. But in the moment of thinking he knew it could not be. He was startled. The reflection was smiling. It was amused.

Even at the moment he remembered another scene, the remembering instant in time of this moment, when he was in the army stationed at Fort MacArthur. He had come out of a Chinese restaurant on the streets of San Pedro. He saw his maternal grandmother, the greatest person he had ever known. She had been dead for several years and yet he could have sworn there she was three thousand miles away from where she had been buried in New York. She was an old woman as she was before her death. She was walking. She had the support of two younger women, one on each side of her. When she saw him she hesitated, faltered. It looked as if she were about to faint. There was no doubt about it, a recognition. He did not understand why he could not approach her. There is no doubt about it, he thought. There was a passing and he was transfixed, inexplicably unable to move.

Here the other was in the smoked glass column, of course a foolishness, Jonathan was thinking. Am I being shadowed by myself? Jonathan was also amused but he also felt a slight tinge of terror and awe. This man seemed to Jonathan to be of the same height and build but he struck Jonathan as being paunchier than he was. Yet this man seemed to be a few years younger than he and Jonathan wondered and he saw that it was not Jonathan, but a resemblance of height, build, age, coloring. There was the thinning of the hair in the same way, the same haircut, the clothes similar but for the tie. The tie is much too loud, Jonathan thought, and yes, there is a wart on the chin. It is not my wart and so it can't be my chin. He turned to the standersby and smiled. Then he turned toward the interior of the boutique and the man was gone.

With the last filter of drops the sun came out and Jonathan was into the street again. Avenida Copacabana was now hot and humid and thick with light. He no longer felt the effects of the gin. That seemed a long while ago. Here was Rio. Hello Rio de Janeiro. Hello morning. He saw the run of the gutter wash over the rat. Ah, well, he thought, I am still here. Hello Mr. and Mrs. Shopkeeper. Hello wonderful shoppers. You're all looking real chic today. Hello, hello. *Bom dia, bom dia*. He stopped short and turned about. There is no one following me, he thought.

Jonathan was carrying on an imaginary conversation as he walked. Jorge, did I not tell you? I didn't tell you. "I'm a very lucky man," Verlande had said. "Right near by there was a cell ten feet by sixteen. There were eighteen naked men in there. They were sitting or standing. At night it was impossible for them to sleep, legs and arms jabbing and poking each other all night, the stench, bodies of sweat, of excrement, of mold, the toilet a hole in the corner where one boy slept. The only food they got was a handful of moist manioc flour and a tiny circle of dried meat. There were whippings and beatings. I was very lucky. I had my own solitary cell."

Hello Mr. and Mrs. Shopkeeper. Hello wonderful shoppers. You're all looking real chic today. Hello, hello. *Bom dia, bom dia*. Hello hatred. How are you Mr. Hatred today. Hatred is an element of the struggle. Verlande had told him that Che Guevarra had said that. Verlande had told him that Guevarra had said that relentless hatred of the enemy impelled you over and beyond the natural limitations of man. It transformed you into effective, violent, selective and cold killing machines. Jonathan remembered the exact words, "Our soldiers must be thus; a people without hatred cannot vanquish a brutal enemy." He remembered the tone of Verlande's voice as Verlande told him about Guevarra. The voice was soft and gentle and carried with it the patience of reasonableness.

Hello, Dom Hélder. Revolution through peace. Hello, hello Sanctity of Love. Dead Ends. Cells. Batteries. Electrodes. Hatred. Doctrine. Love. Poetry.

Where am I? He looked about. There he was. He had walked naturally in the habit worn direction, unaware of his steps, unaware of the pathway people made for him, unaware of their looks of surprise or of amusement or of fear, of one man turning to his male companion and putting a finger to his temple and pointing to Jonathan as he said, "*Louco*." Crazy. Jonathan was mad.

What do you think, hey Professor? There he was on Avenida Atlântica standing at the corner of Santa Clara. He was looking up at the American flag in front of the Thomas Jefferson, the USIS Library. He was looking up and thinking, Harry is right. This is not a safe place anymore. He thought of the good hours he had spent in the library reading and writing and looking out upon the landscape of sand and sea and mountain.

"It's squat waiting for the blow-up one of these days. They're waiting for all that stuff from the Embassy library to be moved here,
waiting for that transfer that'll close the Embassy library. It'll all be in
one place and then on one sunny day the Molotov special at cocktail
time, pow! Closing time! It's closing time, ladies and gentlemen!"

The library or home, Jonathan wondered. What do I do next? The
scar tissue of home. Go home, Jonathan, he said to himself. Where?
Suddenly he saw the car. It seemed to be coming right at him, there
where he stood. "What the fuck!" he cried aloud.

It was a black LTD Ford, tinted windows, headlights on in the sunlight. The car kept coming, ran up on to the sidewalk and jammed to a
stop. Jonathan had to jump quickly aside. He saw the rear door of the
car open and he saw a heavy man with a thick neck and a white polo
shirt sitting in the back seat. He had one hand on the shoulder and
one hand on the waist of an inert figure and Jonathan knew fear. The
man was smiling.

"A remembrance of your trip to Brazil," he said good-naturedly.
"Here, Professor Jonathan, a gift!"

He gave the body a strong shove. The body tumbled sideways and
outward. The blue tattered sleeve of the jacket got caught on the inside
door handle. The body caught. It was suspended and twisted in its
fall, the face upward, the eyes stark open as if surprised. Then the man
in the white polo shirt, still smiling with a cigar stuck in the middle of
his face, said, "A thousand pardons!" He bent halfway out of the car
and with some awkwardness released the jacket sleeve from the handle. The body was free. Then he was back fully inside the car and he
said, "*Até logo*, professor! Enjoy your gift!" He was chuckling at the
joke. He slammed the door and the car sped away.

Under the furling flag, Jonathan knelt at the side of the body. He
closed the eyes of his beggar, his dear Senhor Oleisky. Suddenly and
all at once out of the thick humid density of light there were people
around him. They had simply appeared. Someone covered Oleisky's
face with a newspaper. Someone placed a candle at the head and at the
foot of the body. Someone folded Oleisky's hands on his chest and put
a small crucifix in his hands. Jonathan looked at the crowd and said
angrily, "No, do not do that!" He took the crucifix from the body and
held it up.

"Whose?" he said.

No one would claim it.

"He is a Jew," was all he could think of saying.

2

Jonathan felt slightly dizzy, a bit faint as he stood up. In the brief moment of a startling turn, his eyes came to rest on the figure in the doorway of the apartment house next to the Thomas Jefferson. Jonathan felt the crucifix in his palm.

The shadow appeared. The reflection that had been in the smoked column of glass had materialized, was visible, was smiling, was moving, was taking him by the arm and leading him away from the scene. Jonathan yanked his arm from the grasp but the shadow not unkindly took his arm again.

"Don't be a fool. Why would we do it? We did not touch the old beggar. You know that. Now come along."

"Where are you taking me? Who did it?"

"Away from here. Who does all these terrible things, the fucking pit vipers! I have called for the wagon. I have called for it also out of decency, believe me. It will be here soon. Now please, Professor, come along. I do not want to see you in any more trouble. Please come along. Besides," he paused and smiled, "haven't you noticed?"

"Yes, yes, I have noticed."

"You may call me Roberto," the man said.

Then he said most charmingly, "I will give you a confidence. The wart is not mine. It is false. It is very good, though, is it not? A very good fake. When I am on a job I always put on a trait. A wart, a scar, a see-through patch over one eye, sometimes fat glasses with a hearing aid. And of course a cane for the glasses. Now how do you like my confidence?"

Jonathan, in a daze, had been led off Atlântica and on to Santa Clara. He felt dull in that dense light, almost insensate. The world before him seemed to be going up and down while all feeling was being drained. He felt the blood in his veins ebbing. People were going by in a seemingly endless movement. He could see the Christ atop Corovado in the far, far distance.

Then Roberto coaxed him with gentle concern. "We are at the *Restaurante Arista*," he said. "Have a *caipirinha* and something to eat. They have *vatapá* here as good as you find in Bahia. *Vatapá* is tribal. It is like your American soul food. It will restore you. You are very, very pale."

"Who are you? Why have you been following me?"

"Think of me affectionately, won't you, as your guardian angel sent by the Ministry. I will be with you these last days. I will see you and your family safely out of Brazil. I and the others."

"The others?"

"My relief and the relief of my relief. It is a little known secret that even angels have to sleep. We will be very good to you I assure you for certain. I would not have approached you directly, but the situation, you understand, it required an action. I enjoyed the distance. It was exciting. It provided a mystique between us. It is unfortunate that the situation asked for a direct action. Am I not right?"

"Have you been sent by the Ministry or by the Saints?" Jonathan asked suddenly. Roberto stepped back involuntarily, surprised. Then Jonathan said, "Am I under arrest?"

"Of course not. What would tell you this?"

"I am under custody, then? Under surveillance? Fuck it. Don't look at me in protest. You know what I mean. Your English is damn good. Tailed. Shadowed."

"Professor, nothing is more distant from the truth. You are under guardianship, our hospitality, our protection. Believe me, Professor, I have been lured back to earth for this very purpose, to be your guide. You are very pale. You have been transfixed. Please be seated."

They were now in the restaurant. Jonathan felt his fist still clenched. He released it. There in his palm was the crucifix.

"He was a Jew, you know," Jonathan said putting the crucifix into his jacket pocket.

"I know," Roberto said. "I also know he was no ordinary beggar. Our intelligence is very firm on that. We had much to learn from him alive. You believe me? Alive."

Jonathan thought of his grandmother in San Pedro. He looked closely at Roberto. The wart, he saw, was really pasty. Scar tissue. The foreman has been aborted, he thought stupidly. Oh God, he sighed inside.

"You see," Roberto was trying to explain over the *caipirinha*, "it was the bastard Death Squad. They do these terrible things. That vigilante group is very bad for the reputation of Brazil. The armed forces will not put up with it, I promise you. Believe me. They will not put up with these extracurricular, I say that word for you, Professor, extracurricular activities of a few police who are nothing more than gangsters. They condemn and execute without trial. It is not civilized. It endangers our national security. This is what the Justice Ministry said. You know what will follow. It will be stopped. It is good luck for you that it seems they do not kill Americans. They are all for the capitalists. Besides, they know that diplomacy would require the government to make a prompt and direct crackdown with inevitable, vengeful, even indiscriminate, consequences."

"Why are you smiling?" Jonathan said.

"I always smile," Roberto said. "Even once when I was shot, I went down smiling. No. I joke. You know why I am smiling? It is almost like a mirror, only you are not smiling back. Ah, that was careless of me. I forgot for a moment of your sorrow. I was so intrigued. Please forgive me."

Jonathan surprised himself. His appetite was voracious. He was thinking rapidly as he was eating. This man, this Roberto, then, is my shadow, he thought. He is a pun on my shadow. He is my coffin. He is my double and he is not my double.

But it was not all coincidence or spiritual fate, Jonathan learned. As it filtered through Roberto's talk, in this special assignment the Ministry thought it would not be a bad idea considering all the different disorganized, uncoordinated, blind forces of each upon each, each not knowing what the other was doing, the political police and the death squads and the Rio de Janeiro army and the secret service—and who knew but the *guerrilheiros* might make trouble—each stumbling upon each in a display of power, the Ministry thought there might be a need not only for protection of this important and naive American Professor who was like a son to the American Ambassador, not only a need for protection against this craziness, but a need for a decoy simply because a decoy was at hand. Amusing mother of ducks, they thought, here is Roberto! The amusement had been tinged with a touch of the mystical, given the closeness of the resemblance. It was simply irresistible for them to give to Roberto, the faithful and inexplicable Roberto who for absolutely no reason they could make out loved to make himself up with "traits," as he called them, when on assignment, a wart here, an eye patch there, to give to Roberto the assignment of Professor Jonathan.

Jonathan was alive now, his senses keyed, his imagination soaring. He was catching Roberto's words. Those words were telling him, he was sure, that Roberto was a supplicant of Yemanjá. Yemenjá, her crowned, torch-bearing, petal bearing, flowering, flowing image, a turquoise form in the sunlit veined emerald waters, Yemanjá, daughter of Africa, Goddess of *macumba*, worshipped by supplicants of Catholicism and *macumba*, by the wise syncretists who covered all spiritual bets, so the thoughts and images came upon Jonathan while he continued to consume the *vatapá*.

Tribal, Roberto had said. Lured to earth, he had said. Guide, ah, that was almost technical, Jonathan thought, the words and phrases of *macumba*. Yes, Roberto is a supplicant. I know it, Jonathan thought. My double is a supplicant.

Jonathan let go. Give Roberto the carcass of a goat, he thought. Give him black chickens, give him horned, goateed, satanic statuary in blaring red, give him rice and corn and beans and cakes and nuts and grapes and apples. Let him gaze on the enameled cross. Let him hear the beat of the bone drums and the chants of Yoruba. Anoint my double with pieces of chestnut, twist off the heads of pigeons, give him a bowl of wine and oil, anoint him with breast feathers. Dancers shine with the dance. Let him hear the sound of the crinoline dancers, oh, saint, take up his body. Roberto trembles. His eyes roll back. He has been seized. He falls to the ground. He is helpless. Circle around him parishioners all. This room, this *terreiro*, this clearing in space, has known rapture. And then the black ram, the five white chickens, the drums, the chants, the kitchen knife, the sacrifices begin and the firecrackers sound. We go with God, Roberto.

In this country where parallel streets will meet, where the inconceivable of today will be history tomorrow, cover all bets and think, think shrewdly like a Brazilian gambler, Jonathan told himself. Oh Carol, Mary, Yemenjá, oh Princess, help me to think clearly, to think doubly. Carol will say I am manicky, absolutely manicky. Why this Roberto could even get by on my passport picture! More than decoy, Roberto. Let us go to your *terreiro* where we will consult the Mother of Saints. She will have the solution to all our problems. I will keep you in reserve. We'll strike an understanding. More than decoy, Roberto. Manicky, is it? Why are you smiling again, Roberto?

"You are, if you will pardon me," Roberto was saying, "someplace else. I see the mood in your face, Professor Jonathan, a most active and lively face, filled with expression. Have you been carried off by the White Dove?"

"The White Dove? What do you know about the White Dove?"

"Your Center. Our intelligence is very firm. They say they will build it."

"They?" Jonathan said. "They? No, I see in my mind's eye the black car with the headlights on in the thick sunlight. We sit here and I see the haze of the lights of the funeral car of the assassins."

"You are overwrought because you grieve. I understand. There goes the wagon with the body. I see the tear in your eye for Senhor Oleisky, the tear in your mind's eye," he said kindly.

"No, I shed a tear for the memory of the *Vista Chinêsa* at dusk," Jonathan said.

Roberto looked at him wonderingly. "So much nonsense," he thought. "My double is a madman."

CHAPTER TEN

1

"Wake up," Carol said. "Wake up."

"Why haven't you told me?" he said and in the saying he left it vague knowing that she knew what he was asking. She hated that.

What was she to tell him? Why should she? In what way could she possibly tell him? It was always a question of moment, she felt, like a cloudburst from the sky, from the dark clouds, and it would pass with the shiver of a first breeze.

In what sensible, reasonable way could she tell him there had been two of them? Her friends had given her a birthday party in a brownstone basement apartment a block and a half from Circle in the Square. She was seventeen. She had been escorted by a very nice Brooklyn College senior. There were many people there she did not know. Friends had brought friends and it was a Greenwich Village mix of singers and dancers, actors, writers, composers, sculptors, one architect who was always talking about real estate in the sky, painters, musicians, scholars—noble aspirants and fun-loving pretenders to the tradition and the future of high civilization. She was young among them. She was the child brain, the child prodigy. She was not an aspirant yet, not a pretender to some art or profession.

Everyone agreed, though, that her destiny was to be a marvelous one.

There was almost an anonymity about two of the men at the party. They had walked in together. They were not intellectuals or artists.

Clearly they lifted a hell of a lot of weights. As young as she was, Carol recognized them as third-string muscle-bound jocks. They could have been gate crashers. No one at the party really seemed to know them.

She could see that they scented her ripeness and she could see that their lips were moist. She knew they were watching the effect upon her of the wine and the dimming of the lights. They teased her into having a stronger drink which one of the men made for her. He told her it was a screwdriver. She giggled. Her escort was talking with some people in a far corner of the room. They were discussing cinema.

She was a bit woozy. She had been titillating all week as her birthday approached. She had found herself unable to work, to study. She, who had so beautifully controlled almost without lapse, so she thought, the April florescence of her body, was now masturbating and dreaming on soft rugs under blue lights in front of long mirrors, a passional surrender. She went with the two of them.

She went with them and they had a car and one was in the back with her and they drove the streets. Then they were on a parkway and in the back of the car played on by the stage lights of the traffic she moaned and let it be. It was unreal, soporific, a float of the half torpid, an estate. She moaned and the car quickly, almost abruptly, pulled over to the soft shoulder. They switched and she felt as if she were not there. The car pulled out on to the parkway and she was supine and the second had of her and there she was. As she came, she saw herself rising with the sounds of the traffic, with the play of lights. She was seeing a grinning specter of herself outside of her looking in at her. It is Halloween in the spring, she was thinking.

She was back at the party within an hour or so. Just a couple of quickies, she was thinking. Her friends were asking for her to cut the birthday cake and she stood under the dangling ribbons and streamers and amid the brightly colored balloons. She made the first cut into the cake and then she gave the knife to her escort for the second cut and he kissed her affectionately on the cheek and she remembered thinking how nice that kiss was.

After all these years she would still awaken at night in terror, her body trembling. The morning after that evening, there was no shame or second thoughts other than she felt she had acted stupidly. She thought of it as a base stupidity. When she missed her first period, she became concerned but not frightened. She thought she could not be that unlucky. By now the affair appeared to her to have been wanton and tawdry. She looked upon it as a willful violation of the self. At the same time that she was thinking about the moral dimensions of that evening, she was also wondering if she were not really making too much of it. Then she missed her second period and she became terrified. Her universe had become a nightmare. She wanted mommy and daddy. She was feeling as she had never felt before, stranded, a tremulous waif. Then finally she did what she had to do. She did it on her own and she was enclosed and all confidences of a seventeen year old with bright, chatty friends and lovely spring mornings had ended.

In time she became certain in her mind that she had aborted her daughter, the daughter she never had, the daughter that she saw at times, at different stages, at different developments. As she looked upon the daughters of friends, she imagined here is my baby, here my child, and now the adolescent, brilliant and sensitive and beautiful, her voice spring, her laughter joy, her tears the morning dew, this daughter, her daughter, they, hand in hand, walking the margin of the sea, dazzling the rays of the universe, wildly in love with the glory of creation, my daughter, she would think, and she would feel the welling of tears.

She knew it was nonsense, that she was too rational for this sentimentality. It had happened on a parkway in the back of a car with Tom and Dick and if there had been, there could have been, why not that night, a Harry. Undulant night of soft air and the odor of gasoline, she would think, oh, yes, in love with the glory of creation and, she would think, gang banged.

What kept eating at her and what she could not shake was the bad luck, the foul luck, the incredibly stupid foul luck, she told herself. Life, she told herself, is a lewd smirk. It took all the steadfastness of Jonathan's unwavering love to restore her to genuine grief, to sentiment, and finally, in plowing, furrowing sex, to motherhood.

She also knew this, for Jonathan had joked with her about what others had said, and she knew from the gaze of others, that she carried with her the blessed face of Immaculacy, undefiled, pure, that even as she held the hands of her two children, the world saw in her, Jonathan saying, the wonder of perdurable virginity.

Where are the brown eyes of my daughter that I may gaze into them to find the lost innocence of my heart? So she tortured herself time and again with this kind of question. There had been no luxuriance of passion, not even a rank luxuriance that night. Would you understand, Jonathan, that there had been merely the unthinking, unillumined body in the back of a car? Would you understand this if I told you? I bore a life within a life, dear Jonathan, but one life was all that I could handle, all that I was meant to have then, Jonathan, and do you understand?

Why did they kill Senhor Oleisky? Why did they have to kill this orphan of the Holocaust? She sat alone with her thoughts. She was sitting in the living room waiting for Jonathan. He had called from the *Restaurante Arista* and he had told her about Senhor Oleisky. He had also told her he was with his double.

"Wake up," she had said to him over the phone. She was frightened for him. "Wake up. You are having a bad dream!"

2

Eugenia came in.

"Forgive me, Dona Carol, but is there not something?"

"No, nothing, thank you, Eugenia," she said.

She was thinking of the way he would say, "Why haven't you told me?" Not a question but a cry of sorrow, she thought.

"But you are so sad, Dona Carol," Eugenia said.

What was there to tell and how to tell it, she wondered. What was he saying about a double? Why did he telephone the tragic news? Why didn't he come home? Where was he now? What anguish, she wondered, had produced his float in time? He had so loved the sunlight. "The sunlight of enchantment," he would say. "The magic circle of sunlit reality," he had once said, "is where I live." I am the cause of his anguish, she would think. I am responsible for those dislocations of his in time, she thought, those moments that made her want to scream like a school teacher at the end of her patience, "Jonathan, for God's sake, please attend."

She smiled. Ever since he was a boy, he told her, he had had his one-sided talks with the people of the world. It had begun in his early years when he was playacting in front of his mother's long oval dressing mirror and it kept on going in life without that mirror. He spoke to Lou Gehrig who was dying. He spoke to Joe DiMaggio. There was Rick, Bogart's Rick, in *Casablanca.* Then there had been the run of politicians from Norman Thomas to Adlai Stevenson. Then there was a hiatus on politicians until John F. After his murder, there were no more politicians, well, he had told her, not quite. There was Bobby. Jonathan's tears were sealed in Los Angeles. Martin Luther King was different from all the others and after his assassination, the specter and the voice of King would haunt his dreams.

Urbi et orbi, to writers and artists, that was a different kind of talking he told her. That was not playacting with Gehrig and Dimaggio and Bogart's Rick and Norman Thomas and Adlai Stevenson and John F. and Bobby and the glorious King, but a voice to the city and the world in a deeper sense, that sense being the *annuncio* of his soul to the city and the world. Carol knew the voice of the Professor, the Scholar and Critic of Art and Literature, was a different voice, the voice of communion, Sacred and Scriptural, no momentary leaving of the world to playact in it but an act of breathing in the world itself, the voice of a staying reality. As he would say, that was life, that was his mode of living, the sending of his active voice, his singing voice through time, his sober voice, his whiskey voice, through the path of space and the void of time. "Hello neighbor Homer and how is wrathful Achilles doing today?" he would say upon opening his Homer.

She remembered how one day out of the blue as they lay on their mat at the beach he had said, "I have been thinking. Now in Brazil, it is Dom Hélder." There was something of the wafer in the way he said it, something of the cup. This struck her as the voice in the deeper sense. She laughed when he said it and she said to him, "You are *louco*." "Oh, no," he said only half in jest, "this, too, is what Brazil hath wrought."

"What elth hath Brazil wrought," she teased.

"Elth?" he said.

"Hath," she said. "You said 'this too.' "

"The mulata," he said. "The amalgamation of the races."

"Is that so?"

She could not measure the nuances of change, of his descent from playfulness to seriousness. He could be so up and down, manicky. He was a token of innocence. He was the young man on the bus on a ferrous, rain streaked day. She was suddenly frightened and she looked up.

Eugenia was still standing there. She saw that Eugenia had been reading her. She rose. She came to Eugenia. They embraced. She wept on Eugenia's shoulder.

"Dona Carol, you must trust the Senhor of Good-End," Eugenia said. "You must have faith. Everything will be wonderful if you trust the Senhor of Good-End."

"Everything will be wonderful, yes," Carol said. "I will help you with dinner. Will you bake for us your famous lemon meringue, will you dear Eugenia? It's the Professor's favorite."

3

Harry's sixteen year olds. She would have had contempt and rage for him had she believed him. There were his whores, of course, his frail prostitutes. For that she was sorry. She was trying to listen to Harry who had come to the apartment to mourn. She was listening really for the sliding sound of the elevator door, for Jonathan's footsteps. She sat in silence.

"I was working the nets," Harry was saying. "That's how we met. Oleisky joined the pull one day. He was on the line. He was right behind me on the line. Go down, Moses, like, we were pulling and heaving and joking. We had seen each other around and now we were friends."

"Yes," she said.

"And now he is dead," Harry said.

"Now he is dead."

"The news is in the streets."

She did not respond.

"Forlorn," he said. "pow! and he is lost forever."

"Forevermore," she said with a smile.

"Nevermore. Forlorn and nevermore," he said.

"All right, Harry."

"I'm sorry. No matter how stupid I've got to talk."

"It's all right, Harry."

"I bet you didn't think I was involved in anything anymore, let alone with an old-time Nazi hunter. I know what people say about me. But it's all misunderstanding about me. I have my work and my wife in Rio. She's really here. She is. You got to see that I'm involved. You got to see that by now."

"Yes, I see that."

"Until I find her she's a part of me. She's a part of me in a most unhealthy way. It has made me a kind of hermaphrodite because she's of my nature. Maybe when I find her I'll throw her out. But I can't even think about throwing her out until I find her. Do you get what I'm saying, Carol?"

"I think I do."

"I am involved."

"I suppose so."

We sit upon the dead senselessly, she thought. It is a ritual. We talk and we do not listen and we go around. What was Harry trying to say? What is he saying? Where is the slide of the elevator door? Where are your footsteps, Jonathan?

Sixteen year olds were Harry's way of remembering, she thought. His talk of sixteen year olds was his eccentric way of memorializing his wife. Or was it really a memorial to his youth, to his virgin ore? Harry was just an old-time prospector—she almost laughed aloud at the silliness coming over her—who struck gold once and lost the mine in a poker game. Fatigue, she thought, that is my problem. Will the door please, please slide!

"Not a pauper's grave," Jonathan had said over the phone. "A pauper's grave is too close to Auschwitz. I will not have him mangled and tumbled in the dirt like his mother and father or dumped into an oven. He must have his rites, you know, his poetry, his due. Do you follow?"

"Of course I follow," she had said. "I follow and I follow."

But what could Jonathan do? she wondered.

" 'And you call yourself an historian,' " Harry was laughing.

"That's what Oleisky said to me. The Old Country. I called America the Old Country. I said my friends Jonathan and Carol were coming from the Old Country with their two children. A country very young very old."

Ring around the rosie, she thought. Jonathan going ring around the living room. What madness!

"He knew all about you. I told him. That's how we came to the apartment. He said he knew of a beautiful apartment for the Professor and his family."

"Yes, with a condition," she said.

"With a condition, true. An unknown condition. I thought you knew that. He was so strange this hunter of Nazis. Not strange so much as complex. Not complex but mysterious. Not a condition but a request. Sorry, Carol, for going on like this. The condition was that he might have a request. How could one say no when the apartment was so splendid and the man so interesting? You know Jonathan better than I."

"I'm sure Jonathan thought of the condition as adding to the charm of the apartment."

"This apartment."

"Yes, this apartment. This splendid apartment."

"I am the death pin."

"Nonsense," Carol said stretching forth her hand to Harry's.

Not today, Harry, she thought. Please do not give me your self-pity, not today, Harry. She withdrew her hand. She gazed for a moment on his long and bony fingers. He folded his arms putting his hands under his armpits. They smiled at each other.

"The fingers of lust," he said self-consciously.

"You do pride yourself, don't you?" she laughed. Then she thought a moment. "How many of us end our lives at age seventeen?" she said. "Women, I mean."

Harry looked at her, startled and a bit wonderingly. Then the night was there. Eugenia was in the kitchen watching over the delayed dinner. The children were watching *futebol* on television. Harry was drinking martinis. Carol smoked a cigarette. She felt herself getting hooked on cigarettes again. Slide, she was saying to herself, for God's sake, Jonathan, where is the slide of the door? the footsteps? "Oh," she said aloud, "at last the elevator!"

Harry turned from the window.

"It is not Jonathan," she said fearfully. "It is not his step."

"Better let me take it," Harry said.

He gave his martini to Carol and moved swiftly to the door. "Why, Jonathan," Harry said hesitantly, in surprise opening the door narrowly. "Carol was just saying—why no! Who the hell are you?" he said.

"Ah, you are Harry," Roberto said smiling gallantly through the slowly widening opening of the door. "May I come in? Our intelligence is very firm."

4

So you are Roberto, she was thinking, Jonathan's Roberto. She crossed her legs and pumped her ass and smoked a cigarette. The wart, Roberto had told Harry and Carol in great confidence, was phony. Inexplicably, tears almost came into her eyes. Carol thought, oh well.

Bougainvillaea in bloom in a blue night. It just came to her. She did not know why. She was sitting there pumping and fighting back the inexplicable tears and she was trying to smile and she was thinking of bougainvillaea in bloom in a blue night. She was thinking that in the midst of their red, white, and violet profusion, hidden, there was enmeshed of all things an ancient guitar. The frayed strings unbidden and yet still taut were never to rupture, never to break. Above shone the yolk of the yellow moon bearing a trace of gelatinous scarlet. She smoked and wrapped herself in the dark flowering of night, in the sea scent of a warm and secret breeze, in the spangle of the stars.

Roberto had been explaining. He couldn't help smiling as he looked at Carol. What is he saying? Carol wondered. She heard the words and the laughter.

"You must forgive my rudeness, but in a way you are almost my wife. Is that not interesting? I should be most fortunate among men."

"Do not remove your wart," she said to him.

"Very good. Very good," he said. "I love to sally. It is good for the soul, the laughter. Is that what we are doing? Is that an American word, to sally, an infinitive?"

The sensuosity of death, the darkness of the night and the scent of the sea, she was thinking. I know that Jonathan is by the shore of the dark ocean. I know my Jonathan. I know. I know. He is there now, alone and now.

"Oh, by the Mother of Saints the Saintly Mother," they heard the prayerful murmur. They turned and there was Eugenia standing in the shadowed entranceway to the living room, her body erect, her turbaned head thrown back to a sky beyond the apartment and then Carol saw that she was looking toward Roberto and there was a silent exchange, the slight wisp of a smile passing between them.

Roberto closed one eye.

"So I went with Professor Jonathan to the morgue," he said. "It would not do to have him go alone. Not that there was any danger I do not think. But it could have gone badly without the presence of the Ministry perhaps.

"They had the body in the burlap sack," he explained. "Their policy is record quick time for record quick disposal. They do that like nose tissue, you understand, when the body is from the Death Squad, like a throwaway. But you must forgive me, Dona Carol, because I see and think it is not fitting to give you any more details of this ghastly sort.

"There was a fee as well to reinforce the power of the Ministry. He paid a fee your Jonathan, our Professor Jonathan."

"A bribe, a bribe," Harry said.

"Please go on," Carol said, "please."

"It was really, how do you say, banal," Roberto said. "Ordinary like going shopping into a butcher's refrigerator. It was, like in Portuguese, the same word in American, cataleptic? It was a cataleptic cold. Only for a butcher's refrigerator it smelled of fish, of our cod."

Eugenia, crossing herself, was leaving the room retreating backward. Harry, on his fourth martini, was mumbling something and Carol was hearing it as an undertone, something about a supermarket of bodies.

Now Carol was hearing Roberto saying, "As if a package, a large package, a bag that is, a strong bag like a great sack of dog food or flour or potatoes, Professor Jonathan takes the burlap bag over his shoulder.

"He would not let me help him carry it. 'You get the certificate,' he says to me. 'Yes, I will check the certificate of death,' I say to him."

Carol listening and wondering, how they did get on, Jonathan and Roberto, how it must have been when they laid eyes on each other, even the coloring of the eyes, the complexion, uncanny. She knew it was not uncanny, not for her dear Jonathan. He would say ubiquity. He would say ourselves are out there at least twice and three maybe four times, out there in the world with different names. Oh mystery of life at last I found you she laughed to herself. Out there we are living in different places and different times, he would say. Have I ever told you about my grandmother? Carol would listen again and she would say that may be, your grandmother, that may be, heaven knows I will not quarrel with your divine sentiment. Of all I hear she was a marvelous woman, a saintly woman, but Jonathan, those grand others, those Jonathans out there, you are simply lost my dear in a dimly lit hall of mirrors. You are dancing a times step looking all the while for a spotlight in that dimly lit hall of reflecting mirrors. Image upon self, self upon image. That's show business, dear. Where is Jonathan?

"I must say, no offense of course, but Professor Jonathan is quite mad," Roberto was saying.

"Yes," Carol smiled, "I think he is, too."

"A divinely inspired madness, don't you think? Is he not very persuasive?" he said turning to Harry.

"Pow!" Harry answered looking up as if he had suddenly discovered his surroundings. "Pow! Pow! Think of that. A regular supermarket of bodies. An A and P. An Atlantic and Pacific of bodies!"

"It is all too cruel," Roberto said turning from Harry to Carol.

"Why is your eye closed?" Harry said.

"It is an amusing discipline I practice on occasion," Roberto said. "There. Now I open it."

At the expense of vision, Carol idly thought. To see singly, she thought, and she wondered at the laughter inside her. She thought that what was happening could not be happening, that she was hallucinating, that there was a knot of hysteria inside her about to be untied, a phantom feeling of ghostly silliness about to come out. Even Hollywood has doubles, Jonathan would say. Every star has a double. A top-notch star like Burt Lancaster could have triples. Stand-in, she would say. The stars have stand-ins. He would say stand-ins, doubles, what's the difference? My case rests. Then they would both laugh. That, she thought, had been years ago when they were young and new.

"The playground," Roberto was saying. "I finally understood. The Professor said he had been there earlier in the morning. He told me he had taken a gin and tonic and gone to the playground. 'But why do we take a body to the playground,' I said. In spite of the sad and grisly circumstances, it was funny, Dona Carol. It was very funny, Senhor Harry. I must tell you I was not nice. I was exasperated at this point. It is funny only now.

"I tried to be logical and I said, 'You are a knowledgeable man, Professor Jonathan, but you will admit that corpses have no need of playgrounds and children. And children, who have need of playgrounds, have no need of corpses. You will admit that children do not need to have corpses planted in their playgrounds. Better they should play *futebol*. Please admit this to me. Let them grow up first before they have need of corpses.'

"He sat with the body in the back of my car. He would not let me put the body in the trunk. We had exasperation over this. I said, 'I beg you let me put it in the trunk.' But what was I to do? You understand? He sat in the back with the sack horizontal, the head of the burlap sack resting on his lap.

"I think I go on because so I have promised him. I go on talking to you because I have promised him. What a man is your Jonathan, *hein?* Dona Carol, what a man! Mad! You will forgive me for offense, no offense intended, absolutely mad.

"I thought I understood finally. This is a playground for Jews, for Hebrew boys and girls. I thought maybe this is a rite, some kind of hidden Jewish rite. Ghoulish. How foolish I was! How stupid I was to even think this! I mean no insult on any people. It is only to say how this madness, you will pardon but no offense, Dona Carol, how Professor Jonathan had taken my thoughts to such a point. I mean I was assigned to shadow him. I was sent by the Ministry to guide him by my shadow. I was sent to protect him from the evil sun by my shadow. To build for him a *terreiro*, a clearing of divine safety, a *cordon sanitaire* until you should leave Brazil in the next days. And now do you see what has happened? Now do you see where we are?"

"I see," Carol said. "I don't know how to thank you for looking after him, how to say how grateful I am."

Roberto protested. He was after all a guardian angel sent by the Ministry. It was his function, his virtue by nature. This does not merit thanks or praise, does it?

"Ah, this wart," he said, "this wart always gives me trouble. It is a bad sign. I do not mean to be rude, Dona Carol, but perhaps I need a whiskey for my wart."

"Forgive me," she said. "Where is he now? Please do go on."

"I understood finally," Roberto said. "A parochial school. The playground and the school are part of the church, the synagogue. I have passed it many times."

Her heart lifted. That was the story, then, Carol thought, as she handed Roberto the whiskey. *Bravo!* She wanted to cry out, *Bravo, Jonathan! Bravo, my dearest!*

Roberto paused to turn and savor the whiskey. Then he went on, "Professor Jonathan went inside while I waited in the car. And then in just a few minutes he came out with a handsome young man who was wearing a skull cap. I thought all rabbis were old and with beards. The women must have really liked this Rabbi, no disrespect intended. I am sure the Ministry has intelligence on him, but I did not tell the Rabbi that. The Rabbi looked up and down the street when he came to the car to see in. 'Do not worry,' I told the Rabbi, 'I am from the Ministry and it is all right. Do not worry about anything.'

"The Rabbi looked from me to Professor Jonathan. From Professor Jonathan to me. Maybe he thought we were twins. He was puzzled, very much puzzled, a rabbinical knot, you understand, like they have in that mysterious book of theirs, the Talmud. We have a copy of it at the Ministry."

"It is not mysterious as you mean it," Carol said.

"Right. I apologize. I sometimes think the only intelligence I have comes from the Ministry." He laughed. Then he went on, "The Rabbi showed us where to take the car to an alley side. Professor Jonathan carried the sack again the same way. He will be aching tonight. He brought it into a small room with blackboards and folding chairs and many shawls and many books.

" 'I could not have him mangled and tumbled in the dirt,' Professor Jonathan said to the Rabbi. He seemed to think for a moment and then he said, 'or thrown into an oven.'

" 'Everything will be done in accord with Jewish law for this child of the Holocaust. It will be a Jewish funeral. The deceased is no stranger to us. Oleisky did not go to the synagogue to worship with the congregation, with the community, but he was our brother, may his soul rest in peace.'

" 'And the expenses?' Professor Jonathan says. 'It will cost money.'

" 'You have done all,' the Rabbi says. 'We will take care of it. We will pray for the ascent of his soul. We will say *kaddish*. Now you look very tired. May I offer you some schnapps? And your twin? He looks very much your twin. Is he your twin by chance?'

" 'I understand Senhor Oleisky was a hunter of Nazis,' Professor Jonathan says.

" 'So it is said among other things,' the Rabbi said. 'We will honor him. You are not to worry.'

" 'Here is the certificate of death,' Professor Jonathan says. 'It lists the cause as Unknown.'

"Then the Professor speaks to the body. He speaks in Latin. I am sure of that. He weeps a tear or two. He is a very *sympatico* man, your Professor Jonathan. Then he says and I am sure of this because I am trained to listen to catch words and names. He says, 'Good-bye Sir Thomas. Farewell, my Sir Thomas Browne.'

"I did not want to ask him at that time. It would not have been delicate. Why does he say this? Who is this knight?"

"No intelligence on him?" Harry said. "Just a mutual friend of olden times, that's all."

"Harry, shut up," Carol said.

"I think I am walking where I should not," Roberto said. "It was just an affectionate nickname, then. A calling between friends. I understand. The schnapps was very strong."

5

"He said he would wait for sunset. Then he said he would wait for the fires on the beach. Then he said I must introduce myself to you since I have come out of the shadow. No, Dona Carol, it is not dangerous. I have taken precautions. I have a man. Professor Jonathan thinks he is alone, but he is not. Do not fear. There will be no more trouble today. No more sorrow. He will be here shortly and I have done what he has asked me to do and it is time for me to go. I have come here and told you so that you would not worry and he will not have to speak about it now and I have been introduced, no?

"The sea is where he wanted to be. He said he would throw money into the sea. He said he thought that was the thing Jews did on their holy day of mourning. Or something to prepare for mourning. I am not sure. It is a symbol. At the edge of the sea is the place to mourn, do you not think so? Yes, he has definitely gone to mourn. That he must do alone. I must respect that, do you not think so? Yet I say, Dona Carol, he is protected by my man. You are not to worry."

"I am the death pin," Harry said. He was well slumped into his chair with his martini, so deeply slumped that finally he had one knee on the floor and was kind of supporting himself against the armchair.

I must get out of here or I will go crazy, Carol thought. She began pumping her ass again and smoking another cigarette.

"Won't you please stay for dinner?" she said.

"I thank you," Roberto said, "but I am sure I cannot stay for dinner. Enough of me today! Look for me tomorrow. I will be about. Maybe I will not have this wart and our luck will change. I should like to put on a patch. That is why I discipline with one eye. I confess you can see something through the patch. But it is best for this duty I look like the Professor. What do you think he will wear tomorrow? No, I joke. Then I am off duty now. You will be okay."

Roberto put down the whiskey. He looked at Harry.

"I won't be staying for dinner," Harry said. "Tomorrow night, perhaps? It could be our last night together, the three musketeers of Brazil. One more martrini, I mean martini, and I will be flat on the floor."

"I will help you," Roberto said to Harry. "Let us go. I may have useful intelligence for you."

"For me?" Harry said. "Senhor Oleisky was to find her for me. He was."

Then they were gone. Carol breathed. Eugenia would give the children dinner. Carol told Eugenia that the children could have some of the meringue and that the Professor would surely have a good sized slice when he came home and that she was going to meet him.

As Carol left the lobby and came into the street, she noticed a man in brown slacks and a pineapple shirt and a wide brimmed straw hat. He was standing by the newsstand that was directly in front of the apartment house. She was not certain if he had nodded to her. She thought he probably had. She didn't care. As she neared the beach, the breeze felt good. She felt a quickening of passion. Oh my Jonathan! she thought. She turned but once and saw that the man was trailing her. Another guardian, she thought. Another game. I do not care, she thought.

She crossed Atlântica. The stars were bright and the yellow moon was full and the clouds were lingering in their movement. There was the sound of a guitar coming from one beach fire and she heard a gentle, soft voice singing "Corcovado." It was a woman's voice and it was lovely. As Carol came near the shore, she turned once more. She saw that her guardian had stopped short of the beach and was lighting a cigarette, chatting with someone else by the low-lying stone wall. Both men were looking in her direction and she was thinking that the other must be Jonathan's guardian and Jonathan must be here and she was excited, as if she were fleeing into the arms of her lover, and there he was, his silhouette in the darkness.

He was sitting on the dry sand at the line of the shore. He was still wearing his linen jacket. It was terribly crumpled. His tie was open. He was barefoot, his shoes and socks at his side. He was swigging from a bottle. She looked at the waves, strong and high, and she slipped beside him and placed her shoes next to his.

"How about a swig for the broad?" she said smiling. He passed her the bottle.

"Oh, my God!" she said choking and laughing. "How can you drink this stuff?"

"It's good White Horse," he said to her watching her wipe the trickle from her chin. "Bottled in Brazil."

His voice was tired and his eyes were haggard. He needed a shave. She put her arm around his shoulder.

"It burns inside," she said. "It's a most satisfying burn."

He smiled.

"Then Senhor Roberto was there," he said.

"Oh, yes, quite there."

"He explained."

"He was a perfect stand-in," she said.

"Double," he said.

"Stand-in," she said and they laughed. He kissed her lightly on the lips. She massaged his shoulders. They sat in silence looking outward.

"I was thinking of Whitman," he said at last. "I was thinking of his poem, 'Out of the Cradle Endlessly Rocking,' the sea whispering to him the word death, death, again and again death, the clue from the sea that gave birth to the poet, a rebirth out of the cradle endlessly rocking."

"I remember the poem," she said, "a poem of lament, a song of death and of rebirth."

"Of parting and of loss and of reconciliation," he said. "Whitman was a decadent poet. He knew death was the mother of beauty and like Keats, he was half in love with easeful death."

She took another swig and passed him the bottle.

"We sit at the edge of a continent," he said.

"We sit within the bay," she said with laughter.

They listened to the rolling and breaking of the waves. He took a swig.

"You know," he said in as cavalier tone as he could, "I spoke to Dom Hélder today. You know, kind of, in my imagination."

"Oh," she said, "and what did the good bishop have to say?"

"He said I done good today. He said I done good." She sensed the choke in his voice as he tried to macho it out. "I did do good," he said suddenly, his voice breaking, "didn't I, Carol?"

"Oh, my darling," she said embracing him, hugging him, rocking him as a babe, "you did better than good!"

CHAPTER ELEVEN

1

They returned to the apartment and they loved. They went around the corner of time. At two in the morning they sat in the kitchen, Carol's lips puffy with love. They were drinking milk and eating Eugenia's lemon meringue.

Carol and Jonathan leaned languidly at the window sill of their bedroom. She was swathed in a bath towel and she was warm and soft and scented. Jonathan was in his shorts and he was smoking a cigarette. They were watching the light of dawn, the geometry of light upon the streets and the buildings and the white sills of repose. Brazil, Brazil, she was thinking, light and color, dance and dancer, Brazil, you work miracles of love.

She had reached out to Jonathan and had cuddled him at the margin of the sea. She felt the pride of passion. Cup my breasts, she had whispered to him, the pride of passion at the end of the upright nipple, kiss them, she had said to him, drink of them, oh, drink deeply, she had said to him. She was thinking, Oleisky redeemed, love healing all scars, the adoration of love, the devotion of men, yes, as they came to my apartment, she was thinking, yes, Harry, Oleisky, Roberto, as they sat about, the devotion of man, yes, in the streets, the light-hearted wonder, yes, even in the jokes about my, Jonathan saying, perdurable virginity. She was thinking that through my daughter, through my child that never was I became my daughter, my virginal daughter, she that never was.

She was thinking I give to you by the grace of my daughter and the devotion of man, I now give to you, Jonathan dear, the love I could not have given you as I was then, there, until there by the margin of the sea, I with Oleisky and Whitman and irresistibly you, my darling, who redeemed, who performed your act of redemption, and the burning White Horse. She had told him all about her seventeenth birthday and she even joked and she said lewdly in the darkness of their bedroom, "No more nohow of Tom's Dick that screwed me in the backseat forevermore it almost seemed." Then she said, "I have become trans-figured." He was puzzled. "I don't understand," he said. She strad-dled him. "I am transfigured," she said and she burst out with laugh-ter and joy.

2

Not the two figures on the street beneath the window, the light of dawn bringing them forth from the shadows of the night, could dis-turb Carol and Jonathan's white sill of repose. They, too, their guard-ians, were to be welcomed this new day and Carol and Jonathan waved gently and fondly to them and the men waved back and the sound of their good-natured laughter could be heard and their smiles were visible in the morning air six stories above.

"They must be cold. Do you think they were standing there all night?" Jonathan said.

"I bet they were sleeping in a car or in the lobby."

"So you bet now?" he said smiling. "Do you think so?"

"Yes, I think so," she said smiling back.

"Shall we ask them in for breakfast?"

"No, it is Roberto who shall be here for breakfast. I know."

"A change of shift?"

"It comes with the change of light," she said. Then she said, "Re-member, today's the children's good-bye party to their chums. You will be there, darling?"

"Where are we giving it?" he said. "At the *Clube?*"

"At the *Clube*."

A long car drove up the curb and on to the sidewalk. The headlights of the car were still on. The two men saluted Roberto as he emerged from the chauffeur-driven limousine. Roberto looked up at the win-dow and waved. Then he entered the building.

"Stepping up in the world, chauffeur and all," Jonathan said. "He must have started out in the dark hours. The headlights are still on."

"I had best slip into something," Carol said. "I'm afraid a wrap-around towel just won't do."

Then there was a dizziness in the air, the chimes and phone sounding at the same time, a shattering of quiet morning.

"The door we know is Roberto," Jonathan said, "so I'll take the phone."

"You louse," she said and slapped him on his behind.

She came to the door humming "The Girl from Ipanema." When she opened the door she saw at once that Roberto was smiling very seriously.

"I have come without my wart," he said.

She tried not to laugh. The children came into the living room. They had been awakened by the chimes and the phone. They came in tousled from sleep and they were surprised to see Roberto at the door and then they fearfully heard their father's voice from the study, *Well I'll be a son of a bitch.*

"I suppose your daddy is angry with whomever on the phone," she said laughingly to the children to soothe them, "or he just found out that Flamengo lost their game last night." She was trying to listen to the call while leading Roberto into the living room.

She was looking at Roberto thinking, clean shaven and minus wart he really is a stand-in. She had to admit this to herself with a slight sense of shock, a vibration, Jonathan's other. Eugenia came in in a housecoat. She was taken aback by the flurry, mistaking for a moment in her sleepy-eyed rub Senhor Roberto for Professor Jonathan. Then she realized it was he, Senhor Roberto, the guardian.

Carol saw the funny look on Jonathan's face as he entered the room. His smile was distorted ever so slightly, a bit tight as if he had had a mild stroke. There was almost a wistfulness to that smile or was it, she wondered, a secretiveness.

"Who was that call from, darling?"

"Rather interesting. I'll tell you about it a little later. Let me greet Senhor Roberto here. He was truly my angel guardian yesterday, dear friend, dear Senhor Roberto," he said and he gave him an *abraço*.

"Cartoon time, children, cartoon time," Carol said turning to her sons. "We'll break our code this once. You may eat breakfast in your room and you may watch the set. Will that be all right, Eugenia dear? Then after we will get dressed spiffy and have ourselves a holiday. We'll have ourselves a fun party."

The older boy was staring at Senhor Roberto.

"I want to stay here," he said.

Carol gathered him up in a hug and she looked at him carefully studying his eyes to see if she could tell what he was seeing. Then she hugged his brother.

"I'll stay with you for a while," she said. "I want to see the cartoons, too. I love to look at the color. Come on, come on."

She took them by the hands and they went down the hallway and she sat with them in their room and she was thinking Gaugin and then she was thinking Cézanne and then Manet and then Matisse and then there was Picasso and she saw him blue, his emaciated old man with a guitar. Was this death? Where are the bougainvillaea of home? She was frightened. Something was happening. Roberto and Jonathan. She felt it. Something more was happening.

Maybe not, she thought. Think good thoughts. Think of last night. Think of the dawn. Listen to the children's laughter. Look at the Flintstones. They're speaking Portuguese. Look at the Disney color. Think of the painters. Think of Georgia O'Keefe. Thank Georgia O'Keefe for her flowers. Send your voice out. Do it like Jonathan. Thank you, Georgia O'Keefe. I will pose nude for your lover's camera. Pay attention to the Flintstones, she thought, attend, she thought, what you have told Jonathan again and again, won't you attend? Won't you please attend? Is it the way of all married people to become looney like each other?

Then Eugenia came in with the breakfast tray. Eugenia loved the cartoons and Carol asked Eugenia to stay with the children and enjoy the cartoons.

"I must see to Senhor Roberto," Carol said.

As she came into the living room, Roberto was saying to Jonathan, "Do you have pictures of your ancestors? I am all my different ancestors and yet I am new."

Jonathan waved a kiss to Carol.

Roberto smiled and then he went on, "Does not our resemblance mean a fate?"

"Yes, it constitutes a fate," Jonathan said.

"It is a necessity?" Roberto asked.

"We have to bend to it," Jonathan said.

"It is all a necessity then, is it not, everything?"

"It is, everything."

Then Roberto turned to Carol. She was standing there confused, fearful.

"Forgive me but I will explain," he said to Carol.

She heard what Roberto was saying. The party should be called off because the Death Squad had suddenly "designated" Jonathan. Ah, I was right, she thought with sadness, something is happening. Something more is happening.

"Designated, Senhor Roberto?" she said trying to smile. "I'm afraid that sounds like something fatal. Is it?"

"You and the children will be safe. You are not the mark of the Death Squad. They will not work you that way. I prefer nevertheless that you stay very much in the apartment until departure. It could all be a bluff to scare the Professor out of the country at once, no? Still, I think it is unwise to have the party."

"I've been telling Roberto here that's quite impossible," Jonathan said to Carol. He looked hard at Roberto and said, "The children will have their party."

"I cannot put you under house arrest. How can I detain my friends? No. Be it so then," Roberto said with a sigh. "We will take Dona Carol and the children in limousine under guard. It is bullet proof but I must tell you it is not bomb proof. It is not bazooka proof. It is a limousine, not a tank," he laughed. "There is no cause to be frightened. I joke stupidly. I do not think it is serious. I will go with the Professor in a separate limousine, if that is satisfactory. We will be clever in our route to the *Clube* and we will have a motorcycle here and there."

"Our children," Carol said to Jonathan. "We can't have this. We just can't."

"It's as safe to go as it is to stay," Jonathan said. "I'm thinking of the boys. We're not going to throw away their party. We're not going to end Brazil this way. There's nothing to be alarmed about I tell you. I know. I know it for a fact. Would I put them in any kind of danger, now? Carol, please."

"How do you know it?"

"My intelligence is also very firm," Jonathan laughed. "Listen, think of Billy, that son of that Standard Oil magnate coming to school every-day with a chauffeur and a bodyguard riding shotgun. Shit, that kid was the envy of every boy and girl in the school."

"You're talking nonsense," Carol said. "What I'm thinking now is Captain Spears."

"It's as safe to go as it is to stay. I'm not crazy. I know it for a fact. Take my word for it, once, please."

"But why?" she said turning to Roberto. "I don't understand."

"How could I not respond to the Professor's charm?" Roberto said. "Who could imagine the assassins would make such a fabulous leap, these goons, and think there was a deeper complicity, a deeper conspiracy? Would add one and one and come up with three? What deeper conspiracy could there possibly have been?

"Still, I was not thinking. I must confess that. I should have known they could not understand the act of decency itself. There is no decency these gangsters have not violated. How could they let decency alone but they must imagine a maleficence, is there such an English word?, *uma maleficência*, of the spirit? For them in human nature there is more, always more, a malignancy and a deeper malignancy for these surgeons of the shark."

"You bury a man and you become his accomplice forever," Jonathan said with a laugh. "It's that simple an answer, Carol."

"They believe now that the Professor was not unknowing. They believe now the Professor was active. They believe he was in conspiracy with Senhor Oleisky. Even if they do not believe they suspect."

"Yes, they need only suspicion. They are probably outraged. After all, they gave me the body as a gift."

"I do not understand you, my professor friend. I know only I should not have allowed you. I should have foreseen the end of our journey."

"A burlap bag," Jonathan said. "You could not have known. Besides, we would have done it anyway, wouldn't have we?"

"Do not protest and do not excuse," Roberto said. "I should have seen and I should have thought of all messages and I should have known because am I not related to them? In my line of work, in my calling, am I not a relative? *Que pena!* What a pity! *Que vergonha!* What a shame!"

"They were not to touch an American," Jonathan said good-naturedly.

"It is true they love Americans," Roberto said. "They adore Americans. Americans are capitalists. But they do not understand. They think Americans are *bang bang* vigilantes. They see Western movies, *bang bang,* and they see pussy."

"Possee," Jonathan said.

"Exactly. Are you sure, Professor, you do not have pictures of your ancestors? Would it not be amazing if our great grandfathers had the resemblance?"

"Is it something like having gonorrhea?" Jonathan said.

Carol just couldn't take it anymore. She turned away from them and she left them in the morning of the living room and she went to her bedroom and she entered the dark closet. She stood paralyzed in the dark of her dressing room and she felt alone and afraid and she saw the crawl of crabs and lichens on slimy sea rocks. The glorious morning had become the murky night. Oh God, she whispered, oh God!

Jonathan, too, would go, she thought. He would be in a separate limousine with Roberto. Jonathan was sure. It was a fact. Maybe it was. Maybe it had something to do with the phone call. Believe in Jonathan, she told herself. Turn on the light, she thought. I must turn on the light. I must take care of the day. There is a farewell party for the children, a party for their classmates and friends. Carol, see to that, she told herself. See to that. Turn on the light.

Finally she turned on the light. What to wear? What to wear? Then she smiled. We will breakfast beautifully, she decided, and go on. I will be elegant, she thought, as she reached for a silk blouse. She put on gold earrings that she herself had designed and had made for her by Burle Marx. The scarf was Givenchy, the perfume Chanel No. 5, the eye-shading blue as Egypt, the skirt a rustle of silk, the lipstick a pale silver, her shoes patent, her panty briefs of lace and she wore no bra.

Life on earth, she thought. Her hair was shining and flowing. Life on earth, she thought again. The elegance of life on earth! She fought back the tears. I mustn't let my makeup run. I will be a sight. Oh God! Oh Jesus, oh God!

When the chimes sounded again, she realized that her hands were shaking. She ringed her fingers with amethyst and emerald. She braided her wrists with the languor of gold.

"Good morning, Arthur dear. I thought it might be you at the door. You are just in time for breakfast," she said.

· 3

She moved to the sound of music, a melody of the body and they were stunned and then enchanted and she saw in their eyes love and admiration, luminosity. She kissed Arthur on the cheek and he blustered a bit, dear Arthur, how pleasant a surprise, how dear of you to join us this morning, perfect, how perfect, she said. Airplane tickets, Arthur said, First Class. *Home* she heard him say. *Home* is what she remembered. The plane leaves early tomorrow morning Arthur said and she remembered *home*.

"Goddamn it," Jonathan was saying, "not a pleasant surprise at all, Arthur. Shit! Who the hell wants to go back? Tomorrow morning, hell! Not much notice, is it? You and Roberto, you and Roberto, I see it now, goddamn it. Are you sure you trust me with the tickets? Are you sure of that, goddamn it?"

"The dove of destiny," Arthur said. He was embarrassed and trying to joke. He was embarrassed for the situation and most of all for Jonathan. "The dove of peace. White and rising."

"Yes, they will build it," Roberto said. "It will be bright as a dove. I am enchanted. It must be built in a *terreiro*, a clearing."

"Are doves bright?" Arthur asked.

They sat over rolls and jam and strawberries and papaya and coffee.

"I see it. That you have conspired, that you, Arthur, old friend, and you, Roberto, my friend I thought," and Jonathan smiled his new slightly distorted smile.

"We are your most obedient servants," Arthur said.

"So it has been the Ministry and the Embassy and the Embassy and the Ministry all along in cahoots," Jonathan said.

"What is 'cahoots'?" Roberto said.

"In touch. Simply in touch. I think you might appreciate your friends a little more," Arthur said. "Roberto and I were up half the night with all this fuss."

"Those goons," Roberto said morosely, "and yet to them am I not related?"

"The children's farewell party," Carol said swiftly, "Arthur, dear, you are coming, of course."

"I shouldn't miss it for the world," Arthur said.

"And Harry?" Carol said suddenly.

"Mad as a hatter," Arthur said. "Prudence. We need more in the way of prudence in the world," he began to expound.

"Goddamn it, goddamn it, eat your roll, Arthur, drink your coffee," Jonathan was saying.

"And Harry?" she asked again.

The men were watching her pace about the kitchen. She suddenly turned from the sink and turned upon them.

"And what about Harry," she said and she was furious. "Arthur! Roberto! Is Harry in danger?"

"I'm afraid I don't know," Arthur said at last.

"I regret to say that our intelligence is not firm on his status," Roberto said.

Balloons and streamers. Streamers and balloons. She saw herself standing at the *Clube,* standing under the blue and white striped panoply cutting the cake and she was alone and she was cold but for the bitter scald of her tears.

4

"Oh, by the way, darling, that phone call? You looked very strange after that phone call," she said as she sat in the rear of the limousine.

The children were sitting on either side of her. They were quite excited with the dark tint of the glass and the telephone and the luxuriousness of it all. The smiling stranger up front with the chauffeur had a shoulder holstered gun which Carol and the children could see under the open suit jacket whenever the stranger turned toward them.

Roberto was standing on the sidewalk a few feet from the limousine. He was talking to another man. "He is also a guardian," Roberto had told the children.

Jonathan was about to close the door of the limousine when she had remembered the telephone as the thing to be remembered. With Arthur's arrival and the tickets and the thoughts and images of home, the anxieties about Harry, about her beloved Jonathan, the terror itself of the Death Squad, she remembered now and thought finally as they were to go to the club in separate limos, the telephone, *Well, I'll be a son of a bitch!,* and she said trying to be as casual as possible about it, "Oh, by the way, darling, that phone call?"

As he closed the door, he uttered the word in a low, happy whisper,

"Verlande!" Then he said, "It was Verlande."

Before she could answer he told the chauffeur to move on, that it was unwise to delay like this with the Senhora and the children parked in front of the apartment building. The car started at once and she turned to the rear window and there was Roberto still talking to the guardian and there was Jonathan waving at her and there was that crook of a smile of his, almost secretive, the smile he had after the phone call. That is how he knows it is a fact, she was thinking. He knows because he has spoken to Verlande. Something is happening. She felt it. Something more is happening.

Looking through the tinted glass in the air-conditioned car going along its circuitous route, Carol felt isolated, removed from the amber street outside. All the windows of the car had been secured and the music was playing a soft, samba beat and that which was out there, sights and sounds, was like the sunlight itself, removed, unreal, and she and the children were contained gazing in silence at a diorama of life.

She felt the cramps begin. It could not be, not possibly, she thought, menstrual. She had had her period only last week. But it felt like a premenstrual onset and yes, she was feeling, it was exactly but it could not be and she thought she suddenly felt a wetness, a slight seeping which she was sure could not be and the car sped on toward Leblon and she thought God, I hope I'm not stained.

The man with the holstered gun was paying careful attention to the front and to the rear and to both sides of the street. Occasionally he would bend toward the chauffeur to say something in a low tone, sometimes with a smile or a laugh and a nudge and occasionally the chauffeur in response would turn his head and smile at the guard and once the guard pointed for the chauffeur's benefit quite clearly and Carol saw and couldn't quite believe it that they, her guardians, were simply girl watching.

The *Clube* was on Avenida Afranio de Melo and across the street from the club there was the *favela*. It angered Carol the way the club members spoke of the *favela*, as if it were the nest for the rats and cockroaches and insects that infested the club.

Several times a day women from the *favela*, sometimes men or children, would come with large empty food tins to the spread of the club's entranceway to gather water from the hose faucets, their movement, their gathering supervised by two powerfully built doormen in braided uniforms who themselves lived in the *favela*.

Carol felt the rising scraggly hill almost as if it were an omnipresence, that there was a divinity to the host of colored wood and metal shacks seemingly perched on air, a holy precariousness of the perishable and the imperishable, and rising above it all there was the sound of the samba, the music of their life on the hill. Sometimes from the club's entranceway she could hear the thunder of pain and anger, the wail of grief, a sudden burst of laughter. At night she could see a bare string of poor light bulbs somewhere up there and she could see the small fires burning here and there, this maze, this *favela*, an overwhelming landscape, a scenery, a thrust of nature, she felt, a chiaroscuro, a constant, a value of light, born of the light. In this mood she would then see the squat, narrow building of the club as ugly, as an abasement, as a parasitic festering at the side of the *favela*. She once told Jonathan that the rats and the roaches and the insects came from the *Clube*. She said it was a pity they were infecting the hill where people breathed and had children.

The tennis, because there were no public courts, the tennis and friends had brought them to the club. She had to confess that life in the interior had been pleasant. The children had their tennis lessons and the swimming pool and the tumbling mats and the trampoline. There were billiard tables and the Astroturf putting green and there was the rolling green field where small carnivals would gaily set up from time to time, acrobats and tumblers, clowns and magicians, two or three rides, two or three burros also for riding. Sometimes there would be a caged lion or tiger or other animal or two. There were superb *churrascaria* lunches on the open verandah on Sundays, Argentine baby beef and mixed grill and *farofa* and *salsa* and french fries. There were the movies for children and the Saturday night dances to which Jonathan and Carol never went and the convenience of facilities for parties.

Carol hurried to the ladies room. She was grateful there was no bleeding but as a precaution she bought two napkins from the machine and she placed one and she put one in her pocketbook.

The children were now arriving in force from school and there were a few teachers and quite a few mothers and there was Arthur, and there she was and she waved to him and went to him and kissed him on each cheek Brazilian fashion. She said and she realized she was quite overcome because of the quaver in her voice, "Dear Arthur, dear faithful Arthur, thank you."

Charlie Chaplin ate his shoelaces. Laurel and Hardy chased a piano down a steep street. Buster Keaton wrecked havoc every time he turned with a ladder on his shoulder. There she sat in the rear of the movie room holding Arthur's hand, tears in her eyes shaded by the movement of the brights and darks of the light of the screen, images, she thought, like Plato's cave. Where is reality? There, it was a romp, wails of laughter, Arthur leaning toward her finally saying, "Yes, I think I will phone," and she, releasing his hand, smiled and nodded yes. She saw the lights go on and a waiter was at her shoulder informing her the table was prepared and then there she was under the tent, a broadly striped blue and white panoply.

Who had her by the hand now? It was one of the parents. How lovely everything is, the mother said. Carol gazed about. The tent with its streamers and balloons, its hanging pendants of *futebol* clubs, its colorfully strung banner of *Boa Viagem*, yes, Carol said, it is festive. It is simply divine, the mother said. Yes, that too, Carol laughed. It was as if she were still in the car with the strongly tinted windows, the sunlight removed, that is, life was distant, outside, no, she thought, actual, not the children, not the parents or teachers, not her own children, but Arthur, no, as she saw him coming toward her it was now as if she were seeing him through a mist of crystal fragments as he shook his head slowly to let her know he had no luck. She stood beneath the balloons and streamers. She felt the tears come again with the first cut into the gorgeous cream filled cake. She had to use both hands to control the knife.

A sadness in parting, the parents and teachers thought, as she now held back the tears and carried on in the midst of the unabated joy of thirty-five children who were eating a cake and ices dessert. She smiled at them all and loved them all and what was there to say? She tried to speak to those closest to her but she had no words to say. The words just wouldn't come.

The children took some soccer balls out onto the green field. Carol made her way to the ladies room. She was sure this time and she lowered her brief, her laced bikini and she saw that it was not her imagination. Stigmata, she thought. The drollery of it, she thought. I am endowed. I have envisioned and I have come to see that which came to pass. I stood alone then too under the streamers and the balloons when I was seventeen.

Arthur rode back in the limousine with Carol and the children. He told her she mustn't worry. He was sure Jonathan was fine. He had telephoned the Ministry and the Embassy. He had even telephoned the University on a chance and the apartment where Eugenia had answered. But there was no cause to worry. Roberto was the best. Absolutely the best in spite of his sometimes rather strange ways. It is important that she keep busy and pack, Arthur told her. He would be in touch in the early evening. The men will remain outside the apartment house as a precaution. No need for fretting. Tomorrow at this hour they will be well on their way home. It was a gala party, gala. The children loved it. Until later, then, until later. Yes, she said hearing him, yes.

Alone in the bedroom she was trembling. She changed to a light housecoat and took down the suitcases from the top of the closet. There were many things to be shipped. Arthur had said that he would see to that. Now clothes and drugs and all the goddamn packing, she thought. The suitcases were strewn open on the floor. Goddamn it, she said aloud. I should have told Arthur that there had been a phone call from Verlande. How could I? Betrayal. It would betray Jonathan, wouldn't it? Goddamn it! How could he have betrayed our night, our dawn? She thought, nonsense! I am thinking nonsense! I am at the margin of the world. I am at the end of myself. The nerves are frayed. I can't take much more of this shit. She kept looking at the suitcases and she moaned aloud, Goddamn him! Goddamn you, Jonathan, you bastard!

CHAPTER TWELVE

1

Crabs and lichens and a round yellow moon with gelatinous streaks of red, the tear of the egg, the blood on the yolk. Cry baby! Cry baby! Don't be a cry baby! Come on, Carol! Come on out and play!

Ring around the rosie! Ring around the rosie! All fall down! He betrayed me, damn him!

Double trouble boil and bubble. Talk twice say twice. Toil and trouble. Say twice talk twice. Roberto, Roberto. Jonathan, Jonathan. Stand in bubble double trouble.

Carol say. Say Carol, she said. I am on the edge, she said. Marginalia, she said. No marginalia, she said. Say Carol. Say home. Say no marginalia, she said.

The dusk was across the blind of home, a long, narrow, oblong shadow, a sash of time. I am and will be, she thought, all Carol. All Carol. No marginalia. I will be my name. I will be a song with two sons, two refrains, she laughed.

Has it stopped? Has the bleeding stopped? Jesus, Lord, it has stopped. The cramps have stopped. Get that biological clock on time. No divine interventions. Just divine biological nonstop orderly destiny. No psychosomatic mess. That's you, Carol, okay. That's me? That's you. Take a look at the real moon. Go to the window and take a look at the real moon.

From the window she saw a pure round yellow moon on a soft seascape, a wall of rippling blue and a light light horizon of evening vesper, the pale light of a dying day. Darkness has begun but it has not set in, she thought. It is not time to mourn, she thought.

Too soon to go home, Jonathan had said. Too soon? A refrain. A song's refrain. Too soon. Too soon. A Chinese dish, tu sun.

Two of everything. Two of me. That is the secret of my perdurability. Ophelia upon the water. Jonathan upon the wafer. The daughter upon my bier. The harrowed trough, the eternal cunt. Two children. Two sons. Two lovely wonderful sons. Oh God, let him not be dead. As tender as love, as real as God, I forgive him, I forgive him his trespass. Let him live so that I may love him, Mary, the Queen Mother of Heaven, so that the children may have their father.

2

When the phone rang, she told Arthur that a terrible silliness had come over her, that her imagination was not to be trusted, that it was wrapped in cerement one moment and radiant as the shimmer of Byzantine light the next.

"What are you doing now?" he said.

"I am being divine," she said. "I am sitting in the dark. I am on my bed surrounded by packed suitcases and I am going nowhere."

"For God's sake, turn on the light!" was all he could think of saying.

"For God's sake, I will turn on the light."

"I'll be there in about an hour. Will that be all right?"

Then Arthur wanted to know if she had any ideas on where Jonathan might have gone. She understood. She knew that Arthur understands that she must know at least something. She put him off. She chided him. Are all diplomats as suspicious as you are? she said.

He asked about the children. They were wondering, she told him, but only a little after the excitement of the day and they were also very excited about the long plane trip tomorrow. The children were in bed watching TV, the clown Chacrina, the funny dadist or something clown. They were watching to remember and they were waiting for Jonathan like they were waiting for the Pink Panther.

"You are not to worry," he said. "That doesn't do anybody any good and it doesn't help anything."

"If there is no news, we'll talk a bit about where Jonathan might be," she said.

"In an hour then," he said, "whatever you know no matter how little."

But what do I know? she thought. I know only one word, Verlande. I will tell Arthur that because it is late. I must. I must say it to myself as well as to him. Verlande. He spoke on the phone to Verlande. I will say just what Jonathan said. She got out of bed and turned on the light of the room. She looked at the bed and she thought, the bed linen has not been changed since last night.

3

Harry said, "Have you ever seen Cobacabana Beach at sunrise? I mean at the opening moment when the sun begins to lift from the sea? It's a kind of advent into the horizon. You can see after a very short while that the rays of the sun are blinding the windows. It is as if the bright lights of the apartments were shining out on the ocean. You stand at the quiet shoreline and from there you see those blocks of light on the windows, on hundreds and hundreds of windows, those still shades of blaring light beyond which you cannot see. But the light is mirrored in the pools of the shoreline and on the rippling advance and retreat of the ocean. The beach and the ocean take on its reflection, that is, take on strokes of light not from the sun but from those windows reflecting the light of the sun, take on its awakening from the apartments of Atlântica. Don't you think, Carol, don't you think that's quite interesting?"

His smile, she saw, was distant. Where have you been? she wanted to ask. She forbore. There was a loneliness about him, a *terreiro* of the spirit, a clearing that was almost holy, that one dare not cross. She had gone running to the door at the sound of the chimes and she was thinking Jonathan, it is Jonathan. She was taken aback by Harry. She had never seen that kind of haggardness about him, that weariness, that forlornness as if he had been designated, signed, as if he had been signified, something of the sacerdotal air touching him like a whisper because he stood so alone, so isolate, so individual, so like a man of sorrow that she forbore. Why hadn't he asked about Jonathan? Why hadn't he asked the natural question, Isn't Jonathan home or where's Jonathan? He has not asked because he knows just where Jonathan is, she thought. He knows what is happening. He knows the something more that is happening.

So she let him speak of the ocean and the apartment buildings. She let him claim her with his spiritual desolation, his solitude, his dry, vacant eyes, the sunken and stubbled pallor of his hollow cheeks, the pathos of his stance, of his vestment, the friar's rope about his waist, the extraordinary elongation of the whole of his figure rattling like a skeleton in the looseness of his tattered clothes. She let him speak and she forbore. As he spoke, he tried to comb his hair with his long bony fingers and she would speak but she knew her voice would not reach him where he stood in his own clearing, barefoot in solitude.

He would drink. That he said he would do. She asked him with a lilt in her voice, an attempt at gaiety, if it were the usual. No, it is not, he had said. You just don't want me to mix a martini, she said trying to kid him, to lift his spirits. He just thought he would like a whiskey and he said in a feeble attempt to respond to her cheering spirit, he would like the whiskey straight up and very dry. One straight whiskey straight up very dry she said placing the bottle and the glass on the coffee table in front of him and at last he sat down on the couch. He poured a quick, gulping shot and then he poured again and he raised his glass to her as she sat in the armchair by the couch and she nodded her head in acknowledgment. He took a long sip from the glass and he put the glass down and he leaned back on the couch tilting his head backward and closing his eyes.

She saw his death mask. Time spun on. She thought she could hear the sound of the lamp like the faintest whir of a needle. There we are, she thought. There we are. Harry's on his own floating continent of the self. He will speak when he returns. He will have found the words. Why hadn't Roberto gotten in touch, she wondered. But it all would have been said or will be said, this she now knew, by Harry. Until then, she thought, anyway there we are.

She sat upright with her hands folded on her lap, her eyes studying the painting of reds and blacks above the couch, she seeing, trying to see the painting, its sluggish flow and groping texture. She turned toward Harry. His eyes were still closed, his breathing barely visible. She was thinking now with a smile, he will open his eyes. He will lean forward for the whiskey and as she thought this so he did, his eyes opening slowly, a smile, that forlorn smile and he leaned forward and he poured himself a solid whiskey.

"The Death Squad," he said in a somewhat hoarse voice and then smiling again, "the good guys'll get 'em. They'll get the bastards and it'll be okay. It'll be all right. It will, Carol." He was leaning back again and sloping into the recesses of the couch.

He kept looking at her smilingly and tears came into his eyes. "There isn't a thing for you to worry about," he said.

"That's very good of you," she said at last. The spell had been removed and here was Harry again. "That's very good of you to reassure me. Clearly you've been through quite a day."

"You will have to handle me," he said. "I am not well. I'm even, I might say, maudlin."

"That's a terrible disease," she said.

"So they say," he said.

"You will have to forgive me, dear Harry, if I appear tactless but there are two children in the bedroom waiting for the return of their father."

"Yes," he said as if he had not been listening, "I think I must be handled. I think I'm not well."

"I am truly sorry to hear that."

"Pow," he said softly and closed his eyes again.

She got up and came to him on the couch. Close. She was close as a breath to him. She knew she had to revivify, to lord the process, to give life, to give him her presence, the touch of her hand upon his shoulder, the touch of her hand upon his hand, now the touch of her hand upon his arm, she almost leaning upon him at times as she asked a question, at times almost in a swoon herself as she would lean back, away, wantonly to take in the answer and then to press forward again to open those vacant eyes of his with her presence and he would say something and close his eyes and fade again and die he now knowing and waiting for the alternate rhythm, the surety of her vital power of bringing him back, of reviviscence in the still pool of evening lamplight.

She listened to the float of his lifeless voice and from the listless undercurrent she drew her tone, her voice now an undercurrent as she gently questioned him and he responded and she would occasionally lean away and then she would gain control again and she would place the murmur of a seductive touch of her hand upon him. He shivered at last and the story was told.

4

He had not recognized her as his sixteen-year-old bride, not even her eyes for the fatted lid was too heavy upon them. She gave no sign of recognizing him but Verlande said to Harry, "Speak in English and she will know you."

They were in the Cathedral. She was squatting on a small mound of dirt on the place for the altar. She was like a fat hen, Harry was saying to Carol, and when she stood up she was enormous, her shape the shape of hen, he, Harry, saying this in his lifeless voice. Carol was trying not to laugh and she was trying not to gasp. She was waiting for Jonathan, waiting where this would take her to Jonathan while listening to Harry's immortal moment, he, ragged of skin and bones, bent as a crone before the overwhelming, the sheer size of this woman, Carol listening, unbelieving and believing, sad and comical, the humor of pathos, she listening to Harry as Harry said Verlande said, "Senhor Harry, it is she whom you seek!"

Harry looked at Verlande in terror and he was shaking his head no. Verlande said, "Embrace her!" Harry heard the tolling peal of laughter from Verlande's men ringing throughout the hollow of the Cathedral but Verlande was not smiling and he silenced the laughter and he said to Harry, "Go, go Senhor Harry, it is she whom you seek. Embrace her. Embrace your red bird of paradise!"

In that telling Carol gasped at the sadness, the comedy, the cruelty, but Harry said there was no cruelty, no, not Verlande cruel. Verlande's not the bad guys. But it was not she as Verlande had thought. It was not his sixteen-year-old virgin of hearth and home. Not even Verlande could say so because there was no sign, Harry said, no recognition, no passage.

Carol was thinking of Jonathan, the sad and the comical and the absurd in Harry's immortal moment with the Jesuit's Bird of Paradise, thinking the flaming flower is Harry's hen, Harry's hen is Jonathan's dove, the White Dove of the Center, the Virgin of the Altar, the mulata princess of the samba, she thinking and trying to suppress a giggle, suppress the hysteria of relationship going Jonathanesque through her mind, the surrealism of connection like the meeting of parallel lines at a street corner intersection somewhere, somewhere in the neighborhood.

"Go, go, Senhor Harry, it is she whom you seek," Verlande had said. Carol listened as Harry repeated Verlande's words again and again, the monotone of Harry's incantation, the lifeless litany of love found, found.

"But no," Harry said to Carol, "no, it cannot be."

There was a quick, fluttering note of passion, of voice when Harry said this. Carol knew he said it cannot be because even if it is it cannot be.

"She only smiled. She stretched her smile without showing her teeth. Her teeth must have been very bad, don't you think?" Harry said. "She smiled when I called her name but there was no motion, no passage, no passage, Carol, of anything, no passage at all."

Carol knew his sixteen year old was to remain in his dreams while the hen was to remain a hen on the mound of dirt on the altar of the Cathedral. Harry's sixteen year old still was. Carol had to bring Harry back, reviviscence, bringing him back, his eyes closing and now opening. Jonathan, she thought, you must tell me about Jonathan.

"'Harry? Oh, you are Harry. How nice' That's all she said," Harry said. "'Harry? Oh, you are Harry. How nice.' That voice was not weak. She may have been, been—"

"Impaired?"

"Impaired? Yes, impaired, but the voice was low and husky and all whiskey and smoke."

But Jonathan, you must tell me about Jonathan she was thinking as time spun on, as she listened to the sound of the lamp like the faintest whir of a needle.

Harry thought Malgahães was in the shadows. He could not be sure.

He had seen only his pictures in the papers and there in the shadows with all the dust and debris he could not be sure.

"Senhor Verlande speaks truthfully," the voice said from the shadows. "It is she whom you seek."

Carol wondered. She tried to imagine what it was like, the filtered light of the Cathedral, the light of the dust, the light of the interior. She tried to imagine how this all could be, that broad avenue of traffic, the *Faculdade de Letras* across the way, there, this unfinished Cathedral, Verlande, his men, the man in the shadows, the woman, Harry, the life without, there, traffic, pedestrians on the embankment hurrying by, walking slowly by, sauntering, while there within was the great complicity, carpenters and stonemasons and plasterers and laborers with wheelbarrows, the scaffolding, the scaffolding of light and she was wondering, more sensing anew, divining now that it came upon her, that morning after Carnival now came upon her unbidden and she knew that she had not let it go.

She had insisted that Jonathan go to the Carnival alone. The children had been feverish and she would not leave them and she insisted that Jonathan go. And then that morning, no, that noon when he at last returned, she wondering, said, "You stayed for it all?" and he said, "Just about but I did. I don't know why and what impulse led me, but I decided to look into that Cathedral going up. I've been watching it get along from the steps of the Faculty all these months and I, I thought I'd finally look in there and I rested awhile."

"You rested there?" She had never known him not to tell the truth before.

"There were others there, too, sleeping off the night of the Carnival."

"The homeless," she said.

"The homeless," he said, "and let's let it go at that. I'm bushed."

"Jonathan?" she said.

"Yes," he said and she let it go at that.

"Now Harry," she said, "I want you to tell me about Jonathan. Was he there with you? Was Roberto there?"

"They came," he said. "They came so I could go, kind of."

"Jonathan came and Roberto came," she said to him, "so that you might go? Were you hostage? Do you mean to say released? Exchanged? For God's sake, Harry, please tell me!"

Have you betrayed your friend? she wondered. Have you betrayed my husband? She kept her control and she leaned back and she thought I must find the word to lance his pain so that he may speak to me of Jonathan. He does not want to speak to me of Jonathan. Yes, she thought, and she said, "It is about Oleisky, dear Harry, it is Oleisky, is it not?"

Harry nodded his head and he said, "Yes, yes, it is Oleisky."

"It is Oleisky with whom we begin, is it not?"

"How did you know? Who told you?"

"Intuition," she said smiling and coaxing him. "No one told me."

"Go down Moses. We met on the line. The net line. I told you that, didn't I, once?"

"So you have."

"So it had been. I didn't know Verlande until now. That student came to me, that student of Jonathan's. He took me. He said they found her. We were going to stand on enchanted ground. I didn't know Verlande. I should've gone to the children's party. It must've been a good party."

"It was balloons and streamers," Carol said, "balloons and streamers."

At this she saw the trace of a real smile on Harry's lips.

"Who would've thought," Harry said, "that Oleisky was in with the famous Verlande?"

"Yes," she said soothingly, "who would have thought? But then, Harry, the thing about this apartment, the way it was brought about our renting it, you through Oleisky, did it not seem odd to you? Did he not seem strange?"

"Am I not odd?" Harry said smiling charmingly. "Am I not strange?"

"You? You are Jonathan's Historian of Pow," Carol laughed. "Jonathan now, now Jonathan."

"I mean odd," Harry said. "He was a hunter of Nazis. That is not your everyday occupation."

"Yes, but you knew he was in something."

"If you hunt Nazis, dear Carol, you are in something."

"But you had not known of Verlande. You had not known of Verlande," she coaxed him.

"I had not known of Oleisky hyphen Verlande. I guess as it turned out it was Oleisky hyphen Malgahães hyphen Verlande. I knew only that Oleisky was in something."

"Then?" she said. "And Jonathan?"

"They didn't need me," he said at last. "I was the fake hostage. They could've had Jonathan without me. Verlande knew that. It was the guardian who was the problem. It was Roberto."

"Roberto?"

"Yes, Roberto."

"The day is coming to an end," she said. "It has been the longest day."

"Yes," he said, his eyes closing.

She began again. "Roberto?"

"Now the hands are off the clock. Then again," he said, "she was on enchanted ground."

Carol touched his hand. She said, "Come back Harry, come back, please."

"Sure," Harry said, "sure. Oleisky was the bag man. That's what we used to call it in Brooklyn, remember? The guy who delivers for the mob. He was a bag man and the squad found out and knocked him off."

"Now, Harry?"

"You're right. That's not fair," Harry said opening his eyes and sighing. "Not the mob. The good guys. He was delivering for the good guys. The word was Oleisky. All Verlande had to say was Oleisky and Jonathan would've come anyway. True? That's our Jonathan."

"I suppose so, yes," she said.

"Right," Harry said, "but Jonathan has a guardian. They weren't going to shoot up any of your guardians. They wanted Jonathan. They did not want Jonathan hurt. They needed Jonathan. Verlande wanted Jonathan."

"This is very consoling," she said.

"Isn't it though?" he said and tears were in his eyes. "Jonathan barely knew Oleisky. Why?"

"What is it, Harry? What is it they wanted done?"

She knew the moment was at hand and she thought *Jonathan* and the skies of terror were inside her but she kept control and she managed in the pool of evening lamplight to softly urge Harry onward.

"Verlande is setting up the blind and Jonathan's the decoy."

"You mean?"

"The Death Squad, the ones who got Oleisky. They can't get to Jonathan. It would be too difficult and dangerous to try to get him with all the security the Ministry has set up for you. So Verlande will be getting the word out."

"You mean?"

"The word out will be that Jonathan has slipped his security, his last night in Rio, a girl, to see his paramour for a passionate and touching farewell, that simple, that stereotypically simple for a Latin heart, that he can be had tonight because of his hots for his beloved. Jonathan draws the Death Squad to him but who's really waiting all the time? Verlande. Verlande and his men have set the trap.

"Oleisky's killing has gotten to Verlande and he's serving warning. It will have the support of the people, a big political thing for his group. It will be visible and specific and concrete, that's the kind of talk Verlande uses. It's going to be an example. He will get them when they're about to commit an act of terror. He will get them in the act itself. Verlande believes that since there's no lawful government, since there's no government to deal with the death squads, his group is entering a new phase of action. The death squads, they who terrorize will themselves be terrorized. Yes, that's the way he talks, you know."

"And Roberto? How could Roberto let Jonathan, let it happen?"

"Like I said, I was the fake hostage. They had me. They had me through my hen. They had me through my hen and I was the exchange. Funny, isn't it?

"I guess Jonathan must have convinced Roberto that I was a true hostage, the real thing. I don't know what else. Besides, Verlande promised them safe passage anyway and everyone knows his word is golden. All they had to do was listen to his proposition, his plan. Jonathan doesn't have to act. It's just the proposition they want him to hear, just the damn proposition to get Oleisky's killers. That was the deal."

"And now that they are with Verlande, Jonathan will, will he not?"

"Yes," Harry said rubbing away the tears and trying to smile, "I can't take it anymore. He will, if he can swing it with Roberto in some way, God forgive me, he will act."

"Yes," she said, "I see that."

She took him to her bosom and she listened to his choked sobbing and she held him and she wondered and she was numb and she stroked his hair. She looked out beyond and she was dry eyed and she was gazing into nothing. The waves of the ocean are silent tonight, she thought, and life is a dream.

Chapter Thirteen

1

It had been difficult when Arthur first arrived. The unpleasantness began at once. She found herself standing in the middle of the living room, fragmented and worn after the ordeal with Harry, listening now to Arthur and trying to calm his rage, his fear, his anxiety. *He what?* Arthur fairly shouted at Harry. But good dear Arthur she said and he, cooling down rapidly at the sound and notes of her voice, recalled and asserted the diplomat in himself. Here was a practical matter to be attended to.

No, please, she said to him, no assault upon the Cathedral and she laughed—I am sure they left once Harry left—no, nothing to be done except to wait, she pleaded, or it will make the situation more confusing and therefore it will make it more dangerous.

"It's time for you to be quite simply a noble friend," she said.

"At the least Jonathan should not have done this to the Ambassador," Arthur could not resist saying. "Forgive me, Carol, that was shabby. I do think I should call, though. I must not think of the personal, not of the personal element. This is a potential situation involving two countries. I had better make some phone calls."

"Oh, Arthur, bullshit," she said.

He was taken aback and he said, "I don't know what you mean?"

"Nothing is clearer than the word bullshit," she said. Then she said, "Please sit down and have some whiskey with Harry," and she said this so softly, so nicely that Arthur discovered he was sitting down.

"There are lists to go over, items to be shipped," she said. "You will be helpful?"

"But of course," Arthur said pouring himself a whiskey, "I will be delighted."

But somehow Arthur had to keep going with Jonathan. Why did he do this? How did it come about?

"I don't mean to be unkind," Arthur was saying on his second drink, "but Jonathan, well, as for Jonathan it is too bad there are no huge, ancient, ponderous gates to the City to be moved open for the Processional. He is in the wrong time and he doesn't know what really is can't be wiped away by dreams and by the imagination. I'm a diplomat and what I understand is that which can be negotiated. History is a negotiated reality."

"A negotiable reality," Harry said. "Not for Jonathan, though. Jonathan is a damn Professor of Literature. You want to know why he did this? As his court Historian of Pow, this man I love as a brother, I tell you his reality is symbolic. It is finally a symbolist poem, whatever that is. Arthur, you are unkind because you are unperceiving. The sensitivity of perception is all and everything. In retrieving, in claiming the body, in putting that burlap bag with that heavy weight—for Oleisky was not a slight man—upon his shoulder, he was in the interconnectedness of things that to Jonathan constitutes history, I know my Jonathan, and you won't mind if I pause for another sip of this splendid whiskey—"

"Get it out. What have you got to say? Spit it out!" Arthur said.

"He was carrying the Holocaust in a most personal way, a most intimate way, perhaps the only way to cope in personal terms with its magnitude, carrying by moral choice what could be carried of the Holocaust on his own shoulders and, well, yes, the death squads are S.S. or what have you Nazis."

"Really," Arthur said. "And you, Carol? What do you say to this?"

"Pow!" Harry said and he squeezed his genitals and Carol saw that he was quite tipsy now and she saw that Arthur was well under way himself.

She had been thinking of Jonathan while they had been talking. She was thinking of the time they had been bicycling in the Havana sunlight and how excited he was at the sight of Hemingway's boat, the *Pilar,* at anchor in the harbor. Revolution and love. Cuba. How could she explain this to Harry and Arthur as they sat around the living room like mourners at the bench? He, Jonathan, was seeking the burial rites of the dead, *Irmãos Das Almas,* Brothers of the Soul, carrying the body halfway through the city to redeem, she knew, to redeem and in redemption expiate his own youthful dreams, his own boyish idealism, his own history within the history of a time. She could not, how could she or why should she explain this to Harry and Arthur except to say that Oleisky was one of the world's victims in the time of the assassins. Jonathan felt this deeply.

"As it was for Rimbaud," she suddenly said and surprised herself in the saying, "I think of Rimbaud, that is, history is *le temps des assassins.*" She paused and for the first time in the long evening she felt her heart truly break. "It is the time of the assassins and we just must do the best we can about it."

"What can we do? Is it urgent?" Harry said.

"Where is Jonathan?" she said.

"History is a fat hen on an altar of mud," Harry said. He wiped away the saliva from his lower lip and his chin and he closed his eyes.

2

She left them in the living room along with the whiskey. There were things to be gotten together to be shipped, she told Arthur. She said there were two paintings, you know that lovely seascape, Jenner's *Yellow Day in Bahia*, and the *Genero*, the one that was so brilliant in color that he had done as a design for a tapestry, remember, Arthur, Harry, yes, and some small odd sculpture, some sandstone, a hard glazed, remember, Arthur, you were with us at the time, ceramic, and there are a couple of tapestries, a Renot and a Kennedy, the Kennedy for the children who loved the red mystical bird among flowers that have eyes, and some special silverware and some platters, it is, I'm afraid too much to ask of you, Arthur.

Arthur was saying I will have a crew here and I will personally supervise the packing and shipping. I will be delighted. It is no trouble at all. I will sing my way through it knowing that all of you are safe at home, back home and out of trouble, and your paintings, your tapestries, your sculpture, your *objets d'art,* will be safe home with you as well. If you have a harpsichord, I will send it to you. If you have even, even a clavichord, I will send it to you. I will send the harpsichord and the clavichord through diplomatic pouch. Aha, you think I jest. There, Carol, you smile, you smile and my heart sings. Have you ever seen a diplomatic pouch? he said while beginning to open his shirt buttons.

You have more than made up for your bad behavior and if you go on like this I will be delighted to kill you, she said and she left them with the whiskey. She knew they were trying to make time pass for her, to cheer and comfort her now, and she was amused that Arthur was getting high. It was the first time she had ever seen him drinking this way.

She sailed out of the claustrophobic sea, the lamplit float of the evening, into wider waters and she could hear herself breathing and in the dark of the bedroom she thought of the bougainvillaea in bloom, a hidden guitar, her hero, Jonathan of the night, as she thought and she was thinking, oh how we dress the bones of reality in the straddling of the flesh, in the straddling of the mind by the wild whisper, the lovely breeze of a dream. It is I, she whispered to herself laughingly, it is I, Jonathan, whom you seek.

Then she turned on the light and she took down the two paintings and then she paused and she left the paintings on the bed and she went into the children's room. Chacrina had long since gone and the boys were quite drowsily watching a *novela*.

"Soap opera?" she said.

"The Cabin of Father Thomas," the older boy said.

"Don't you think it's time for you *meninos* to go to sleep? It's been a long day. It will be a longer day tomorrow."

"Who is out there?" the older boy said. "They sound like Uncle Arthur and Uncle Harry. Are they *embriagodo*? They sound drunk."

"They are a little noisy," she said, "having a good time."

"Where's dada?" the younger boy said.

"Dada is so busy with final arrangements for our trip that you had better not wait up for him."

"Is Eugenia coming with us?" the younger boy said.

"No, but she may follow. She has a large family here. We'll certainly see that she comes to visit."

"Good," the older boy said.

"Good," the younger boy mimicked him.

"Shut up, Sam," the older boy said.

"My name isn't Sam," the younger boy said. "Your name is Sam."

"My name is Frank," the older boy said. "Your name is Lothario."

"Lothario?" Carol laughed. "Where did you dig up the name Lothario?"

"My name is," the younger boy said, "my name is," and then he began to giggle. "My name is Sweetie Pie."

"That's what little chubby Helena calls him, Lothario," the older boy explained. "She doesn't let go of you, Sam."

"Luther-Rio! Luther-Rio! That's what the girls call you, Luther-Rio!" the younger boy tried to taunt him. "I'm Sweetie Pie."

"Now that's enough. That's quite enough," Carol said laughingly. "It's beddy-bed time, *meninos*. Beddy-bed time!"

The hug of life and the air was sonorous, a slightly awkward hug, his awkwardness, for the older child, a lingering hug for the younger.

Lights out and life is resonant, ah, the children! she thought. She felt herself gliding forth, a new movement. The music is jazz and she felt herself played on by all kinds of colorful lighting, shadings of yellow and orange and blood red in the black hallway. Yeah, she *feels*, yeah, she says to herself yeah, and she uplifts her head and dangles her arms and tilts her shoulders and suspends her body, unmoving and precipitate, yeah, she feels, a curvaceous vase, an urn for gray ash, a hot incendiary for a circus of thought. She faces the full length oval mirror of her bedroom and she smiles. She remembers saying tenderly, Carolinha. You were then Carolinha.

Carolinha comes out of the mirror. Yeah, memory, take me by the hand, Carol says, and we'll wait together. Here, I'll take this crepe and put it over the lamp and we'll turn off all the lights but this one. We'll let Arthur and Harry, we'll let the men and the whiskey wait in the yellow light. See what the crepe does? We'll wait for Jonathan here, here in the soft blue, in the cerulean light, no, we are bathed in indigo, it is, it is mood indigo. There, take the paintings off the bed. Place them carefully against the wall. Now lie down softly, better, good, there. I will let you stroke my hair. I will let you kiss me. I want you to sing me me a song, lyrical and loving, of days gone by.

No, Carol says to Carolinha, no, please no. She is breathing heavily and she is pumping and she is squeezing her thighs and she feels memory's warm lips upon her breast and hot fingers trembling downward and under the waistband of her panties and there, there she is tumescent and warmly wet and she is moaning and arching and she is seventeen and the waves are silent and she sees the arch of her body on the slate horizon of a strange and distant and awful sea.

She extended her hands outward and there was no one there. Jonathan, Jonathan, she whispered.

Seventeen years of age. She smiled and she laughed a little. Was it all so very long ago she was thinking sixteen years ago when I was supposed to be so bright, the prodigy and progeny of colliding stars? The doe-eyed valedictorian of dreams? Yes, it was a very long fancy time ago, she thought. The sun had not stood still. The moon rose and the dogs howled at bay. In that rank, brown office outside of Philadelphia in the ammonic twilight she knew she had been born. Until then, she knew now, life had been imagined.

She had not been living with the bread and stone of time, she was thinking, but within a Shirley Temple kind of dream of the good ship *Lollipop* sailing under cotton candy clouds on a sea of ice blue glass, a toyful dream along with the other toys of childhood that kept you dreaming, the *brincadeiros*, the playthings of youth, seemingly divine and eternal. Then in Philadelphia, she was thinking, I got myself born with the daughter that never was. Tears came into her eyes. It was not the child but the mother who got born. I got born into the bread and stone of time.

Poor Jonathan, she thought, how he put up with me! She laughed. I've been such a lousy lay. There he was not knowing more than any of the other men the real mystery of my virginity. Oh God! An alabaster figurine, a gypsum virgin, that's what I was, the hoofer in the dotty sailor outfit from the good ship *Lollipop* who had gotten herself all fucked up. And how! No more. I don't think anymore. No more.

Upon the bier of Oleisky Jonathan created the royalty of form, she was thinking, the dominion of spirit, the shape of a kingly phantom on a puppet screen. What else is real? she thought. He had taken her back to Jerusalem, so she thought, to climb the Mount of Zion, to listen to the tambourines, to begin again with all the ghosts he memorialized, all the evil he wanted to expiate, to begin again in a passionate fit of baroque relation, all, she thought, the abortion itself, by so stately an act of bestowal, by so stately an act of life this bearing of a body to Zion she unsuspecting, taken by surprise, the sea within her, life and death, her Jonathan grieving at the shore with his White Horse and his thoughts of Whitman, herself surprised at the trembling of her flesh, her body redeemed, at the joy of at last, at last, at last the sound of tambourines, the sound of tambourines.

Yes, she thought, I have come out of it with the actual real loving husband, the wonderful children oh Lothario and Sweetie Pie, stone and bread and bread and stone, she thinking, remembering. She sighed. Then she was smiling, turning her head from side to side on the downy pillow in the deep violet, in the violet blue light.

She rubbed her eyes and yawned. She rolled out of bed and went to the window. She looked out below and there under the streetlight were the two security men, the chauffeur and his partner, smoking and leaning against the black limousine. She removed the crepe from the lamp and turned on the ceiling light. She went into the bathroom and doused her face with cold water. She sat at the dresser brushing her hair. She went down the hallway to the children's room and she was happy to see them sleeping soundly. She returned to the bedroom and picked up the paintings and went down the hallway again into the living room. There was a note by the drained bottle and two glasses. It was in Arthur's script with the time notation of 9:00 on the upper right corner of the napkin. *Dearest Carol, Didn't want to disturb you and all that. We are out for the air. We'll bring back a pizza. Took the brash liberty of checking the fridge and you have the beer. Love, Arthur.*

She went to the front door and opened it. There was another security man, the one of the night before, who had been wearing a pineapple shirt and who was now wearing a strawberry shirt, a profusion of strawberries. He was sitting on the stairs and smoking and reading a comic book. He looked up at her and smiled sympathetically.

"Good evening, Senhora," he said in a soft and gentle Portuguese. "Is there anything I can do? I do not think it advisable that you go out tonight. You understand that is what I have been told by the rainmaker."

"Oh," she laughed, "you mean Senhor Roberto."

"A very important person."

"I am sure he is. May I get you something, something to eat or drink, a coffee perhaps?"

"I am very well disposed," he said patting his stomach, "but I thank you."

"Are you sure?" she said looking about into the lonely, the desolate stairwell, their voices echoing.

"Senhora," he said, "please forgive me for being too forward but you know our hearts are with you. We like your family. All the security likes your family. You are very *simpatico*. There is something good about your family."

"That's very kind of you."

"So you forgive me please for intruding when I say I do not know anything but do not worry. The boroughs are clean. All is blue. The rainmaker will see to that. Senhor Roberto has a knack."

"The men below? Would they like something to eat?"

"The chauffeur," he laughed, "is very strong. The other is not so weak either. They are well fortified."

"Well, then" she laughed, "if you wish to avail yourself of the services of the apartment, do not hesitate to let me know. Do you promise?"

"You are most graceful, Senhora."

"Well, then, good night," she said.

"Good night, Senhora, may you dream in gold," he said.

She closed the door softly behind her. She went back to the bedroom and began to collect the objects they had bought here and there and so she went back and forth from the bedroom to the living room and there were the two tapestries but the Kennedy would have to wait until the morning because it was hanging in the children's room and she did not want to disturb them. Then she brought into the living room three ceramic pieces from the kitchen and *cafèzinho* cups and saucers, silverware setting for eight, a hammer for pounding meat which she had not seen in the States, a cloth coffee strainer. The all purpose electric frying pan that she had brought with her from the States, that she decided she would leave for Eugenia. It was difficult and expensive to come by in Brazil. And so she gathered and then she went into the study for a few more objects and for a pencil and pad. Before sitting down in the living room to make up the list for Arthur, she poured herself a gin and tonic.

She began writing and she was nearly overcome by a terrible loneliness but she kept on and she smoked a cigarette and she felt that her heart was weeping and she was trying not to imagine the possibility of horror, the possibility of a tragedy, of a loss so overwhelming, no, she would not, there, the White Dove, Jonathan's White Dove, his Center rising like a white dove. They will have us back for the dedication, she was thinking, sunny skies and blazing sunsets, the White Dove, that is what she will say to him on the airplane, silver wings, her power, she, Carol, feathers like gold, oh but the disquieted heart, the fear of a death, fearfulness and trembling, the horrible dread, and I am being overwhelmed, she thought, overcome by the dread.

There the list, get the list done, the door, get the door.

The pizza man, the pizza man Harry and Arthur said in unison. They were both still slightly high and they went noisily into the kitchen and they got the beer and Eugenia came in puzzled. She was wearing her glasses and she had a newspaper in her hand. How proud she was that she could read and good reason for the pride, Carol thought. Carol was saying now Eugenia sit with us and Eugenia, smiling with embarrassment, was saying oh I cannot Dona Carol and Harry took one arm and Arthur the other and they led Eugenia to the table singing she's a jolly good fellow and they sat her at the table and so Carol had her last dinner, pizza and beer, in Rio de Janeiro.

CHAPTER FOURTEEN

1

She was not certain whether or not she had been sleeping. She was exhausted. She had sprawled on the bed after Harry and Arthur had gone. They were reluctant to go but she told them she would be perfectly all right and she promised that she would let them know at once of any news. They were to return early in the morning—they were sure Jonathan would be back soon, certainly—and they would go to the airport in gala fashion they said, with champagne and caviar and they would be sure to have some *guarana* for the children. She was nodding yes and smiling, wanting to be alone, wanting to wait it out with her own thoughts, her own feelings. She was afraid that Harry, she did not want to be hard, was to begin again to speak of his sixteen year old wife, his beauty, and then of the hen, the impossibility of relationship between his sixteen-year-old wife and the hen as if the beginning and the middle and the end of life were somehow organically connected. She was sympathetic to the plea in Arthur's eye as Harry was saying to him, "Let's find a nice café table if you don't mind helping an old friend and we'll sit into the night and I will tell you all because I am not well, you know."

Carol managed to get them to the door with some grace and she heard their voices mingling pleasantly with the voice of the security guard and she turned out the light and then, exhausted, she had sprawled on the bed, a tired spirit haunted by the movement of the clock and the blackness of space. She remembered seeing a collage of a white dove in still flight against the blackness and then she did not remember until there was a touch upon her shoulder and she bolted upright, startled. What is it? she said to the crimson darkness.

2

Exú was dressed in black that night. He was suave in top hat evening attire, a necklace of red and black beads about his collar. He had high-boned hollow cheeks and he was smooth, tightly skinned to the skull. His eyebrows were heavy and arching toward his temples, his eyes blue and almond shaped, his eyelashes black and long and thick, his nose acquiline, his lips full and curving, a lurid red, the demon himself of the *Umbandistas*, a devil who could do an awful lot of good work as well as evil.

And there was his whore, Pomba Gira, wearing a golden crown upon hair black as the raven, a diamond on her forehead, her red and gold cape parted upon her naked breasts, breasts most sensual, round and bold, parabolic, nippled in the purple grape, bold, brazen, her smile glistening of nectar, of the lascivious juices of the world. Between her breasts was a silver chain holding Solomon's Seal, gold within a gold circle.

They were regal and erotic, royal and base, an androgynous couple, two headed, partnered, male and female, sometimes with one lower body with the trunk bearing man and woman. They came from the shadows these two, from the decaying and decadent gray walls of cemeteries and ancient pavement stones, devil and whore of the same sustenance and of the same flesh, summoned from the cemetery and the walls of Inhaùma itself at the foot of the Serra da Misèricordia, the Mound of Mercy. At midnight when the breeze is desolate over the barren lots, the ashes of cinders, the *favelas*, Exú and his whore of the world are summoned forth into the night by beefsteak and popcorn, by whiskey and a cigar, by the blue rivulets of *cachaça* fired by the flame from the votive candle, the flame creeping among the fragments of glass from broken bottles, Exú, the guardian of graves, receiving his sustenance from the slaughtered carcass of headless chickens, from the eyeless heads of goats soaking in the juice of their blood, smoked sausages, onions, tomatoes, the stench of burning wax and *cachaça* and butchered meat in the sightless night, the night of ghosts, of spirits, the African chants, the sounds of mystery, the language of a remembered homeland of rain forests and of deserts, of mountains and plateaus.

Carol did not know if she were awake or asleep. Somewhere she heard the sound of maniacal laughter there from the shadows, from the walls of the cemetery Inhaųma at the foot of the Mound of Mercy.

What is it? she had said to the crimson darkness. Eugenia was whisper-ing to her, calming her, soothing her. She had been startled into the night and after that moment of awakening, it had been as if she were drugged.

Had she been into the night and she knew yes she had. There was Eugenia's voice in the dark, there was the *figa*, the charm of the clenched fist with the protruding thumb to ward off the bad spirits, the *figa* between her breasts. Upon awakening her, Eugenia had slipped the pendant about her and it was there and that had hap-pened.

There was Eugenia's voice, its soft, melodious rhythm reaching her through the daze, explaining gently and carefully how it had been arranged with the security guards below because they were *Umbandis-tas* and though they knew Carol was not an initiate into their cult what harm, they said, she and the family were very *simpatico*, a good bet to cover all bets, and Eugenia leading her out of the apartment through the servant's entrance, through dim and wavering light, she dazed, drugged she felt, she, looking down at her feet and remembering that Eugenia had put her shoes on for her, she riding down the servant's elevator half leaning against Eugenia, her head resting on Eugenia's shoulder, Eugenia stroking Carol's hair and humming and chanting softly in a language Carol did not know. Then they were in the base-ment garage and there was an old beat-up Ford and a thin young man with taut skin behind the wheel and she remembered riding up the ramp into the night, riding north, to the *Zul Norte*, and she remem-bered that the security guards had smiled and waved to her as she looked back to the front of the apartment house and she cuddled into Eugenia's arms.

She knew she had come somewhere, there, where Exú was, the wall of the cemetery and there was a family, a mother and three children all expensively dressed, lighting candles, setting out *cachaça* and food for the spirits and Eugenia said and Carol remembered her saying that they had come for the woman's husband and the children's father who was deathly ill in the hospital. In the flickering light, the odor of burning wax and slaughtered carcass, Carol saw there people of every class and color, whites and mulattoes and blacks, and someone was laughing from the shadows, this she remembered, and then she did not know and there was a votive silence and the passing of a gust, the desolation of a breeze, a guitar hidden somewhere among the bougainvillaea, where was she, was she awake or dreaming, what was happening, why did she find herself raising a bottle of *cachaça* to smash it against the pavement stone? She stared transfixed at the flame as it mingled and trailed along the rivulets of sugar-cane rum and she raised another bottle at the whispering, the urging of Eugenia and she smashed it and a third bottle and she smashed it on the pavement stone and she felt weak and faint and she was not sure now this was really happening to her and she thought afterwards was I there, was I in a trance, and she remembered whispering Jonathan, Jonathan, Jonathan, spirits, gods, demons, please, please, my Jonathan and she felt the lingering spirit of her love possessing her and then Eugenia had taken her back to the car.

How long she had been at the altar of the wall at Inhauma she did not know and she had been there, yes, she thought, for she remembered clearly that as Eugenia helped her into the car and they were driving away, that the flames moving along the spilled *cachaça* had streamed like a current from the pavement stone to the gutter and, catching the refuse, there was a fire at the curb.

This, too, she knew that was not a dream, not a trance, the driver turning his head to the back seat where Carol was nestled in the arms of Eugenia, the driver smiling broadly saying it is good, Senhora, look, look at your hand, see what you are holding. Through glazed, half-opened eyes she looked at her left hand and she saw she was clutching a white rose.

They rode through the night and when they were near the apartment house, the car stopped at the corner, the crossroads of Rua Souza Lima and Avenida Copacabana and Carol began to laugh and she said no, Eugenia, please, and Eugenia said no more, this once, Dona Carol, and no more, and she gently and carefully helped Carol out of the car. For your Eugenia, Dona Carol, and no more, she said. They were kneeling on the earth at the base of a bare tree. Eugenia took out from her shopping bag a bottle of *cachaça*, a cigar, three candles, a box of matches. Dona Carol, this is our private offering, our *despacho*, Eugenia said. Place the three candles in a row, Dona Carol. Good, she said, very good. Now light them. Good, she said, very good. Carol was tired. She was very tired and she felt the emptiness of the dark streets within her and she could scarcely move her arms. Do not be surprised, Dona Carol, Eugenia said, but I have brought this photograph of you. It is very nice, don't you think? Oh, Eugenia, Carol said, I am weary. *Estou pregado.* I am exhausted. I need to rest. Please, Carol said, please.

Soon, Eugenia said tenderly, soon it will be all right. We must summon the good saints. Now write on the back of the photograph, there, she whispered, giving Carol a pen as she held Carol's trembling hand. Jonathan, Carol wrote, and she held the photograph as Eugenia told her what to do. She held it over the center candle and the photograph began to burn and the flame curled close almost singeing Carol's face and Eugenia said, it is good, Dona Carol, you and the Professor will be together very soon as the flame joins you now. You will be together very soon, she said again, and she was hugging Carol and tears of joy

were coming down her cheeks. They left the bottle upright, the burning candles, the box of matches and the cigar there at the base of the
tree.

A security man waved to them as they drove down the ramp. The
security man who had a gun in his shoulder holster raised the garage
door for them.

"Well," he said good-humoredly to Eugenia, "I was waiting for you
to get back so I can get some food."

"I will bring you food," Eugenia said.

"Good," he said. "It is after midnight more or less and I am purple
with hunger. This night air gives you a good appetite. How did it go?"

"I, too, am purple with hunger," the driver of the car said.

"I will bring food for everyone," Eugenia said looking at Carol. Carol
nodded her head and said, "Yes, please do, Eugenia."

"And how did it go?" the man said again as Carol, supported by
Eugenia and holding the white flower in her left hand, moved slowly
toward the service elevator.

3

She clasped the *figa* at her breast and felt the after calm of sacrifice
before the deities of the night, so she thought of it. She saw divinity in
the white rose in the glass of water upon her dresser. Next to the glass
lay the cross which Jonathan had emptied from his pocket the night
before. Oleisky's cross he had called it. She lay propped up in her bed
dreaming of an auroral celebration, a dawn of wings, as she fancied it,
that would take her and Jonathan and the children across the undula-
tions of land and sea, there, downward, that uncertain light of ivory
upon the flesh, the chambered nautilus, to home.

She finally went once again to the closet. The clothes on the hangar
in the otherwise emptied closet were for Jonathan's change when he
came home. She checked again and she was sure these were the
clothes he would want to wear on the plane. She went to the window.
She leaned out and the security men below catching her form waved to
her. She waved back. She would wait for the light to come up the
street. There would not be a great deal of time but the time was ample
before departure. Time enough. Jonathan will be here. She would wait
for the light, she thought, and she would wave to Jonathan as he got
out of the car with the *manda-chuva*, the maker of rain, the dear Senhor
Roberto, the man, the guardian of resemblance.

CHAPTER FIFTEEN

1

The whistle sounded above the noise of hammers and buzz saws. The men, half naked in their rags and invariably short and muscular, were balancing small rickety wheelbarrows of cement as they skillfully walked the planks extending from the outside of the Cathedral to the scaffolding of the interior. They were moving more quickly now that the whistle had sounded. The buzz saws had stopped. The carpenters were checking their workbenches, the artisans with trowels and a flourish, rapidly and with care, their last strokes. The whistle, having stopped for a few minutes, sounded again. Then there was some laughter and a sound of voices in the hollow Cathedral. There were sighs of weariness with the last sound of the whistle and the further rise of laughter, of voices, and some of the younger men, whom Jonathan noticed over there not far from the jeep, were dousing themselves with water from a hose. They were washing under their armpits and down the length of their arms. They were rubbing water on their chests and joking about women. Then some of them were taking off clothes from a line they had set up earlier in the day with two forked sticks and a cord. The clothes had been drying in the filtered dust and the men were changing into the clothes for their big evening.

The men were not paying any attention to the waddling mass of a woman sitting on a mound of dirt where the altar was to be, sitting and staring into space, into, Professor Jonathan thought, the calvary of dust. He could tell she was listening to sounds that she did not seem to fathom, her eyes taken every now and then by motion or by movement, by the rising, he saw, of Verlande's arm as Verlande was pointing to the ceiling of the Cathedral.

Verlande was saying, "See this Mayan Temple, how the walls rise and the roof is blunt at the top? See, we are in a pyramid and the outside walls will be terraced like steps and the rise of the entrance wall will look like a broad stairway leading to the razed top."

"Do we not have as Brazilians our own descent?" Roberto said. "What magician of logic would build a Mayan temple for a Cathedral in downtown Rio de Janeiro? What is wrong with our own descent?"

Verlande said, "It is good to embrace our spirit through time, to make chronology timeless, to embrace the Indians. Someday we'll build for our own Indians of the Amazon. This Cathedral is our *abraço* for the Mayan Indians, our oppressed brothers in time. Besides, it is modern, it is current, is it not, Professor, like your Mr. Frank Lloyd Wright? He was brother to the Mayans in his architecture if I am not mistaken."

Before Jonathan could reply, Roberto said, "I do not know about this countryman of yours, this Mr. Wright, and my apologies for that, Professor, but I give this volcano, yes, a volcano, my yellow smile."

Verlande said, "You must not say this anymore than you would about the hunchback and the woman." He turned to Jonathan, "She was gypsy, was she not gypsy, Professor? And Senhor Hugo, was he not a revolutionary perhaps? On this occasional camping ground of mine I am now building my Cathedral. That foreman, that last lamented foreman, has been replaced by this new one who is one of us. It is my permission that allows all to go forward so that it is funny, no, that I who was to be a Jesuit am at this moment something of a builder of a Cathedral whose work proceeds through me. I, a man of the Church, I, Verlande."

Jonathan was startled. He saw Verlande in a state of almost religious possession, of pietistic rapture. Jonathan was trying to get the connections, if there were any. Perhaps Verlande was simply mad, insane. He was trying to understand what Verlande was saying.

Verlande said, "I am sowing the dragon teeth of revolution even here, on this, my occasional camping ground from which will spring stories, hey Professor, like Notre Dame de Paris. This is a volcano, so the good Senhor Roberto would have me believe, but I say no. It is what I make it to be. It is a ground made sacred by the stories I am giving to it, hey Professor of Literature. Is there not artistry to my design, do you not see?"

Jonathan did not answer. He was looking at the grandeur of Verlande's smile and he could only turn toward the altar. He recognized his voice was strained and tremulous as he said, "And what will you do with Esmeralda, with the gypsy on the mound?"

Jonathan saw how her fat-lidded eyes had followed upwards as Verlande pointed to the blunt shape of the top and Jonathan saw her smile that was not a smile, a smile that stretched her lips and gave to the edges a slight upward curl, the kind clowns paint on, the whole of her rounded and red blotched face assuming, so Jonathan thought, in that moment a mask of mirth and his heart went out to her innocence and what he felt must somehow be her despair.

When they had first come into the Cathedral and Jonathan saw Harry, he felt that somehow Harry had never seemed more helplessly frail, Harry standing like a puny planet alone in the soaring universe, his back so rounded, so bent that it would seem his bony shoulders were to touch in front, his head bowed, his eyes welling with tears when he saw him and Roberto, the palms of his hands upward and outward stretched, his fingers crooked and stiff as if painfully arthritic.

"I am not well," he told Jonathan. "Why did you come? They would not have hurt me. Why did you come?" He turned to Senhor Roberto and he said, "Goddamn you, why did you let him? It was all a fake."

Then Jonathan embraced him and two men led Harry away, Harry shuffling, half turning, tugging at his genitals, muttering goddamn, goddamn. Then suddenly shaking himself from the two men and turning about to face Jonathan and Verlande and pointing to the altar he shouted, almost in a falsetto, "She is a fraud, a cruel trick! A cruel trick! Senhor Verlande, you have torn my heart! You have put electrodes to my soul!"

He was visibly trembling and as Jonathan came toward him he raised his hand to stop Jonathan and then remarkably as he had his hand raised so he gave to Jonathan the sign of the cross and smiled weakly at the blessing he had bestowed. He turned and with one *guerreiro* on one side of him and one on the other he shuffled most pitifully toward the cavelike opening of the Cathedral and Jonathan could see that he turned once at the opening for a backward glance. Jonathan waved but Harry did not seem to see and then he was gone and the three men stood alone by the jeep.

Verlande then said, "Yes, you may go as well, the two of you." Then he said to Senhor Roberto, "Yes, your resemblance, your resemblance to the Professor is a true one. It is not empty and it gives me confidence and I see, I see how clearly the Professor was able to persuade you to come. Our plan is a good one, is it not? So simple, very simple and we will have Oleisky's murderers, a simple decoy. The word is out, the time and place set. They will be there. The hunter cannot believe that he has become the hunted. We will deal with the death squads for the people by executing a very specific, a very concrete example, hey Professor? We will get them in the act of trying to murder. Is that not a poetic justice? Do not worry, Professor. We will see that you are safe. We will see that you are on the morning plane. What do you think Senhor Roberto, Senhor Guardian? I knew the Professor would persuade you to at least listen to us, yes, with Harry here, for did the Professor, did he not persuade you to restore Oleisky to the community? That is what you have done. You have not allowed him to disappear and so I know you are of the true resemblance, I say, not empty, not empty at all."

2

"Now I will tell you what I will do for the woman and what I will do for Senhor Harry. I will deliver her to Senhor Harry personally."

"Then she is really the one?" Jonathan said.

"Whether or not she is the actual woman is not the issue, is it?" Verlande said with a slight smile. "It is not, as you might say, the point."

"Surely you're not going through with this. It's not a good joke."

"Senhor Harry needs her," Verlande said. "She will be his salvation. Do you not see that I am still a terrible, terrifying Jesuit? Senhor Harry must make good somewhere must he not, she whom he corrupted? It is the theology of the thing. It is basic morality. It is the idea. It is kinship."

"It's bullshit."

"Ah," Senhor Verlande laughed, "that it is. You do not see that I am joking? How could I, even I, deliver her? And how does she feel? And how could I force him? I was playing my game. You are here. But it is proper to remind him as well."

"What will you do with her?"

"We will make her our Patron Saint, that is what we are going to do with her. How well the poor creature sits upon the altar!"

Jonathan looked at Roberto who was very much amused and who now closed one eye.

"If this Mayan Indian," Roberto said, "returns the stolen cars in prime go away condition and with the gas full, would he not at least return the woman with her tank well filled? I think so, Professor. I think she will be well paid."

The jeep stood there with its mounted machine gun carelessly covered with canvas. Verlande was off to the side talking to one of his men and pointing to the woman and then he returned and he winked at Roberto. At his wink Roberto shot open his closed eye and they began laughing. They played the game again with the shut eye and the wink trying to time it perfectly. Jonathan shrugged his shoulders and also laughed. Then the foreman came over to say the men were going.

Jonathan saw that almost all of the laborers were carrying a bundle or a parcel of some kind and occasionally someone would glance at Verlande's circle and then wave a farewell on parting.

The foreman said to Verlande, "Maestro, the architect and contractor will be here soon, usually at the hour after the men are gone. It is perhaps an accommodation. The guards are in place and I think it is wise that we go."

"Yes, our business is done here," Verlande said, "and we have stayed too long. But first quickly, the courtesy, the honor is essential. It will fortify our Professor and it will take only a moment."

The foreman, glancing at his fob watch, was nervous. Verlande clapped him on the shoulder and said, "Do not worry. I say it will be only a moment more or less. Are we not on Brazilian time? Here, keep Senhor Roberto company. Sit in the jeep. I have whiskey in the compartment. Drink. It will be but a moment to pay our respects."

Then he said to Jonathan, "You will now come with me if it pleases you."

Senhor Roberto made a motion to accompany them but Verlande laid his hand gently on Roberto's arm to restrain him.

"We are only going over there to meet someone in those shadows," he said, "see that rounded corner, there, yes, there. A Brazilian experience for the Professor, that's all.

"You do not want to go, Senhor Roberto, Senhor Guardian. You do not want to meet this person because it would place something on you, at worst an action that we would all regret and at best a compromise you do not want."

"It is his Excellency," Senhor Roberto said very quietly.

"I do not forget the delicacy that you are of the Ministry," Verlande said, "a delicacy I most gratefully appreciate, and while we are all fine and in balance right now, I tell you you do not want this for a concern, no."

Jonathan, seeing the hesitation on Roberto's face, a grim and even dangerous hesitation, said, "Let it be, my friend."

"Then again, it may not be his Excellency," Roberto said at last. "It may not be the big fish."

"My whiskey is very good," Verlande said.

"Well, well. That good?" Roberto said.

"That good," Verlande said.

Roberto got into the driver's seat of the jeep. The foreman, in the passenger seat, opened the compartment. He took out the bottle and handed it to Roberto. Roberto looked at the label and said, "It is very dry and dusty in this god-forsaken volcano. I think I will have a drink, after all. I will toast our oppressed Mayan brothers. But I tell you, my eyes will be upon you."

Then Verlande and Jonathan began to walk toward the farthermost point of the shell, to the tantamount edge from where they were.

3

Jonathan was thinking that he would not have been surprised to find a cow in the shadows. He felt he was walking on the ashes of reality. He wondered if it were the lunar dust and the amber light and the sheer hollow shell of space that made him feel almost weightless, as if he were a citizen of another country walking on the sacred ground of the afterworld while there on the jeep he was thinking he had really remained humanly imbruted in the form of his double, in the body of his stand-in, who was swigging whiskey.

Then Jonathan saw an indistinct figure in the round corner and then he saw that the figure was seated on a chair and next to him, sitting cross-legged on the ground, Jonathan was now able to make out, was his student. His student had an old American M1 rifle cradled in his arms.

"Professor," his student said cheerily, "I am very happy to see you."

The man in the chair got up and he was tall and tanned and very handsome, strikingly so. He had a touch of graying hair at the temples and a warm and friendly smile that made Jonathan smile back. He was very fit and he reminded Jonathan of a younger Christopher when Christopher was about forty-five. He was wearing a blue boating jacket, an open collar shirt that was light blue with a touch of silver, white bell pants, miraculously immaculate in the dust, and the softest loafers. There was a dazzling blue gemstone ring on the pinky of his left hand and he said in superb British English, as he extended his hand in a firm handshake, how very pleased, really delighted he was to meet the Professor who so kindly and generously had taken such splendid care of his apartment in his absence.

"I must apologize for the untoward circumstances in which we meet. Someday under more favorable circumstances and conditions, we will walk the aisles of the Cathedral together in supernal light," he said.

While Jonathan was still struck by the words "untoward" and "supernal," Senhor Malgahães was asking him about his wife and children.

"I trust your wife and children have enjoyed the apartment in spite of the more recent," and here he paused and said, "inconveniences of late."

Jonathan assured him it was a splendid apartment from beginning to end, no inconveniences at all, and then he went on to say, "Mr. Secretary, legend has it that you are quite a swimmer."

Senhor Malgahães laughed and said, "We Brazilians are amphibious, moving with ease from air to water and back to air again, like those excellent divers off the highboard. There is something ecstatic about it, is there not, in the plunge from air to water and the rise from water to air? It gives us a double life, does it not? We cling with our sun filled bodies to our beaches, to our sea, and so," he said laughingly, "we are made immortal by forever reduplicating ourselves from air to water, from water to air. The double life, the amphibious life, Professor. But, as we were saying, there are, ah, in this particular life of the land at this particular time, inconveniences, but these inconveniences in the end may be really certain opportunities for which we, in the long run, will be grateful."

"I'm not quite sure about what you've just said, but it was said well and it sounded substantive. Clearly you must be a formidable politician," Jonathan said.

At this Senhor Malgahães laughed again, a hearty and strong laugh, and turning to Verlande he said to him in Portuguese, "Didn't I tell you that the Professor is one of earth's noblemen?" Then he said in English, "Professor, you must return here with your family. You must have your children grow up here. Brazil is the country of the future—and we will always remain so."

"The future?" Jonathan said. "You'll pardon me if I say that the future strikes me as somewhat remote and theoretical at the moment."

"Now you sound like a Professor!" Senhor Malgahães said good-naturedly.

"I incur the risk," Jonathan said.

"It is, perhaps, a moral risk you speak of?"

Jonathan was stunned by this bit of perception. "Yes," he said, "I don't believe in violence. How am I to stand before the world ever after, the future? There will be, must be an alteration of all relationships. I think you've got the wrong man. I'll probably freeze when the time comes. Besides, I'm about to do just what I protest about my own government, interfere in the affairs of another country."

He felt a shiver in his spine as the words of Dom Hélder came to him, "Be revolutionary like the gospel, but without wounding love." He thought with shame how he had turned away from these words. They did not make sense, he thought. They did not cohere. There was an inconsistency about them. Pulpit talk, he had thought. Now the words came to him with sweetness and power and Jonathan was thinking I cannot go on with this. I cannot.

His imagination was stirring and he was in a state of momentary transport. Carol, he knew, would tell him to attend. But he could not seem to find reality in the moment and place where he stood. There was a dream vision taking hold of him. There was a pomegranate garden with a fresh spring and a flowing fountain, a garden of myrrh and spice, of aloe and honey and there he was with Carol and the children. They were hand in hand in the garden of living waters, a family breathing in the scented air of freedom. But Jonathan knew the flow of the air was circumambient and that terror there sooner or later would be breathed in here, north wind and south wind, east wind and west wind. He knew the spring could be shut and the fountain sealed. But with blood on my hands, he was thinking, how am I to walk hand in hand with my family, ring around the crimson pomegranate, dark ruby hands the signet of my complicity? What will happen with the first firing? What will happen with the first throw of the molotov or petrol cocktail? What will happen with the first toss of a hand grenade?

"My dear Professor," Jonathan heard Senhor Malgahães saying, "you are not an outsider but a member of the community. You are not interfering in the affairs of others. In claiming the body of Senhor Oleisky you have performed the rites of the community and whether you want it or not the Death Squad has conferred upon you membership in the community. I bestow upon you a lifelong honorary citizenship in our community. If it were in my power I would bestow citizenship itself upon you."

Then he laughed uncomfortably and said, "Alteration is but another word for change, is it not? The question is always whether change is for the good or for the bad."

He laughed uncomfortably again. Then he went on, "Reality is elusive and there are moral discriminations to be made between terrorism and armed action. We deplore terrorism. But enough of this weighty business. I am afraid it is time to count time," and he gave Jonathan an *abraço* and then stepping back gallantly he turned to Verlande and warned him to take good care of the Professor.

"Return to us, my friend, return to us soon," he said.

Jonathan moved through the dust and the debris and glancing backward through the amber light he now saw the indistinct figure of Senhor Malgahães as a shade in the shadows. He heard the merry voice of his student saying something and he heard Senhor Malgahães laugh, a short burst of laughter.

Now that's the color of reality, he was thinking, olive green, the jeep, time to count time. Roberto was saying, "Revolutionaries have very good whiskey, Professor." Then he said to Verlande, "Tell me honestly. The troops drink bad *cachaça* and weak *chope*, do they not?"

"Senhor Roberto, I will go first in the jeep with three of my men and the whiskey, if you do not mind. You and the Professor will follow in your bullet proof car. I would enjoy, Senhor Roberto, to steal that car someday. It would give me great comfort to have a bullet proof car."

"You travel with your comfort," Roberto said raising the whiskey bottle. "How much more comfort does a man need?"

"We will have a red Simca behind you," Verlande said. "We will have two motorcycles who will go in and out, who will trail and be with us. Does this, Senhor Guardian, strike you as strong and proper?"

"The street police?" Senhor Roberto said. "If they glance even with one eye they will see the mounted gun."

"They will not see," Verlande said. "Why should they? They are not ready to die for this government."

"And where are we following you?" Senhor Roberto said.

"Why, it is the Professor's last night in Brazil. We have prepared a *feijoada* for him," Verlande said.

"You cannot. It is not Saturday. *Feijoada* is served only on Saturday. Today is Thursday. Where do you find a *feijoada* on Thursday?"

"This makes it all the more special," Verlande said. "It is our offering to our American friend. If you cannot imagine having a *feijoada* on Thursday, Senhor Guardian, then clearly you will never understand what our revolution is for."

"If it is *feijoada*, then I think it must be Saturday," Roberto said. "Yes, it is Saturday, then."

Jonathan laughed and the driver started the jeep and Verlande walked the nave with Roberto and Jonathan. Just as they were leaving the Cathedral Jonathan turned and he saw three of Verlande's men walking toward the shadows where Senhor Malgahães was seated, toward, Jonathan thought, the rounded corner of history itself. He heard the full strong voice of one of the men saying it is growing late, we must move forward, your Excellency. Then he saw another two men, the last two of Verlande's *guerilheiros* left in the Cathedral. He saw them moving slowly toward the altar, toward the woman on the altar.

Then he was outside in the air where the jeep was waiting by Roberto's car and by the red Simca that had not been there before and at once Jonathan felt a deep sadness come upon him, a nostalgia as he felt the softness of the breeze, the gentleness of the light of early evening, a nostalgia for the most pleasant normalcy of the street, of the passersby going home from a day's work.

The small caravan moved down República do Chile and on to Avenida Rio Branco and they had crossed Avenida Presidente Wilson. It was not quite dark as they branched out on to the broad and lovely expanse of the *atêrro*, the beautiful landscape taking on a silhouette form in the twilight. Jonathan thinking, looking at the sailboats and the yachts in the Bay of Botafogo, the first lights of evening coming on, Jonathan thinking of Carol, thinking of the children, thinking of love, trying to free his thoughts from the dread of the oncoming night, but he could not. His thoughts were haunted by the figure in the shadows. They were summoned forth by the beckoning specter of the charming Secretary of State in exile.

CHAPTER SIXTEEN

1

Senhor Roberto was cursing furiously as he drove the car, cursing in low muttering tones in a mixture of Portuguese and English, saying I must be an imbecile, I must be crazy, an idiot for the hanging, a fucking dog with a kerosene tail. Why look at what kind of country this is anyway with that goddamn poster communist perched like a parrot, a goddamn macaw taking in the sights in that open jeep and that goddamn obvious machine gun not even barely hid with that goddamn naked barrel pointing right at us and we like two fairies, forgive me Professor, following that enormous goddamn perforated metal penis like two goddamn, forgive me Professor, fairy fags, and no one giving a good goddamn. Look at that patrol car passing us like a sleek shit-assed sylph! That's what you get for building a fucking city at the edge of the jungle, the *jaracaca*, the fucking pit vipers.

Roberto caught his breath. He smiled. He said, "I am embarrassed, Professor. Excuse me. I apologize for saying bad things about fags."

Jonathan hadn't been quite listening to Roberto. He was preoccupied and finally he said, "The parrot perch. Do you know about the parrot perch in a violet room?"

"Yes," Roberto said, "I have heard much about that room, with the walls of violet cloth, the *sala roxa*."

"That's where they had Verlande."

"Then I must apologize for my words about him," Senhor Roberto said. "Who knows what is to become of anyone who has been in the purple room?"

They moved on for a while in silence and then Roberto said, "You have been to Bahia, to Salvador of course?"

"*Bahia de Todos os Santos,*" Jonathan said, "I love it as much in its own way as I love Rio in its way. And of course, Rio is home."

"Bay of All the Saints," Roberto said, "there was a man. Do you know that little park in the upper city, the one with the small café and that mansion that is a police station? You can see from that café the lights of the lower city and the view is wonderful."

"When I was lecturing in Bahia, my wife and I were taken to that very café by a cultural affairs officer and his girlfriend."

"I remember one night," Roberto said, "the grain elevator, the Lacerdo elevator that rises from the lower to the upper city? That elevator also has a spectacular view. Have you ever been there at the top and taken it to the lower city?"

"Planned on it, but I never did."

Roberto's voice was soft with sadness. "Have you ever noticed sitting at that café those high voltage wires running into the mansion?"

"Yes, I know. The aide pointed it out to me."

"I was once assigned to shadow a prisoner just released from 'interrogation.' You understand what I mean by 'interrogation?' I was outside and I have never been in that mansion. I have heard stories but I have never been. When this man left the mansion he was wild. I had trouble staying with him even with his jacket open to the wind. He moved strangely with his arms outstretched high up to the sky and his bad limp. I never saw his face, only his back. His hair was very long and tangled but I don't know what expression he had. For that I thank God.

"I do not know if his eyes were gleaming. I do not know if he was clean shaven. I know only that the tail of his shirt was hanging below his jacket and he moved so fast, never looking around, never looking back, never looking to see if he was being followed, how do you say *desajuntar* in English, disconnected, is that good? He was disconnected, in shambles, a very big, a very big man, like a bear. It was very funny too because I had on my fat glasses and hearing aid and cane disguise thinking that since he had just been 'interrogated' I was going to have a very slow man coming down those steps of the mansion, not a wild one. There I was trying to keep within distance of him and I could not understand how he could be swift coming from the mansion and I managed to stay with him but in the end I could not reach him Professor Jonathan.

"He began shouting over and over again *I am a man I am a man* just like that running along the walk by that grain elevator and I could not reach him. He was shouting *I am a man I am a man* over and over again turning my blood cold and I could not reach him and I could only watch him through my fat glasses as he threw himself over the barrier into the space of all those lights of *Bahia de Todos Santos*. It was something, huh, Professor Jonathan?

"I could not go down to the body in the lower city and it was very funny, wasn't it, the way I had put on my disguise? Who knows about Senhor Verlande? Once he has been in the *sala roxa*, who knows? Who knows him now? Not even his mother!"

Jonathan could see the tears in Roberto's eyes. The limousine was moving rapidly along the *atêrro* and then Roberto cleared his throat and he took a handkerchief from his breast pocket and wiped his brow and his eyes and blew his nose and glanced sheepishly at Jonathan. Then he said in a joking tone, "It would be a great prize to get that leftist Senhor Malgahães, His Excellency. You do not suppose he was hiding in that rounded corner, do you suppose, Professor?"

"I do not suppose," Jonathan said looking out the window.

"I see," Roberto said sympathetically, "you are time out of time. You are somewhere else. You are on some sidewalk, hey?"

"I am on the sidewalk in front of my apartment house."

"We should have stayed there. We should have gone to the party. Anything but this. This is not your work."

"It is not my work."

"This work with thugs is not real for you."

"This is not real for me."

"I see you have entered the sidewalk. I am talking too much, no? I will leave you on the sidewalk."

"Thank you, my dear friend."

Jonathan was thinking that it was as if Verlande had been on the sidewalk in front of the apartment house listening to them. It was uncanny. Verlande knew the claim that Jonathan could and would make upon Roberto. Knew it for sure.

Jonathan said, "Do you think Verlande is a genius?"

"I do not know about genius. I know only he has concentration. He concentrates well. It is a deficiency that he is a communist. How can he be a genius if he is a communist? But enough. He has been in the *sala roxa*. Look, he is turning to wave at us. We are going over the lane into Atlântica. The Simca is following. I think we are going to become strong in Copacabana. *Feijoada* is a fortification. To make it well you need a general to marshal the troops. But where but where? I smell the ocean. It is a beautiful night. Look at those motorcyclists. Some protection! They think they are in a ballet."

"I mean," Jonathan said and then he stopped and he thought of Verlande's word, "empty," Verlande saying to Roberto, "I know you are of the true resemblance, I say, not empty, not empty at all." It had been as if he were on the sidewalk listening to Senhor Roberto weakening under Jonathan's persuasion, about to give up.

On the sidewalk Roberto had said, "Without our doubles, without our semblance, we are empty, my Professor, empty. Yet what am I to do?"

"But they have Harry."

"We are going to the *Clube* under the protection provided. Besides, Professor, with all respect, how are we to miss our children's party? Our, for are we not our ancestors?" Roberto laughed. "As for Senhor Harry, he is not in danger. Why should they touch him?"

"They say they have his wife."

"Now *that* I find interesting, a most interesting love story," Roberto said.

They had been standing on the sidewalk, Jonathan thinking my heart is breaking as he saw Carol looking at him through the rear glass of the car, her tenderness, her wondering, that lovely oval, high browed virginal face, the red lips pursed, forming the question born of confusion and hurt, the question in the word, *Jonathan?*

He could see the questioning in the beautiful and deep softness of her large brown eyes. He could see the car beginning to move away slowly and he could still see the query, the wounded query, the dove listing in flight, *Jonathan? Jonathan?* He tried to smile and wave as he turned away from the car. Then he took Roberto by the arm, Roberto who was giving last minute instructions to one of the guards who was to remain at the apartment house.

"Senhor Roberto," Jonathan said, "I have received a phone call, that call when you came into the apartment."

Senhor Roberto looked at him and said, "Am I to divine the phone call for we have given you the courtesy and ourselves the economy of taking you off the tap as of twenty hours more or less last night."

Jonathan said, "It is a courtesy I appreciate, believe me. Maybe Senhor Verlande knew about it because he made the phone call himself. Even if the phone had been tapped you wouldn't know where he is and you'd know only that they have Harry and I am to meet him at our place where I met him before."

"Where is our place?"

"You'll come with me and I'll show you."

"I have not been sent here for Senhor Verlande and Senhor Harry and I do not care about Senhor Verlande right now and Senhor Verlande will do nothing to Senhor Harry and we must take our precautions against the Death Squad in an event that is unlikely, no?" Then he said, "We are going to have a good time at our children's party, are we not, Professor? Under the protection provided?"

"Have I dreamed you?" Jonathan said. The two men stood facing each other squarely, looking into each other's eyes. Senhor Roberto, for the first time since Verlande's name came up, began to smile.

"Have I dreamed you?" Jonathan said again.

"The world is real," Roberto said.

"What we must do, we must do then," Jonathan said.

"You mean it is a necessity," Senhor Roberto said. "I look into the mirror and I see you."

"Yes, a necessity."

"Well then. I always say yes to necessity. Our ancestors would approve."

"That is the only way."

"Yes," Roberto laughed, "it is the only way to have your skin."

He told his driver to stay guard at the apartment. Roberto got behind the wheel and as the car moved away from the curb, Roberto said, "This necessity is a wonderful grandmother, do you not think? Although she is very old she still has strong teeth like a shark and she will always take good care of us, do you not think?" Then he said, "I must tell you, Professor, with all respect, that I thought when we first met actually that you were mad to begin with. I think I was right. Now will you tell me where we are going, this *our place*, because since I am driving this also is a necessity."

"República do Chile."

Roberto, astonished, said, "To the *Faculdade de Letras?*"

"No, across the way."

"There is nothing across the way except that architectural abomination they build to God."

"Yes, the abomination."

"You mean the Cathedral!" Roberto said and whistled. "But it cannot be! Where are we truly going?"

"The Cathedral."

"The *guerrilheiros* are in the Cathedral? I cannot believe that."

"You don't have to believe. You're going to see for yourself. Now is Verlande a genius or isn't he a genius?"

"Only in Brazil," Roberto said and whistled again, "only in Brazil, no, only in Rio, well, I, too, will be a son of a bitch!"

"Maybe in Bahia?"

"In Bahia, too, everything is possible except the Cathedral is very old and it is not an abomination."

"In Recife? Maybe in Recife?"

"No, not in Recife. In Recife we are talking of Archbishop Dom Hélder."

Jonathan began to laugh.

"Why do you find this comical?" Roberto said.

"Sorry," Jonathan said.

"This is a *bagunça*, a complete mess," Roberto said. "How can this all

be? How can the *guerrilheiros* be in the Cathedral? That is Brazil for
you. That is Rio. That is a good one for the *carioca*. I listen to the
amusement. I listen to the jokes now. The *carioca* will have many sly
jokes."

Roberto pondered matters for a moment, shook his head, paused
and said, "This we have to be thankful for. God, as you have heard, is
a Brazilian. Everything then must work out in the end. We do not have
to worry over the confusion if you just remember that is natural with
God since He is a Brazilian."

2

There is no narrative in time, Professor Jonathan thought, we only
pretend to succession. He felt the minutes as they drove in their
isolation along Atlântica, there in the bullet-proof, air-conditioned,
black limousine. The traffic was heavy, stop and go. The cafés were
starting to fill and he could see the breeze in the flutter of awnings, in
the float of the palms. He could see the *futebol* games that were still
going on under the endless light of the beach. All of Rio seemed to be
playing or taking a stroll under the crescent moon. He watched the
passersby. He was thinking I am only minutes from my apartment.

"Maybe if I go by your apartment I will turn sharply into your
garage," Roberto said. "How would you like that, Professor? Dona
Carol is waiting."

"You're reading my thoughts," Jonathan said. "Harry should be
there by now."

After a long pause and a sigh, Jonathan said, "What difference
would it really make if Senhor Malgahães had been in the Cathedral?"

"Ah, you do not want to think about your apartment," Roberto said.

"No, I do not want to think about my apartment."

"Then I will help you not to think. I will explain to you. It would be a
great prize to get that leftist, His Excellency, once again. It would be a
great prize for the Ministry. In Brazil with a fish as big as His Excellency, it would be a triumph. It would be very good for our score. It
would also be very good to have a *chope* with our friends and say we
got the big fish back again."

"If you caught the big fish, then what?"

"I am happy my explanation has your interest."

"It has my interest."

"Then we photograph him. We measure him. When it is convenient
we let him escape again or we just throw him back into the sea at a
convenient time so he can swim away."

"Aside from the brownie points and bragging rights, why bother? I mean it's a strange game."

"Brownie points?"

"I can't think of the Portuguese for that. My Portuguese is not good enough. I wish it were as good as your English. To look good and brag about the score. Let us go back—it's a game then."

"Not a game, but a sport, my Professor. Fishing is not a game but a sport, is it not?"

"You're right."

"Now, then, I will explain further and I will give you an examination afterward, Professor, so you must pay attention. You must not enter the sidewalk again."

"I am paying careful attention, maestro," Jonathan laughed.

"Well, then, that is why we are here because the big fish brings with him and needs all the little fish. Senhor Oleisky, for example, is one of our little fish, no? I mean he is little from a political point of view, you understand."

"I understand."

"They want to swallow up the little fish because that's where the trouble is. The big fish do not attack each other. They do not devour each other. We do not have violent revolutions *bang bang* in our government. We are famous for that, no? It is not customary for the big shot coming in to shoot the big shot going out. They take care of each other like this. It is not customary to even touch their property. The waters are always changing and shifting. They are never certain. Even if it looks clear and calm, there could always be something, an undertow."

"I can understand why there is no *bang bang*, but why the little fish?"

"The little ones are the pilot fish. Those in power hope that by getting the little ones who are attached to or swim around the big one, they will not be able to guide the big one back into power. The big one must have the pilot fish."

"Or the whale will be stranded on the beach," Jonathan said.

"I think of shark instead of whale. If they get to the beach, yes. That is the idea of the sport."

"It is some sport, all right," Jonathan said.

"There are new elements. Did you not expect us to catch up with the world? Did you not expect us to modernize? Verlande. The death squads. The DOPS. It has made the sport very grim, no? These terrorists fragment our soul like a grenade."

"Yes, yes," Jonathan said softly, "terrorism makes for the fragmentation of the soul."

"I do not hear you, my friend."

"I was just agreeing with you."

"And now that we have modernized and become a modern part of our modern century, everybody in this country has power and nobody has power. Everybody is in control and nobody is in control. If you wanted to make a phone call to God, you would find you could not locate Him."

"Everybody sets up shop for themselves."

"It is a funny American expression," Roberto laughed. "What you say is so. Verlande does what he wants. The DOPS do what they want. The army does what it wants. The death squads do what they want. The secret police, ah, the navy, where do we stop, my Professor?"

"It ends in the Jewish Cemetery."

"It is so. There is many, many a sadness, a terrible sadness, a very modern country now, no, but look, there is our Verlande coming from the Cathedral on an evening ride in an open jeep on this Avenue of the world, Atlântica, and here we are behind him! What a country of marvels this Brazil is! *Hola!*, we do not reach your apartment. There he turns on to the sidewalk drive. My God, I have always wondered," he said.

"I have passed here a hundred times and I have also wondered," Jonathan said.

"They say this is where the little old grandmother lives with her husband's ashes under her bed. It is twenty-five years now and she never sweeps under her bed. Have you heard that?"

"Yes, I have heard that," Jonathan said, "only it was fifty years that I heard. Has anyone ever seen her?"

"Nobody has ever seen her leave or go. They say sometimes the gate opens for a maid or a workman. I do not know why I never checked with the Ministry on it. Their intelligence is very firm."

"That is because you like a mystery."

"I like a mystery. Mysteries are necessary, do you not think? I would like to own this property and clear the mystery. An old house like this on half an acre, more or less, of Atlântica, what do you think it is worth? It is worth millions of American dollars, no?"

"Yes. I'm never quite sure how to answer your 'no,' " Jonathan said.

"The Simca does not follow. The Simca waves us farewell," Roberto said as they followed the jeep through the gate at the end of a long, high wall, a stone wall with spidery cracks and ancient fissures. The wall was wantonly hung, scattered with trumpets of begonias, at least a dozen hues.

CHAPTER SEVENTEEN

1

The earth rich and warm seemed to glow in the night beneath the foliage of vines and large leaved plants and there were coconut and banana trees in fruit. There were passion vines climbing over the low-lying house with the tiled roof, the house whose scabrous brow Jonathan could see when he used to pass it on the street. From the street he could catch the upper glimpse of the Venetian shutters, a distempered white, peeling and warped.

Here within there were crimson flowers strewn among the leaves on the pavement stones, stones of deep ochre, tints of vermillion, and there by the wide verandah was a cascade of shrubs and vines, of philodendra, of scarlet leaves of poinsettias and a profusion of begonias blue and yellow. The garden was more like a rain forest, a wilderness untrammeled in which Jonathan could scarcely breathe in the thickness of the air. There was a broken fountain with stagnant water in about a quarter of the basin and a crumbling memory of a statuette, perhaps St. Theresa, Jonathan thought, noseless and armless, adorning its beaded top. Jonathan said to himself this is the Fountain of the Breathless Rosary.

There was a cluster of three palms, one straight and smooth as a stone column and it was higher than the other two which had a slight and graceful sway. There were two giant trees, one bare of foliage at the top with branches and leaves climbing along its trunk. The other tree was thinly crowned at the top and almost bare along the trunk except for coverings of green, giant parasites winding about the tree like an immense serpent, the coil of the anaconda. There were very thin vines, like the gauze of bridal veils, climbing to the summit to floss and flutter down against the purple night in a silver shimmer of garlands, down to earth. At the base of this tree there were orchids of unbelievable beauty. Jonathan looked about for jaguars and tapirs in that ancient garden but he saw only a horned lizard and a fat-bellied toad and some chameleons. When he had entered the garden he thought he had stepped into a primeval century. He realized, as he made his way through the garden, that he was really standing on the poise of decay in the last moment of time.

The verandah was lit by two poles with kerosene bunting at the top. There by the Moorish entranceway under the shadows of the flickering light, Jonathan could see but not hear through the tangled growth Verlande and two of his men. His men had rifles and Verlande had a holstered gun at his waist. They were fixed like a group of wax figures in a museum beyond which the interior of the house beckoned, dimly lit, a phosphorescence and a conjuration of a chamber of dark mirrors and a draped, dust-laden foliage of velvet curtains streaked with the green of mold.

Verlande now spotting their approach called out in a loud and hearty voice with just a little spice of unction to it, "It is time to dine, gentle-men, a virtuous wedding feast."

"And where," Jonathan asked as Roberto and he came up the stone steps of the verandah and hesitated by a Corinthian column, "where is the bridal bedroom?"

"After dinner you will have bridal bedroom enough," Verlande said. Then he said it again in Portuguese to his two men. They broke out in laughter.

"Is this not where the little old grandmother sleeps?" Roberto said wonderingly.

Verlande looked at him a moment and said, not unkindly, rather gently, "The one with the sharp teeth?"

The two men had been left outside on guard and there was no maid, no serving girl on the inside. They were the only ones in that grand chamber of gilt and antique, of stuffed sofas and chairs with their intricately carved backs and arms and legs and their frayed, fading upholstery. There was a grand piano, chipped and peeling with yellow keys, and there were two rocking chairs, both with broken spines. There were portraits that seemed laminated in the phosphoric light, nineteenth century personages with ruffles. There were two land-scapes of the country around Lisbon, of *Lisboa* of the last century. There were drawings and lithographs of *fazendas*, of rubber plantations and cacao plantations, of slaves and masters, of Amazon Indians, maybe those of the Xingu basin, Jonathan thought. There was a grandfather clock of brazilwood whose gold pendulum was still and whose hands were missing. There was a stuffing of crockery and china on end tables and coffee tables. There was a mantle with no hearth beneath. There was a scattering of threadbare rugs on an old, scuffed, worn, loosely planked floor. There were dim mirrors and the velvet curtains were streaked with mold and there were cobwebs on the curtains and there were cobwebbed corners. One mirror, above the mantle, was covered with a white sheet. There were three paneled walnut doors in the high room, one on the far side and one on each side, doors to open up on. Jonathan wondered to open up on what? Which one to the bridal bedroom?

In the cove of the chamber there was a large round rosewood table around which twelve could easily gather. At its center there were three waxen tapers unlit in their golden holders. The feast was spread out on the table and the odor of the *feijoada* was an incense for the musty air.

Jonathan smiled at the devout look on Roberto's face as they stood hostage for a moment before the stewed black beans, dried meat and smoked meat, loin, tongue, thick pork sausage, tripe, smoked bacon, white fluffy rice, roasted manioc, orange, kale, onions in a sauce, hot peppers, the *batida* with which to start the meal, whiskey, beer, wine, cognac, *agua mineral*. They sat down to the feast with ample space between each from the other.

A large rat came through the open door, a rat pursued by one of the guards who got it with the butt of his rifle. He lifted the rat by the end of its tail and he smiled. He said excuse me but this rat is very stiff. Then he said good appetite and he said I think I close the door.

There was an old Victrola and Verlande put on a record of a soft samba, a tender and gentle sighing of love, of love lost and love found, of love dreamed about, of ideal love, of sensual love, of remembered love, of the death of love. Verlande told them that the singer is now an old man, that he had once been an anthropologist, that he was playing the guitar as well as singing, that the old man had great versatility and great skill and great feel with the guitar.

"Do you not think so?" he said. Then, looking up from his plate, he said, "Would not Heitor Villa-Lobos himself compose A Fugue Without End in honor of this *feijoada*?"

In the soporiferous light of the room, amid the food and the drink and the samba and the lyrics of love, Verlande was on his way in a flood of words, talking, talking as if he had a great deal to explain to Jonathan, talking not of revolution or of what was to be, talking to explain something to a fellow intellectual. He was explaining that Brazil does not produce great thinkers nor great philosophers. "No Kant, no Schopenhauer, no Hume, no Descartes, no even, William

James, no, that we do not produce, no great musicians except Heitor Villa-Lobos, A Fugue Without End. No great mathematicians, no great scientists, ah, but we are great in plastic surgeons, in *plasticos.*

"In the body is where we are great, Professor. We have a genius for the body, a genius for the sensual, our pop music, our writers, a genius for the apple round bottom of a woman, a genius for the pear shaped bottom of a woman, a genius for movement and a genius for relaxation, a genius for bed, a genius for sex. We are the sun worshippers of sex. We are celebrants of the body. The mulata for whoring, have you not heard what we say to foreign social science professors? The white woman for marrying, the mulata for whoring, the black woman for working. Banal but it gives the social science professors something to go home with and write about in their country and so they all write about the same thing.

"A genius we have, Professor, for the streets, *o movimento,* a genius for the crowd, the mass, we celebrate the body. That is how we know ourselves, the one body, the Eucharist, we partake of the Eucharist between the sheets. Better than the mind. The mind divides. A better celebration to eat, to taste, to feel, to feel with the heart, to smell, to touch, to hear, to see, to divine."

He was becoming more and more excited as he went along. He was saying, "We are the samba, we are the bossa nova. It is not a musical artifice of studied language and art and composition but a music of the genes. We *are* the samba. We *are* the bossa nova. We are its experience. We are experience itself. Professor, look at the *sinuosidade,* the sinuosity of the ground we walk on, the undulating stones of Atlântica, of Copacabana. Can you walk the waves of those patterns for long without realizing life is a rhythmic undulation? a sway? We are all children of Christ. Nowhere but Brazil, all day and all night in infinite variation partaking of the body, the memorial of the blood, we know the mark that is upon us. We are secure in our knowledge of a special dispensation—God is a Brazilian and we are children of the Eucharist."

Verlande was now laughing, laughing broadly. His hands were shaking and he was having trouble pouring the after dinner cognac. "A toast," he cried out, "a toast to your last night, to the dinner of your last night in Rio! A toast to the Angel of the Ministry, to the counterparts of ourselves, to the holy duplicity of our semblance, to the soulful whore in the mirror, the one covered with the white sheet." There were tears in his eyes from the laughter.

Roberto stared at him saying, "*Guerrilheiro communista,* forgive me, but after the *sala roxa* does your mother know you or are you lost forever?"

"I see you do not approve of my portrait of Brazil," Verlande said.

"It is, of course, of Rio you speak and even there," Roberto said leaving the sentence in the air. "Minas Gerais, for example, is very different."

"Oh, Minas!" Verlande laughed. "I will explain to the Professor."

"The Professor is not a tourist," Roberto said.

"You think me a pagan?"

"You are a communist."

"I paint the colors of life," Verlande said. "Is it so bad then? What is so ascetic about the Eucharist? Are these unlit candles not memorials? Does the rosewood of our table not glow? Do we not sit here in a state of communion? Among the sounds of the samba and our words, do you not hear the sound of the distant dove? Is it howling or is it sobbing? The flesh is sad, is it not? That is not for the tourist. This the Brazilian knows. This we do not say to our foreign social science professors. The flesh is sad. Is that better, Senhor Angel? Is that better my friend?"

"Yes, Jesuit, that is our knowledge," Roberto said.

"We live too close to the yellow sun," Verlande said.

"This is a tragic fact," Roberto said.

"The flowers are our poverty," Verlande said.

"This, too, is true," Roberto said.

"I know of a young girl who killed herself because her dress did not arrive in time for her to dance in the Carnival," Verlande said.

"We are a people of ghosts and enchantments," Roberto said.

"We hide the fact," Verlande said.

"We are a supernatural people," Roberto said. "We are a people of the veil."

Jonathan had seen it before, so often before, *saudade*, the Brazilian longing, the homesickness for the immemorial, the blues. Not a modulation but an unexpected coming on, not swiftly but suddenly there would be a turn of the head, a wave of the hand into the air and a shrug of the shoulders, a wistful smile, *saudade*.

Now Verlande and Roberto rose from the table and they came to each other and put their arms around each other in an *abraço* and then they stepped back from each other and were blowing their noses and wiping their eyes in memory of the young girl.

If there were not that black limousine with the yellow glare of headlights in his future Jonathan thought he would have smiled with tenderness but he could say only, "I don't mean to be anxious, but isn't it time?" Then he said weakly, "I have a plane to catch."

He saw Roberto and Verlande looking at each other in silence and it seemed as if they were speaking to each other without words and then, having spoken in their silent language, Roberto finally said with a forlorn smile, "Senhor Communist, the Professor is right to remind us. I have a very smart double, no? There is much to do, is there not, before the moon leaves the night sky?"

2

Her body was hollow. The pale pink coverlets seemed to rest on air.

"I was once a wench. I was lascivious," she said in perfect English by way of introduction, smilingly, her teeth white and young, her face very small, very old, shriveled, her eyes barely discernible, slits rather than eyes, white lace covering her head, not a wisp of hair to be seen except for the tuft of hair at the end of her nose. She was half propped up by two large pillows. She wore a dangle of earrings and there were silver vines of jewelry around her slender throat. There was a full water basin on the table by the bed and pink blossoms were floating on the surface of the water. There were no mirrors in the room. The bed was canopied and curtained with bridal lace. The large room was spartanly furnished except for the luxuriousness of the bed. They had taken hard-backed, untufted chairs to sit at the side of the bed. There was a stark black cross on the bare wall opposite from where she lay and she said, "My heroic children. *Nossa Senhora, Nossa Senhora.* And how was the music, A Fugue Without End?"

"*Ótimo*, dearest Grandmother, *ótimo*," Verlande said. "When is your *feijoada* not fit for all four movements of a fugue? When is it not fit for the Maestro, for Heitor Villa-Lobos himself?"

"And our heroic children, did they ride the elephant in the garden? Have they spotted the eyes of the owl? Have they wrestled with the juggler's bear? Did they free the lion from the net? Have they found the golden snake? So many questions for an old woman, so many questions and so few visitors, you must forgive an old lady, but I am anxious for news of the outside world."

"It is a fiction," Verlande said turning to Roberto and Jonathan. "You see how she plays with us? Grandmother knows that the whole world is where she is. It is the rest that is story. Is not this so, Grandmother? Are you not our beautiful necessity? Do we not exist only for you?"

"Yes," she said, "I was once a wench. I was lascivious you know. I am still lascivious but I am vacant."

"Why are you such a faker, Grandmother? Why do you make believe you are such a ghost?"

"I can float," she said flashing her teeth, "but I cannot eat."

"You would have us believe you are a witch," Verlande said. "See how she plays with us?"

"I was once very wicked," she said. "Men worshipped me at the altar." Her tired and croaky voice broke and she cackled violently. For a moment it seemed to Jonathan as if the face were an old worn and faded yellow sponge that had been squeezed. He saw those brilliant teeth glistening with spittle and the word "infernal" crossed his mind. When she came to rest she said, *"Nossa Senhora, Nossa Senhora."*

They had come to her after dinner. Verlande had been joking with Roberto saying, "This time you may come and although as you say there is much to do before the moon leaves the night sky, we must pay our respects to our hostess."

"But there is no one here," Roberto said. "The house is alone and with all respect I do not think I have ever been in so empty a house."

Verlande, sweeping the grand chamber with his arms extended and his hands outstretched, said, "How can you say this is empty when it is filled."

"There is not a soul," Roberto said. "The *feijoada* must have been cooked in heaven where it is always Saturday and delivered by an angel."

Verlande laughed and said, "There is a regiment in the house. Is not the *feijoada* proof enough of this? Does not every Brazilian know that it takes a general and his troops to make a *feijoada*? There are soldiers everywhere in this house at the service of the hostess who is our grandmother."

"Ah, how truly sad it is that a Jesuit like you is a guerrilla communist," Roberto said.

The walnut door at the far end of the room opened upon a dark corridor, a long dark green corridor at the end of which Jonathan could see a dull bar of light that seemed to be coming from under a closed door. Verlande was saying smilingly, "If you feel and hear a crunch it is nothing but tropical beetles, another army. They live in the hallway. They are squatters. This is their *favela*. This is why the green color. It is their iridescence. You must be sure to let me lead the way because there are alligators in this passageway and we must be careful, no? I see you do not believe me. I admit I exaggerate about the alligators. I do not exaggerate about beetles. Grandmother now lives her life in the bridal chamber and she is very old and this the beetles know. Have you ever tasted beetle broth? It goes well with a good helping of parmesan cheese and french bread. I would recommend a dry white wine. Shall we pay our respects? If we keep this door open we will be able to see a little into the passageway. You may be able to see other doors and hallways coming off this passageway. Stay close and do not get lost. Shall we then?"

Jonathan felt the brush of a web and then another. His imagination got going and he was thinking they were not going to visit Grandmother but the Great Spider who inhabits the room at the end of the corridor, who devours beetles and lord knows what else. He thought he felt the snap of one beetle underfoot and then another. Then he had another funny feeling. In the glaze of that mossy darkness he felt he was naked and swimming through space, like swimming alone underwater on a warm, moonless night and being touched by currents he could not see. He was shadowless. And then his fancy took hold again in that long dark corridor and he suddenly felt like a phantom dressed in tails and he saw himself prone in the roll of a billowing coffin. There were crabs and jellyfish in there with him. He thought aeons could pass for all anyone knew or cared and eternity itself could come to an end. There you still are, he thought as he groped his way down the corridor, with the crabs and the jellyfish.

Now he saw himself as a swimmer breaking to the surface of the water. He was surrounded by the vast desolation of silent stars and the watery world was devoid of humanity. There were no houses, no light except that of the desolate stars, no shore. There was no horizon. The world had become the sea at creation and he was its only swimmer. Jonathan knew he was scared.

He was thinking now of orange clouds drifting through a starlit sky. He was in the puffery of a romantic death, cotton candy and revolution and love. He was thinking, I am the eternal adolescent. I live in the fiery tallow of dreams. The tallow is melting and running off into the gothic like turrets of wax from a candle.

Then Jonathan is thinking, the mirror, the frame of the mirror, narcissism, no whore under the white sheet of the dim mirror, no, it is I, Jonathan, I am there. My picture is inside the frame, he thinks, my double and what is a double but a form of narcissism? At first it is a pretty picture of reality, an innocent look into the otherness of reality, the games of childhood played before mother's oval dressing mirror. Now the static, cold, uncanny and magical professorial consciousness takes over, he thinks, changing nothing, isolating us each in an individual world in which there are no hands on the clock. I am in the loneliness of a timeless world. I want to talk to the world, he was thinking, but there is only the image in the mirror to talk to.

He was remembering his first glimpse of Roberto, his feeling that he, Jonathan, was the image in the mirror. The image had become his reality. It is Roberto, he thought, who is in the life. I have looked at him, he was thinking, and it is he who has emerged from the smoked column of glass and it is I who have entered it.

This I know, he was thinking, if I'm to get out of that damn smoked column, I've got to do something. I've begun. No heroic posturings in the mirror. That must come to an end. I've begun with Oleisky. Didn't Verlande and Malgahães say I have performed the rites of the community? Roberto and me and Oleisky, my first true action in the politics of time. I must meet the black limousine with the yellow headlights. I'm scared.

He imagined that moment of the meeting as a moment in which all of time, like the still photograph of a building in the process of demolition, would collapse into that one soundless act.

Set fire, he told himself, to one random moment of time and you'll be alone and lonely no more. You will be brother to Oleisky and Roberto, to Verlande and Malgahães and you will have put an end to distraction, an end to the pale narcissism of the isolate consciousness. For where does the shaft of darkness lead, he asked himself, death itself but to a dull bar of light at the end of the corridor at the foot of the door?

3

"You may look for the ashes," she said.

Roberto and Jonathan looked at Verlande. Grandmother was laughing again, the laughter turning into a deep, violent, hoarse catarrh. She was catching the phlegm in a large cheese cloth. Verlande was bending close to Grandmother stroking her arm soothingly and with concern. Then he was smiling at Jonathan and Roberto. He was amused and offered no sign.

"Everybody wants to see if there are ashes under my bed, heaven knows what for," she said. "But you must kneel or bend or prostrate yourself. That is the only way to see under the bed. You must be careful the golden snake doesn't get you on the nose, though. That would be too frightful."

"I must explain," Verlande said, "that the golden snake is the guardian of the urn. Is that not true, Grandmother?"

"And there are only two of you?" she suddenly asked looking at Roberto and Jonathan through the slits, the blinds that were her eyes. "Are there not three or four and five and six and seven of you? Fifty-two of you?"

"I agree, Grandma," Verlande said. "If there are two, then there must be an eternity of them. But they are your heroic children, Grandma, and so that is good. They are all their own sons and fathers. It is interesting, is it not, Grandmother?"

"Yes, yes," she said. "They are all their own brothers. I agree with you, Senhor Commandante. It is interesting. Are they to spend the night here?"

"No, Grandmother," Verlande said. "They must wrestle with the hyena tonight."

"Oh, that is good," she said. "I never did like hyenas. They are ugly and they have the smell of death in their nostrils. I do not like their hides. Their hides are cruel, do you not think? We have never let them into the garden, have we, Senhor Commandante?"

"No, my dearest, we have not."

"And we never will," she said. "Promise me."

"I promise."

"Then you will spend the night here to be sure," she said.

"But I was here last night, Grandma. Do you not remember?"

"Oh, I remember now that you mention it," she said wonderingly. "I have read about you when I was very young. You are the grand King and you must sleep in a different chamber every night. That is how you trick your enemies who would kill you in your sleep. Why do you not instead get two three four five six seven fifty-two like these gentlemen have? That way your enemies will not know which one is you. It must be tiresome to move from chamber to chamber every night. When I was young," she went on to say, her voice fading as she began to nod, "I was very silly. The boys found that very attractive. I do not know why. And then I grew up to be a wench. I was lascivious but there was only one I truly loved and he died. He went away by dying. Please," she said with a tired smile, "you may look for the ashes. I do not mind."

And as she was fading into sleep she mumbled once again, "The ashes."

Jonathan spoke for the first time. He said gently, "You must sleep, dear Grandmother. Perhaps another time?"

They heard her whisper *Nossa Senhora, Nossa Senhora* and Verlande kissed her on the forehead and in her sleep she did not seem to be breathing. They left the room, Verlande leaving the light on and quietly closing the door. Jonathan looked down the corridor with a smile.

When they returned through the door that had been left ajar they found that the rosewood table had been cleared. On the table now was a bottle of Benedictine brandy and a canister of cigars and a box of matches and a slender, elegant vase with a long-stemmed white rose. There was an old photograph in a gold-leafed antique frame arranged next to the elegant vase there in the center of the table. The tapers had been lit and they were flickering gently.

The photograph was a portrait of an extraordinarily beautiful woman, a young woman with an insinuating, Jonathan thought almost wanton, or artful, smile. Jonathan thought he would never forget that smile even if he were to live beyond this night for a hundred years.

Verlande was saying to Jonathan as he raised his glass in a toast to the woman in the picture, "You are right, Professor Jonathan. You are also hypnotized. You are in a trance, no? It is she. It is our hostess, our grandma!"

CHAPTER EIGHTEEN

1

As he walked the streets unattended that night, the crowded streets to the apartment of his paramour, Jonathan found himself in a high pitch by the events of the evening. He was carrying on an animated, flushed conversation with Dom Hélder. He felt the presence of the Archbishop of Recife at his side, in the flesh, a slight figure in priestly vestment as if he had just come from service. Jonathan was completely unaware of the passersby, who gave him a very wide berth.

"Now this is more like it at last," Jonathan was saying.

"You have told me you are an admirer of Sir Thomas Browne, you and Senhor Oleisky."

"Yes, Dom Hélder."

"Yet you did not get on your knees or bend nor would you prostrate yourself to determine if in fact there were ashes in an urn under the bed."

"That is true and I begin to see what you're driving at, Dom Hélder."

"As a professed lover of Browne, you might have thought at least of the possibility that there is an urn of dry bones rather than ashes under the bed, a minor monument. Had you thought it, then I suppose no one could have dissuaded you from looking for this historical accident as a possibility."

"Yes," Jonathan said excitedly, "dead bones older than the living ones of Methuselah, an accident of time, a failure of art in the service of time to turn all things to dust. I must have been beside myself, Dom

Hélder, to have forgotten Sir Thomas, the flight of his soul in *Hydriotaphia.*"

"Or? Or?"

"Yes, *Hydriotaphia or Urn Burial,*" Jonathan said, "or *A Discourse of the Sepulchrall Urnes lately found in Norfolk.*"

"Very good, Professor. And the time?"

"1685," Jonathan said.

"Now tell me, Professor, have you meditated upon his *Christian Morals?*"

"Yes, Father, I have," Jonathan said.

"I will begin the passage, then. 'Let *not the sun* in Capricorn *go down upon thy wrath,* but write thy wrongs in Ashes. Draw the curtain of Night upon injuries, shut them up in the Tower of Oblivion, and let them be as though they had not been.' Now, Professor, complete the passage, if you please."

" 'To forgive our Enemies, yet hope that God will punish them, is not to forgive enough. To forgive them ourselves, and not to pray to God to forgive them, is a partial piece of Charity. Forgive thine enemies totally, and without any reserve, that however God will revenge thee.' "

"Very good, Professor. Very good. He was, you know, not a great scientist like Harvey. He was not a great philosopher. He was no Descartes. In matters of religion, he was no Pascal. Yet, he was all of these, was he not?"

"Yes, Father, he was," Jonathan said.

"He was a devout man, was he not?"

"Yes, Father."

"He was a physician and a scholar and a husband and a father. And he was?"

"Yes," Jonathan answered, "he was a consummate artist."

"Very good, Professor. The lesson is over. Go home in peace!"

"Go home in peace?"

"Yes, my son, I have said it in English, now go home in peace! Shall I say it in Latin? Shall I say it in Portuguese?"

"But you can't," Jonathan said, "not yet. You can't go. There's still time. Don't send me off this way! Don't go this way! There's still time!"

At this juncture Jonathan stopped dead in his tracks. A young couple stumbled into him from behind. Jonathan whirled and they got out of the way rapidly as if they were being threatened by a dangerous madman. Jonathan was aware now of his surroundings as he found himself whispering the shout that was within him, whispering at a slight figure retreating from him, "It is you who are going! I remain! I'm staying! I will do what I must do! Come back, Dom Hélder, come back! Listen, Dom Hélder, listen!"

He looked about and saw that he was standing in a charmed circle. There was no one within twenty feet of him.

It is a funny feeling to be funny, he thought. Well I'll be a son of a bitch. Then he was thinking if I do not attend I will be dead.

Jonathan walked on. He noticed that up one side street there was a group of children seated on the sidewalk and there was a handful of adults standing behind them. They were in front of a television store and they were laughing and a sideward glance told him they were watching Chacrina, the clown in the funny clothes with a whirling flower attached to his plaid cap. Thinking of his children, thinking of Carol, perhaps she was nestled in bed with the children watching Chacrina, he moved on, the corner showcase lights at the end of the next street his destination. That is where I really turn the corner of time, he thought. Teacher, scholar, father, husband, he thought.

2

He had come to the corner showroom facing on Atlântica and the side street, all glass and brightly lit, the BMW models polished to their ultimate gleam. This was the showroom designated by Verlande as the place for the ambush, the urban ambush, he had joked, not very natural, he had said, but ah well, we are concrete and glass, are we not? There were two snappily dressed yawning salesmen on the inside, the day about to close but not quite. Jonathan pretended to be looking in at the machines and one of the salesmen waved good-naturedly for him to come inside. Jonathan shook his head no and smiled back.

He turned on to the side street, pausing at the apartment house next door, observing with a feeling of wry comfort the small truck, a three-quarter-ton he thought, shielding the entrance. He glanced furtively up and down the street and felt a bit silly. He took out a key and studied it in the bad light to see if it were the right one. Turning the lock, entering the dimly lit lobby, no doorman or *porteiro* to nod to, the elevator with a tarnished folding grate door waiting, he pressed the button for the fourth floor.

He slid open the grate door of the elevator and turned to the right down the long faded green hallway. It seemed to him like all the hallways of his public school days. His right hand was in his pocket. He was feeling for the second loose key under the dull yellow bulb of the hallway, the bare ceiling bulb protected by only by a mesh of wire. In that hallway he felt there could be no moon, no stars, no sky beyond.

Verlande had told him to turn the key and enter. He decided to knock first. The sound of his knock in that grim hallway, he smiled, sounded to him like the opening bars of a hollow fate. There was no answer. He turned the key. There was no entry or foyer. He was directly in the living room. He called out. There was no answer to his hello. It was a small room modestly furnished.

As he looked about the lamplit room, his eyes came to focus on the sofa and he felt a momentary palpitation, was she asleep? There was a figure reclining on the sofa, unmoving, not a stir. He closed the door behind him quietly, almost reverently, for he sensed at once that he was in a presence. He came slowly toward the sofa and as he was about to speak he saw her fully and there she was and the laughter of Verlande and his two men washed over him and he shuddered and for a moment he felt his balance give way.

He remembered Verlande saying, "You will have bridal bedroom enough."

There she was, a crown of gold, her parted cape exposing her bare breasts. She was bejeweled and she was smiling through her painted lips and her cheeks were red and rouge, her hair raven, and there was a hyacinth fragrance about her, larkspur and iris, and there was, so it seemed to him in the lamplight, almost the touch of a glow, the tint of a faint reddish orange about her, an emanation, his paramour, Pomba Gira herself, he thought, the Whore of Whores, Exú's Own, the Whore of Verdant Mystery. He touched her arm and her arm seemed resilient to his touch. He sat down on a soft chair and he looked at her and he said aloud to her, Babylon. He said it with affected hoarseness as if he were playing a game. He said I don't know much about you, Pomba Gira, but were you ever in Babylon?

He felt his hands trembling and there was a twitch going beneath his right eye and he was laughing a little and he looked around the room and there on the wall above the sofa was Solomon's Seal, the Star of David. On the coffee table by the sofa there was a bowl of fruit. He became aware of a very low beat, it was a samba, and his eyes followed the barely discernible sound to the stereo. The stereo was on a bookshelf which didn't have any books. Scattered on the shelves were wooden, metal, and plastic ornaments of *figas* and fish, of vessels and grapes, of tambourines and drums and there was the ornament of a guitar and there were ornaments of flowers and vines.

There on a shelf on a tray was a bucket of ice and a bottle of scotch with a grand label, Verlande's own. Jonathan smiled appreciatively. There was a bottle of carbonated water and there were two glasses. One was half filled with a pure looking liquid. He smelled it. It was *cachaça*. He put it down and he poured a straight scotch into the other glass. He thought about it for a moment and then put in some ice.

He turned up the stereo slightly and he turned out the light. He opened the window blinds and as he craned his neck a bit he could see the corner sidewalk and on the sidewalk a block of light from the showcase window. The living room was light enough from the lights of the apartment building across the way. He took off his jacket and threw it over a chair. He loosened his tie and sat down in an armchair opposite the sofa. He put his feet up on the coffee table and he lit a cigarette and he said to Pomba Gira, seductive and real in the shadowy light, he said the vigil of my dreams and then he said well, my love, there is nothing for us to do now but wait until we are called, wait until the curtain goes up, show time, and he breathed deeply and then he said how thoughtless of me. He went over to the bookshelf and got the glass of *cachaça* and put it on the coffee table and he said I think it's in easy reach and he bowed to the mannequin and he said, your devoted servant, Madam, your devoted servant.

3

To the Princess of the Carnival, to the Colombian Lady, to the Hen of the Altar, to the Grandmother of the Urn, to the Virgin of *Nossa Senhora de Copacabana*, to the Whore of Verdant Mystery, and to Mrs. Calabash wherever you are. Amen. He sipped. To Adam and Eve, the androgynous, the hermaphroditic body, two out of one, one body two souls. He sipped. To Saint What's Her Ass Everywhere in the Habit of the Bikini. He sipped. Then he noticed how dark the room had become and he saw that the lights in the apartments across the way had been turning off. He went over to the lamp and turned it on for a moment to look at his watch. The bold black eyes of Pomba Gira were staring up at him. He felt himself hovering over her. An icon for red tapestries, he thought. It was a little after eleven. He turned off the light and he was in a blurry darkness. There were streaks of light on the unwashed window. His eyes adjusted. He went to the window. Verlande had good-naturedly warned him not to stick his head out the window like a giraffe or it could be awkward. He pressed against the window and he saw that the block of light at the corner had disappeared. A couple were standing in a momentary embrace where the light had been and then they proceeded to walk up the street.

A little to the right he could see the truck still there by the entranceway. He saw as far as he could up and down the street and he saw that the line of cars were miraculously parked along the street like a barricade.

"You must understand," Verlande had said, "that they just about never shoot from a moving car. They will stop the car and they will get out and fire. It is a more careful way of doing it. They want only their target. They also delight to see the face. They like to say a word. They are very sociable. They may even want to apologize to you because you are an American, no? It is so simple, particularly with the truck we have parked at the entranceway. That is a nice touch, do you not think so? They will see clearly that their opportunity is at the corner. No cars can be parked there. When you come out you will be a little, how shall I say, rumpled, no? After all, it has been quite an evening with your, your paramour, no? You will breathe deeply the fresh night air and you will stagger slightly and wipe your lips with a handkerchief, just a touch, a touch for the theater, as if there were traces of lipstick to wipe away." Verlande laughed at this.

Then he said, "You turn toward the corner, not too slow and not too fast. They will be watching your every movement. It is just a few steps, you will see. Listen carefully to your director, Professor. I do not want to lose my star. A few steps but you act a little drunk, no?, cumbersome and a little drunk. That will make the scene more interesting and it will relax them. They will laugh and know that they have you easily. They will even make lewd jokes among themselves about how fortunate you are for your last night on earth. They will see you knocked out from the gymnastics of the bed, an easy drunk, a perfect set-up, a perfect opportunity, what a mark! The car will come swooping down. They think that they get you at the corner on the side street and then they turn right on to Atlântica and they are excited, triumphant, laughing and passing the bottle and talking about the expression on your face at the final moment. That is what they think.

"It is quiet at that hour. Not too quiet, but quiet. When is it ever that quiet in Copacabana? Now listen carefully, my dear Professor. I want even your bones to listen. When the car pulls by to stop, you stumble, Professor, you hold your stomach as if you are about to puke. You stumble and you fall and I mean Professor you fall quickly and you fall flat on the sidewalk, very flat, an unexpected moment for them, no? The sliding glass door is open and they will not have time to observe in the dark and they cannot see anyway because it is all glass anyway and you will have distracted them. We are there very happy with the BMWs. It will be so tempting to steal one. Maybe some day. When they stop and you fall, we will be very careful on the inside of the showroom. I give you my complete and total word that we will be very accurate and we will make a glow, like a sunburst, a splendid magnificent glow of just the right scientific quantity, a work of plastic art, no? Anyone who manages to be alive and steps out of that painting of a blazing limousine, steps out like a dazed Moloch after dinner, we will be there with our submachine guns. That is how simple it is."

"I do not like this," Roberto said. "I do not like this at all."

Jonathan at the window looking down was attracted suddenly by a burly man in a white polo shirt puffing away on a big cigar. He was walking slowly and casually and Jonathan sensed, an instinct of memory, this is the man, this is the man who pushed Oleisky's body out of the car. Jonathan secured himself in the shadows and he saw the man slow down by the truck. The man walked to the corner and he walked back to the truck and this was deliberately done as if he were measuring. Then he kind of circled the truck as if he were looking it over to buy it. The street was now fairly deserted and he went around to the driver's side and got on the running board and he pulled out what was probably as Jonathan could see a pocket flashlight. It seemed to Jonathan as if he were looking to read the registration. Then he flashed the light around in the interior of the truck. Then turning off the light he went back to the sidewalk. Facing the apartment house he leaned at ease against the right front fender of the truck. He looked about him, occasionally casually spanning the floors of the apartment house. Then Jonathan could see that the light on his cigar must have gone out because he stood erect, cupping his hands, lighting his cigar and tossing the match with a flourish. Then he went back up the street from where he had come and now he was beyond Jonathan's sight.

Then it is for real, Jonathan said aloud and he knew it finally in the coursing of his blood, and he said with a kind of self-amazement, it is really for real. There are things in life that you thought would never really happen, but you did them. You did them, spinning the web, so he thought, thread by thread, filament by filament, and then they happened. You wrote a book that way, Professor Jonathan thought. Dream takes you on to dream, romance to romance, illusion to illusion, image to image, and then, always, there was something to pay. That something to pay, he thought, is reality. Reality may be surreal and it may be magical but it is still reality and if you have been spinning the web, the dreams and the romance and the illusions and the images, then it happened whether real or surreal and magical. What do you think, Dr. Pomba?, Jonathan said aloud as he came back to the sofa and settled once more, quite calm now, into his armchair. Then he thought with amusement, I should be on the sofa and you should be in the chair. I am the patient. Then he wondered for a brief moment, *Go home in Peace!* He knew it was too late to even think about, too late anyway. They were on the street. Then he leaned over and touched Pomba's hand and he said dead ends house the sanctity of humble love. Then he leaned back and relaxed in his chair with his scotch.

4

The time that had been set was midnight more or less. Jonathan thought of Brazilian army officers in combat synchronizing their watches and saying we take the hill at twenty-four hours more or less. Brazil, Jonathan was remembering the beautiful War Memorial you could see from the *atêrro*, had fought gallantly with the Allies during the Second World War and he was thinking twenty-four hours more or less.

"If I fall asleep," Jonathan had said to Verlande, "then? I mean will the woman in the apartment see to the time?"

Verlande laughed and said, "The woman in the apartment will see to the white egg of eternity itself."

"If she is careless of time? If I am careless of time?"

"Do not worry, my friend."

"Why not just have someone call me on the telephone as a kind of check and say, 'Now. We are ready now and you go now.' "

"That is impossible."

"Why is it impossible?"

"There is no telephone in the apartment."

"Then I am not to call my wife?" Jonathan said surprising himself with the thought.

"But then there is no telephone," Verlande said. "I sleep there from time to time and there is no telephone. I do not miss it. I do not need it. You know how expensive telephones cost in Brazil? Do not worry. No one will be careless. Without a telephone it makes us more thoughtful, more careful. Do you not agree?"

Verlande had offered him another brandy.

"Who is this paramour, my woman?" Jonathan asked.

"She is the sweetheart of us all," Verlande said. "She is the great granddaughter of our grandmother. I met her in the apartment of a friend of mine many years ago when I was a student. I was staying in his São Paulo apartment. He had just returned from the Amazon. He had brought her and her twins to the apartment."

"Triplets? You mean triplets?"

"Like grandmother said, are there not two or three or four or five or six, no?"

"But isn't that the story," Jonathan said a little alarmed now, "the story you told me that affected you so deeply, the prostitutes? I mean—"

Verlande, interrupting him, said, "It is possible because I tell so many stories, like Senhor Hugo."

Jonathan turned to Roberto for support. Roberto had been standing in the cove gazing upon the picture.

"Senhor Guardian," Jonathan called trying to get his attention, "Senhor Guardian!"

"This picture torments me," Roberto said looking up. Jonathan saw that Roberto's eyes were moist.

"Why is this so, my friend?" Verlande said.

Roberto quietly answered, "Because I cannot grasp it. It is as if she is looking into a mirror. This picture was taken not of her but of her image in a mirror. It is the picture of a reflection. That is why she is smiling so. I think she sees that she is only a phantom and that is why she gives us this phantom smile." Then looking at Jonathan, he said with a little smile, "I, too, am a phantom."

Jonathan stumbled for something to say.

"I think it's an artful smile," he said.

Verlande, trying to joke, said, "Are not all the secret agents of the Ministry phantoms? Is this not what makes you secret? Is this not a requirement for your job?"

"The meaning is not to be grasped," Roberto said, "and it torments me. Not if I would dive into all the mirrors of the world would I grasp it."

Then Roberto smiled, a most charming smile.

"This picture has changed my thinking. It changes my mind. I have an idea I like the plan. I have an idea I like the plan very much. Do not worry, Professor Jonathan, I am your *manda-chuva*, your maker of rain. I am your guardian. I am, if you will permit a bad, small joke, your very own phantom." He said this while looking all the while at Verlande.

Jonathan, puzzled and disturbed, saw again that look of *simpatico* and of communion between the two men that he had seen earlier in the evening. Jonathan knew he could not be privy to the silent language between the two of them and he knew it would be graceless to try to intrude upon the unspoken word.

CHAPTER NINETEEN

1

A s he lowered and closed the blinds and turned on the lamp-light he found himself staring into the gaze of Pomba Gira. He was thinking there is a question. He looked at his watch and it was 11:40. Time to count time, he thought. More or less, he thought. A question, he thought again, as he sat down in his chair to sip the last of the scotch in the glass, there is a question of moment.

He wondered if he should see the rest of the apartment, the chamber where this mythical king, Verlande, sleeps from time to time in his nocturnal quest for surety in sleep. No, the question, he thought, stay with the question.

Roberto. Roberto, he thought, was entranced as he himself had been, with the portrait of grandmother that had been taken long before any of them had been born. The question had something to do with Roberto's conversion, his turnabout, his consent to the arrangements as if he had been overcome by the table altar of picture, candles, vase and rose.

Roberto had not been willing to agree to the arrangements, not at all. *I do not like this at all,* he had said. It was as if an invisible influence had descended upon him, as if he, Roberto, had been visited by an impression, perfumed by an emanation, whispered to by a deity, touched by a phantom image. Jonathan smiled slightly thinking about it. Roberto had looked at him and then Jonathan realized that Roberto was not looking at him but through him and beyond him. Jonathan remembered thinking that there is something happening. Something is taking place. You could almost see it in the distant glaze of Roberto's eyes. Narcissus sees the flower, Jonathan thought. Death by transfiguration. The time is upon me and there is a question of moment.

Jonathan looked into the light of the apartment and the lamplight that had seemed so soft, that had so warmly suffused the living room when he had entered from the grim hallway now appeared dull, tarnished, a faded and dingy yellow. He looked at the wondrous Star of David, the pendant of Pomba Gira on the wall. If it had not been for Roberto, Jonathan thought, could he, Jonathan, have borne Oleisky?

The questions that come like shadows, Jonathan thought, are spooky. He and Roberto had been looking at each other, he now felt, each from the other side of a mirror. Only Roberto had known it all along and he had not. It was like a pool of still, shiny water. A pool of still, shiny water does not exist, he thought. It exists only as a mirror. Only when you burst through the water or even if you just cast a fly upon the water when you're fishing for trout, only then are you aware of the underworld, only then are you aware of the other side of the water, only then when the surface is shattered, when the mirror is shattered in some way, does the water come into existence, come into being. You could see that in the best paintings, he thought. Something has happened. He felt it. Something is amiss. Something has gone wrong. One of us exists. One of us has been identified. One of us is free and one of us is in the mirror. Oh shit, he thought, what crap am I thinking?

He thought of the carefree way Roberto had taken a cigar, peeled the wrapper, lit it, puffed, looked after it, and said with a sigh, "So it is arranged then." There was Verlande nodding his head in cheerful agreement and Roberto then said, "It is best I drive the Professor."

Jonathan unaccountably felt himself stiffening, a little pissed off, feeling as if he had been left out of something although he felt he was the one who was putting it all on the line, said, "No, I walk. This is a condition. I walk to the apartment by myself, alone, no shadows, nothing."

Roberto looked at Verlande. Verlande nodded his head yes, it's all right, and then Roberto smiled and turned to Jonathan and said light-heartedly, "Professor, you may be free of all of us. You may be free to walk with your thoughts, no?"

"I need to collect my thoughts and to breathe the air," Jonathan said.

Verlande said sympathetically, "There is no danger now. We will give you an hour more or less to get into the apartment and our contact will make the call. He will notify the Death Squad. He will notify them where you are. They are waiting for the call in a café in Botafogo so there is no problem. They are very comfortable. He will even describe what you are wearing so there will be no mistaken identity. We do not want an innocent lover killed in the dark, no?"

"I don't quite know how to take that," Jonathan laughed. He turned to Roberto. "Are you staying or what? Where do we meet? At the airport in the morning?"

"Do not worry, Professor, I will be around, maybe with a cane and a patch, what do you think? Please forgive me all my sins," and with that Roberto gave Jonathan a warm *abraço*.

If anything should happen to me, Jonathan had been on the point of saying and he was glad he had not said it, that he had not said anything except *áte logo*. Roberto nodded his head and Verlande said with a smile and a wave, "Until midnight, more or less!"

That was all there was and Jonathan waved to the two guards on the verandah and he moved rapidly through the garden not noticing, thinking I am moving through the end of time and there is no looking back. He went past the jeep and the limousine and he opened the ponderous gate just a little and he sidled through into the street and he was on Atlântica and he breathed as if he were free.

2

As he raised himself from the chair, he felt that somehow he had been left out of something in the end, as if it were Roberto and Verlande in touch with each other and he wasn't part of it and he felt ashamed at his feeling petty about it. Still, he felt as if he had been put upon somehow and he thought what the hell it'll soon be over. He walked into the hallway leading off the living room and he found the bathroom. He pissed and then he washed his hands and he let cold water run on his wrists for a while and then he walked on down the hallway to the bedroom which had one small bed, an armoire, a little desk, and three straight-backed cane chairs. He went into the living room and picked up Pomba Gira and took her carefully down the hallway and into the bedroom. He took off the bedspread and he put Pomba Gira on the bed covering her waist high with a sheet. "Good night, sweetheart," he said and turned out the light.

He went over to the window and looked carefully through the blinds. The street was as it had been. Still time for a quick one, he thought, great scotch. Better take it standing up. Don't want a little snooze to get me past the time. What a goddamn arrangement. At least if there were a telephone. Carol. What was there to say? Had it been only a night ago? He took a shot of scotch. Love lies a-bleeding, he thought. Something is amiss. He felt a sense of panic. Something is wrong, he thought. I feel it in my bones. Carol. The room whirled for a moment. Steady, he told himself. Must not think of Carol. Must not think of night, of last night. Must not think of the boys. Must not think of my boys. Ring around the rosie. Fall down flat. Fall down right. Now. Time now. Something wrong now. Do it right. For God's sake do one thing right! Time now.

He was in the elevator and he felt he was all right. He looked at his watch. 11:57. Yes. Carol. Yes. I am all right. Not a tremor. He took out his handkerchief. He crumpled it. He walked through the lobby. Take a breath, a deep one. Wipe the lips. Remember. Stagger a little. Yeah. Do not think of Carol. Carol. You are not to think of Carol. Carol. Out of all my tangled dreams now you, only you, now Carol. God now! In a moment. Just a moment of eternity. Turn the handle of the outer door and one moment of eternity. He turned the handle and he stepped into the night air glancing up the street from where the car would come.

He breathed deeply in the night air and he put the handkerchief to his lips and as he did so he heard the explosion, a shattering boom and in the time that he heard it there was a sudden burst of the sun and he staggered, my God, yes, and the world had become a world of glowering forms and shapes and he thought this is the underworld, this is hell and he ran toward the corner, toward the flaming car, wrong, oh, my God, wrong, and he heard the windows of the apartment houses being flung open, lights illuminating the street and the street had become dusk and his soul was crying out in the eerie light and he heard the swelling surf of murmur and then noises and shouts and then he heard wailing and cries and the car was blazing and the doors of the car were all open and there was a body half out the rear door and it was in flames and there was another body lying in its blood in the gutter between the curb and the car and he heard the sound of the flames and he smelled the smoke and the gasoline.

One of the two men kneeling over Roberto on the sidewalk was Verlande. There was another of Verlande's men standing up and he had a camera and he was rapidly snapping pictures and seeing Jonathan come upon the scene he turned to him and he said cheerfully, "I take one for your scrapbook, hey Professor, no charge!"

3

At the corner on Atlântica there were the two motorcycles and the jeep and the red Simca. Verlande had wanted his men to link their hands and forearms, he was showing them how, for a stretcher. Roberto would not have it. He said he could make it. There was blood on the front of his shirt and on the lapels of his jacket and along one sleeve. He leaned on Jonathan and said to him, "I do not know exactly where I am hurt. Is that not funny? When I saw the elevator begin to come down from the fourth floor, I left the lobby. My timing was almost good. I now feel pain in my shoulder and here and there around. That is almost good. I do not want to be numb. That is not good, Professor. When you are numb you send for the rabbi, no? Just a trifle second more or less, Professor, and those bastards would not have had the chance I think to raise the gunfire. They only about raised it and it was sunrise, no? But I am well protected, am I not? I am protected by the *feijoada*. It is an armor inside me, do you not think?"

"Don't talk," Jonathan said. "For God's sake, please do not talk."

They got Roberto into the back of the Simca and they stopped Jonathan from getting into the car and Verlande said, "Go home, Professor. Go home in peace!" Jonathan was startled.

Verlande was smiling. He said, "The fire engines will be here soon and then a little later the police will come. They will not rush to a car bombing. They have disappeared from the area and they will wait until they think it is safe. For this government, why give your life? Then the DOPS will come and it will be very serious. It is necessary that you go now. Listen to the Jesuit, listen to me, go home in peace! Go home with all our blessings dear friend. The service is over. Come to us again when the Cathedral is finished."

At that Verlande got into the car with Roberto. Roberto was sitting upright, very still, and his face was very pale and Jonathan said, "I must go with you."

"Do not worry my friend," Verlande said. "Our surgeon is the best and he is not far away." He suddenly winked and he said, "The stars are ours. Do not worry. It has been a great night. The future of history belongs to us. Ah, we will have stories to tell! We will have wonderful stories to tell just like Senhor Hugo! What do you think, hey Professor?"

Verlande shut the car door and Jonathan was left on the sidewalk.

Roberto turned his head slightly toward him and made the sign of victory, a two fingered V. Verlande was putting a blanket around him and the motorcycles started up and then the jeep and then the Simca and Jonathan said, "Roberto! Roberto!"

Roberto said in a voice still strong, "When you come back, Professor, you will kindly remember to bring pictures of our ancestors, will you not? Tell the Senhora, tell her grace the lovely Dona Carol she is not to worry. Do this for me, my friend. Tell her," and he thought a moment, "tell her not to worry because my intelligence is very firm. She will like that. It will give her a smile, no?"

Then they proceeded to move. The ragtail army was proceeding to move out and Jonathan watched them, he watched them moving swiftly now along Atlântica and they passed a red light and they were gone. Jonathan hunched his shoulders and put his hands in his pockets and without looking back he began to walk after them and he was overcome by a feeling of vast desolation, a spiritual loneliness, intense and filled with a mournful sadness. The wide Avenue was fairly empty but for a hurrying passerby or a straggler here and there. Suddenly he was aware of a touch on his arm, of someone beside him.

As if in the leafy haze of an autumnal dream, he raised his head and looked into the beautiful face of a mulata. She was smiling and she put her hands on his shoulders and she said, "Do you want to see a show tonight? Come to my place." She was laughing now and in high spirits. "I have the best show in town," she said.

Jonathan kissed her on the cheek and hugged her affectionately. "Another time, another night, love."

She said once more, "The best show in town."

"Thank you very much, love," he said, "but not tonight."

"I will be here tomorrow night at this time more or less," she said.

He smiled back at her and walked on.

4

He watched the fire engines go by from the verandah of the old Hotel Miramar. He was only a block from his apartment and it was 12:30 and he wondered that it was a bare thirty minutes since he had left the apartment of Pomba Gira. He fingered the rim of the cognac glass. It wouldn't do to call now and disturb the children and he thought he needed just a few minutes to compose the self that was to be at the apartment, the self that was to embrace his love, he, at home at last, the voyager among the sirens of Brazil, a free man bound, a discoverer only of loss. He saw himself standing at the door, a charcoal self that had been sketched upon his flesh and blood, a pig's snout and a top hat and strumming a guitar, no, better than that, he, Jonathan, teacher, scholar, father, husband, and pretender to thrones and princesses and a doctrinaire of the sun and mist, of the meadows of the dove, and he, Jonathan, thinking, the vulturism of flame in the shadowy air, the gun barrels oiled to a polished shine and the charred bodies with skulls of a smile and a landscape of patience sitting upright in a burning car, he, at home at last, the innocent and ignorant voyager among the sirens of Brazil, the Princess of the Carnival, the Hen of the Altar, the Grandmother of the Urn, the Virgin of *Nossa Senhora de Copacabana*, the Whore of Verdant Mystery, and oh, he thought, yes, the Lady of Columbia, her torch held high and he with a limp hard on, love's body, the flesh and blood, the bread and wine, to be consumed, love's body transubstantiated, incarnated and consumed, the final composure of the self vested with the loincloth of humiliation, returned with the ritual of return to Penelope Calabash, to the loom of last night's loving, he, Jonathan, the prisoner of the mirror of the horizon, the hermaphroditic form of an echo of a silent world but, he thought, coming along, getting along and coming along and there, walking the clouds his decoy, the decoy of the decoy, show time, stand-in, the double decoy, Roberto among the clouds, my starry semblance free and among the clouds.

"Professor, I trust the Senhora is feeling well," the waiter said breaking in on his thoughts. "And the children? They are strong?"

"Yes, they are very strong, thank you. And you?"

"I have been up to Urca today," the waiter said. "I had a beer and sausage up there. It has been a very clear day."

"It's funny that I've never been up on Sugar Loaf. Did you take the cable car?"

"I do not trust the cable car. I have not lived well enough to trust the cable car."

Jonathan laughed. "Has a car ever fallen? I've seen them stalled."

"The cable car, Professor, is waiting for me to enter and then you will hear the wires snap one by one. It is waiting for me like the Finger of God, the *Dedo de Deus*."

"How far can you truly see from there?"

"You can truly see from the rock in Gávea to Itaipu beach and to Niteroi. It is very impressive, Professor, a view like that. But that Finger of God, I know it waits for me to go in the cable car."

"But you can't see the Finger of God. Isn't it in the Organ Mountains? Isn't it in Teresopolis? The Finger of God is not in Urca. Why worry?"

"It would make no difference if it is in China," the waiter said. "What man can see the Finger of God anyway, hey? Six hundred feet of granite in the fog, Professor. Yet I know it waits for me to enter the cable car."

"Well, my friend, I will not tease you more about this Finger of God. I have enjoyed the conversation and the cognac. It is time to go now. We are off for the States in the morning."

"I understand but I am sad," the waiter said. "I will miss you and your wonderful family. I think you are homesick by now. It is natural. You have *saudade*, is that not true? That is the way I think you looked coming up the stairs tonight." He paused. "I have relatives in Rhode Island. Do you know Rhode Island? They fish the cod there, do they not? They speak a very strange Portuguese in Rhode Island. Is this true?"

"I do not know Rhode Island well," Jonathan said stretching into his pocket for some *cruzeiros*. "I have played golf there in the summertime."

The waiter held his arm. "I cannot take money for this on your last night at the Miramar. The father of such beautiful children cannot pay for this. You will give my remembrances please to the Senhora? When you return, your first drink will be here. Is that agreeable? I will have for the children the true Amazon *guarana*, direct from Manaus."

"It is most agreeable," Jonathan said shaking his hand.

"*Boa viagem*, Professor. Do not forget us."

"*Até logo*," Jonathan said trying to smile.

There were only three or four lights at sea. Burt Lancaster, he thought, where are you now?

The air was cool and the streets were nearly empty. He saw two guards leaning against the boarded up newsstand in front of the apartment house. I guess no one's told them, he thought. The party's over, he thought.

He looked up. There was Carol leaning at the window. He could see that she was tentative. I better identify myself, he thought. She is thinking I might be Roberto.

He waved to her and then she began waving and waving and he heard her voice six stories high calling his name out into the night.